RACHEL ALBERT

QUEST TO TELOS

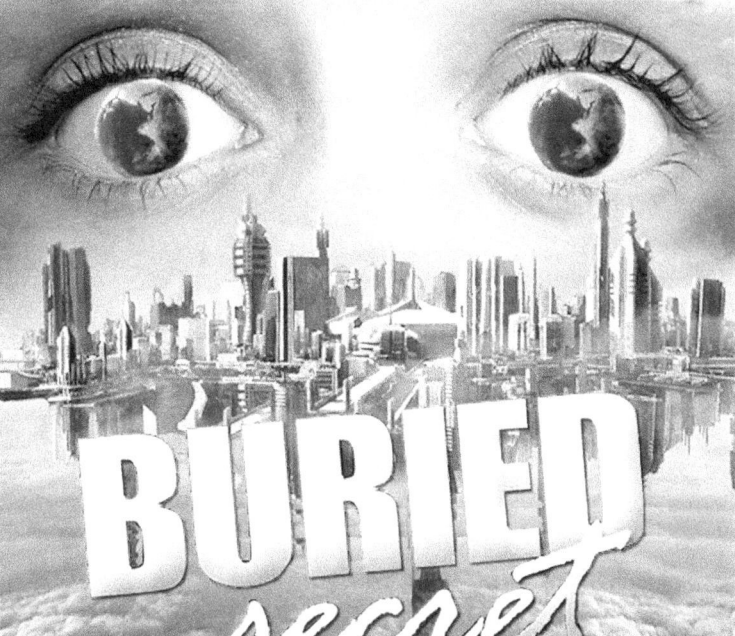

BURIED
secret

Quest to Telos
BURIED SECRET
(Book I)

By Rachel Albert

Written for
the children
of the world—
our hope for
the future.

ISBN 978-0-615-44628-8
Copyright 2012 by Rachel Albert

Printed in the U.S.A.

Published by New Icon Books, Inc.
Miami, Florida
(786) 55-TELOS

For more information contact:
Rachel@QuestToTelos.com
QuestToTelos.com

Cover designed by Eric Farley
Cloud in the Sky by Alex Popescu used with permission.
Typeset by Juan Sebastian

CONTENTS

Learn more about Lemurians, Telos, Nikola Tesla, Admiral Byrd's Polar adventure and more at QuestToTelos.com.

Acknowledgements

This book is dedicated to my Creator who gave me the courage to follow my dreams. A special thanks to my biggest fans, including my husband, David, my mother, Shoshona, and my kids, Esther, Rivka, Adina and Ari.

Grateful acknowledgement to these special people for their encouragement, input and inspiration: Robin Alexander, Ken Atchity, Ariella Cherniak, Peretz Goldberg, Ilonka Harezi, Tanya Hastada, Toby Katz, Leba Levy, Deborah Mills, Tamar Segal and John Silver.

Author's Introduction

At first glance this may seem like just another adventure fantasy novel; however, some of the places and famous people mentioned in this book are based on recorded historical events that happened within the last hundred years. Most of our generation has never heard of any of it.

Since the beginning of our time dimension, almost every civilization has told incredible stories of an ancient race of super-advanced beings that live in an inner-earth city called Telos. Many explorers have tried entering this hidden place, but all failed—except for one American pilot, Admiral Richard E. Byrd.

It is believed that in 1947 he wrote a secret diary about his flight to the mystical city of Telos that occurred shortly after the first atomic bombs were dropped over Japan.

My personal quest to Telos instantly began after reading his diary where he describes his amazing voyage and the urgent message he was asked to deliver to our world leaders—a secret buried from the public... until now.

Even though I admit his diary is hard to believe, it's even harder to ignore.

You are invited to enter a place where reality and fantasy meet and anything is possible!

Rachel Albert

Chapter One –

Operation High-Jump: The Secret Battle

I write these words in secrecy so that some future generation might someday know the truth—the truth about the incredible battle that took place in that God-forsaken, frozen wasteland where the sun shines four months long.

I was a part of a 4,000-member crew on a top-secret expedition for the navy called Operation High Jump. Waiting for the pilot to arrive, I was standing next to a twin-engine plane that was ready for takeoff. It rested on the navy's largest aircraft carrier ship, named the U.S.S. Philippians Seas.

I stared out at the icy water shimmering in the sunlight. There was an eerie calm, considering I was surrounded by our entire naval armada of 42 warships, when without warning all hell broke loose.

About twenty disk-shaped, black-colored flying machines, maybe forty feet across, just popped out of the ocean all around our ships. They flew low at incredible speeds, never making any kind of noise. Not a sound.

What in the world was happening? Then one of them hovered not far from me, shooting a brilliant red beam that hit my ship's forward deck guns, which melted into a pool of hot, molten metal.

Totally stunned watching all this, I couldn't believe my eyes.

When the other ships' deck gunners finally reached their stations, they began firing continuous rounds of bullets at the deadly, flying machines. After a few minutes it became apparent that nothing we did had any effect on them. An invisible shield seemed to surround them.

I watched helplessly as one of the flying machines fired at our lead battleship, the U.S.S. Destroyer Murdock. The red beam cut right into her forward ammunition room, instantly igniting the stored explosives. A second later an enormous fireball shot skywards, reaching hundreds of feet into the air, accompanied by an ear-shattering explosion.

Then suddenly, everything went quiet, except for emergency alarm bells ringing everywhere...

Riiiiiing!!!

The afternoon school bell reverberated up and down the hallway of lockers while students hurried to their classes. The annoying sound startled thirteen-year-old Adam Mason while he read about that unbelievable battle scene that was written in someone's personal diary. It was tattered and yellowed with age, mysteriously appearing on the shelf of his bottom locker when he opened it after lunch.

Adam crouched down and swapped out the things from his backpack, grabbing his math book. He threw the diary into his locker, wondering how the heck it had gotten in there, glancing around for possible clues. He was about to stand up when a pair of silver sandals, partially covered by a white dress, appeared right next to him.

Adam cocked his head upward to see the girl, but the glare from the ceiling lights made it hard to see her face. He could only tell that she had long, blonde hair and seemed to be about his age.

"Here, Adam. This paper fell out from that book you were just reading," she said in an odd accent.

"A book? What book?" Adam asked lamely.

"That," she said, pointing to the old diary inside his locker.

"Oh, that thing? It's not mine, but thanks."

"It must be. This paper has a little note attached with your name on it," she said and smiled brightly, handing the paper over to him. "I must go now. I'll see you later."

Utterly mesmerized by her presence, he forced his eyes down to the note that read:

"Adam, may this diary help you discover your mission as a great leader."

"Great leader? Is this some kind of prank?" he said laughing, standing up to get a better look at the girl and ask her if she knew why it was in his locker.

But to his dismay, she had vanished. Instead, in her spot stood Nathan Marcus, one of Adam's least favorite classmates. A real bully type. Adam looked left, then right. No sign of the girl anywhere.

"Where'd she go?" Adam asked Nathan, as if he had forgotten they hated each other.

"What?" Nathan replied in a nasty tone, accompanied by a cold stare straight into Adam's bewildered eyes.

"The girl that was standing right here just a second ago talking to me," Adam said enthusiastically. "And she gave me this," he continued, showing Nathan the note as proof.

"You freak. What girl would talk to you?" Nathan said, slamming his locker shut. He walked off sneering, "Dreamer, dream on."

Adam was thankful that today was his last day

at this school so he wouldn't have to deal with kids like Nathan teasing him anymore. Since girls generally steered clear of him, he was dying to know who that girl was. He was certain that he had never seen her before, but she sure knew him.

Adam unfolded the paper in his hand. It was a newspaper clipping.

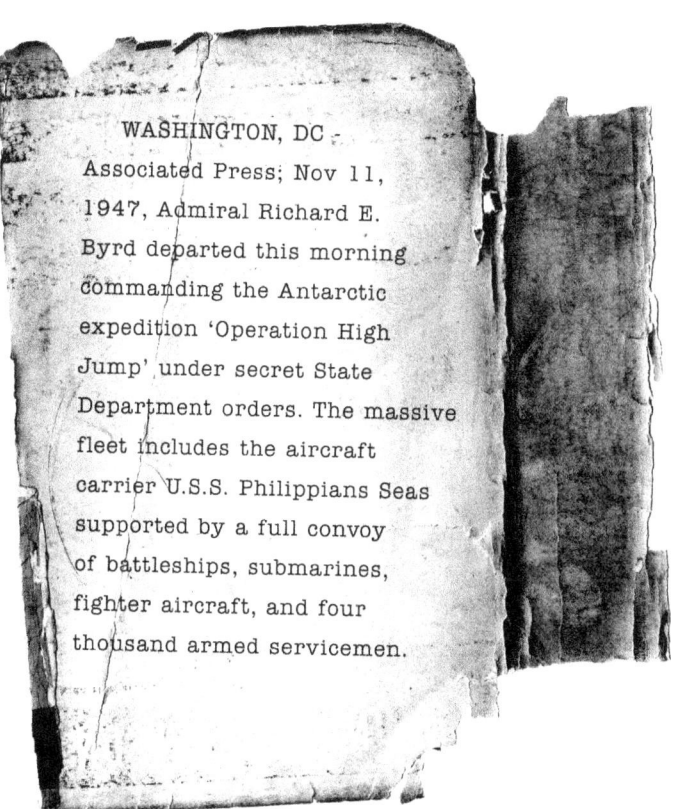

WASHINGTON, DC.
Associated Press; Nov 11,
1947, Admiral Richard E.
Byrd departed this morning
commanding the Antarctic
expedition 'Operation High
Jump' under secret State
Department orders. The massive
fleet includes the aircraft
carrier U.S.S. Philippians Seas
supported by a full convoy
of battleships, submarines,
fighter aircraft, and four
thousand armed servicemen.

Adam realized that this newspaper clipping was somehow related to the battle scene described in the strange diary, but what did any of this stuff have to do with him? He slipped the clipping between the pages of the old diary and shut his locker door.

Walking to his math class, he contemplated who had written that bizarre story about flying machines in the Antarctic. After all, if something like that had really happened, he would have read about it in some history book. Right?

Chapter Two –
The Pet Shop

A dam was cleaning out a snake's cage on display in the window at Nicky's Pet World, his after-school job a few blocks from home. His mind drifted off to the flying saucers and the naval battle scene. Operation High Jump? Battleships in the South Pole? That strange note with his name on it? No apparent connection registered in his mind, except for a faint memory of hearing that his great-grandfather had disappeared on some secret mission to the Antarctic, never to be heard from again.

He couldn't wait to read more of the diary, but for now he had to finish his work at the pet shop.

Carefully returning the copper-colored snake into its clean home, Adam heard a high-pitched bark from one of the metal cages on the floor directly across from him. He walked over and peeked through the bars.

Smiling, he bent down and unlocked the latch, reaching his hands inside the cage. A little brown and white Yorkshire terrier began licking his fingers. Adam scooped the dog into his arms, its excited little body instantly curling up into Adam's dirty T-shirt.

"Hey there, little doggy. Where did you come

from?" he asked, like he was expecting an answer. As he looked straight into the dog's bright yellow eyes, for an instant they seemed to radiate a light, like a camera flash. But he must have simply imagined it. Perhaps his mind was playing tricks on him at the end of his long day. He tried to look away, but his attention was strangely drawn back to the dog's big eyes. Adam blinked and shook his head, feeling a little dizzy. Without meaning to, he dropped the dog onto the floor.

It yelped in pain.

Just then Nicky, the pet shop owner, finished his last sale of the day, turned off the "We're Open" neon sign and walked over to Adam.

Nicky picked up the dog and scratched her chin. "A real cutie, isn't she?"

"Yes, but there's something weird about her eyes," Adam said, trying to figure out what had just happened.

"Gypsy just arrived this morning. She seems to really like you. Maybe you might want to adopt her?"

Adam reached over, petting the pooch on her little head.

"Thanks. I really wish I could. I would give anything to have a pet like Gypsy, but, you know, my dad would never let me."

"Too bad," Nicky said, disappointed. "She's growled at everyone else who tried to even get near her today. See, even Gypsy knows you're a special kid."

Adam managed a half smile. "Yeah, sure, Nicky," he said, glancing at the old clock above the cash register. "It's after six. I'd better head home for dinner." He stroked Gypsy one last time. "Good night, little doggy. See you tomorrow, Nicky."

"Looking forward to it," Nicky said, putting the dog back into her temporary home.

Adam smiled, grabbed his book bag and headed out homebound.

Whining in her cage, Gypsy put her head down, staring out through the bars of the cage door. Nicky turned to the dog, "Don't worry, Gypsy. It's not the right time yet, but very soon your journey and this boy's future will come together."

As Nicky locked up the place, a tranquil peace descended in the store. Gypsy whirled around in a small circle on the fresh newspaper covering the bottom of her cage until settling into a little brown and white ball, nose tucked under her tail.

Gypsy's mind wandered off in thought about what she had agreed to do here on earth and she was eager to get started. The first step was completed. She had met Adam.

Yawning with boredom, she closed her eyes for the night for a much needed rest. She desperately wanted Adam to take her home already. This dreadful cage was really the pits.

❀ ✳ ❀ ✳ ❀ ✳ ❀

The highlight of Adam's day was working around all the animals in the pet shop. Birds sang, cats meowed and dogs barked for attention whenever a customer walked into the store. Adam cherished the ruckus because in his head everything was at peace. The attention they gave him was all the appreciation he needed in exchange for cleaning their homes.

Adam considered Nicky to be like his adopted grandfather. Nicky's gentle manner and fine facial features made him look younger than his long, graying sideburns. Nicky really appreciated Adam, with his quirks and all.

Adam had a special gift, although he considered it more of a curse. He could sense how other people were feeling simply by glancing at their faces. So he learned at a young age not to reveal his knowledge to anyone—except Nicky, of course—because when he did, people typically acted defensively. It was a heavy burden for any thirteen-year-old kid to carry. He became a loner, and he liked it that way.

The only advantage of just turning thirteen, as far as he could tell, was that he could get away with being old enough to know better, and yet, too young to really care.

He often inspected himself in the mirror for any signs of manhood. A single facial hair would have made him incredibly proud. But all he ever saw was peach fuzz. He was a good-looking boy with intense blue eyes and an awkward charm, but his hunched posture reflected his feelings of insecurity.

A little mole on his left cheek didn't help to boost his self-confidence either. He hated that thing.

Adam's family lived in a small brick home in a modest part of Beverly Hills, just on the border of the famous 90210 zip code. This allowed him to attend Beverly Vista Middle School, which most kids considered a real privilege. But Adam couldn't wait to move since many of his classmates came from wealthy and famous families. His family wasn't either of those—just weird as far as he could tell.

Adam wasn't book smart like his mom and dad, Suzie and Larry Mason, but he made up for it with a different kind of brains. His taste for adventure often led him to some outlandish mishaps quite unappreciated by his hyper-critical parents.

Like last year when he wandered off to the edge of town, following what he thought was a lost dog. It looked hungry and perhaps injured. Adam trailed behind the scared dog as it roamed aimlessly down one street and up the next. He followed it into a warehouse, unwittingly setting off a silent security alarm.

A few minutes later, he froze when the police showed up with guns pointing at him. Even though Adam thought it was so cool riding to the police station in the backseat of the car, his dad sure didn't.

Adam's face dropped when he overheard his dad on the phone yelling to the policeman, "Something's not quite right with that boy. I think a night in jail will teach him a good lesson."

Of course his mom refused to let this happen and insisted on picking him up. Thank God for mothers.

Finally arriving home tired and late for dinner, Adam was greeted by his father's righteous rage.

"So besides lousy grades, now you're a juvenile delinquent. Congratulations. How are you ever going to get into college?" he screamed at Adam.

"I wasn't doing anything wrong. I didn't even—"

"What were you doing there, then?" his dad interrupted.

"I was just following this dog—"

"What's wrong with your head? Why don't you think first?" his dad interrupted again, not even paying attention to his son's attempt to explain.

Adam hated his dad for making him feel stupid. He wasn't a bad kid; just a spaced-out explorer sometimes.

He constantly questioned his life and loved to explore his world. He knew there must be something powerful that made the universe, even though his family acted like there wasn't.

His dad often proclaimed he didn't buy into anything he couldn't scientifically prove, and that especially applied to religion. He was proud that he didn't fall into the trap with all the other brainwashed worshippers.

"Besides, look at all the suffering in the world," his dad would say, shaking his head. "Only a fool would believe in something he can't see with his own eyes and touch with his hands." He was a hundred percent certain of this belief, or lack of it, and he used it as a badge of reason to avoid following any spiritual path.

How do you argue with that? Adam would think, never openly questioning any of his father's philosophy.

Chapter Three –
The Crystal Dream

A dam could write a book about the amazing
and vivid dreams he dreamt. He was fast
asleep when one suddenly dropped into his
mind.

Wiping the sweat off his forehead with his shirt
sleeve, Adam leaned against the wall of a cavern
illuminated by a huge stalactite crystal hanging
from the ceiling. Just next to him, a stunning,
aqua-colored stream flowed through the cave. On
the ground next to a huge boulder Adam spotted a
treasure chest overfilled with glowing crystals and
sparkling stones. His eyes widened with delight.

"Wow! Hey, Dad, look what I found!" he shouted,
glancing off to his side.

As the words left Adam's mouth, in the center
of the stream a white light pushed a glowing orb
upwards. He watched in wonder as it slowly moved
toward him, floating a few feet from where he stood.
Inside he could see the face of a young girl. Locks of
golden hair, adorned with a small crown of crystals,
framed her almond-shaped eyes and warm smile.

She gently beckoned to him, extending one hand
and softly speaking but a single word, "Adam."

Without any consideration, he reached out to

meet her hand. Just as their fingers were about to touch, the orb disappeared in a flash of light.

Bewildered, Adam looked around for the girl. Not finding any signs of her, he walked outside the cavern. But instead of finding her, he came across a golden ladder that appeared to stretch into the heavens above.

He began climbing upward, but the ladder seemed to go on without any end. So he stopped.

As he gazed off into the puffy clouds, his hands lost their grip on the ladder. Panic set in as he fell down through the clouds.

Below him, green trees and pastures stretched as far as he could see. He surveyed the surrounding landscape and noticed a column of black smoke rising from a large house directly below him. Flames leaped from the thatched roof, smoke engulfing him.

"Help! Help me! Dad, where are you? I can't see you! The smoke is too thick...I'm falling ... I'm..."

Abruptly waking from his strange dream, Adam's body jerked up in his bed. His arms were outstretched in front of him, ready to break his fall. Breathing hard, he tried to clear the cobwebs in his mind.

This was a bizarre dream. What could it mean?

Calming down a bit, Adam saw that the clock on his dresser showed it was almost three in the morning.

He rolled out of bed and tiptoed down the hall

towards the kitchen. He passed his dad's den and noticed him hunched over his computer, typing away, oblivious to everything around him. Hardly ever in bed, his father liked to brag that sleep was a waste of valuable time. That might explain why he was always so cranky.

Usually his dad was totally immersed in his scientific research, chasing his dreams. In particular, he was utterly obsessed with Vril power. He considered it the most potent energy in the universe, and whoever knew the secret of how to use it could control the world.

Recently, his dad had joined an ancient lodge that was known to use the Vril energy in their secret rituals. These meetings often took even more time away from family life. The idea of work became a negative thing in Adam's mind, regardless of possible fame, power or fortune.

After getting a drink of water, Adam returned to his room and opened his laptop. He made sure the sound was muted so he didn't wake up his brother Mark, who shared his room.

Opening his search page, he typed "The meaning of dreams." After reading a few website descriptions, he came across one dealing with dream interpretations.

He eagerly typed in "treasure; ladder; fire; falling," intentionally leaving out the mysterious girl, because in real life girls never looked his way.

He waited impatiently. Finally, a page loaded with the results and he read one of the links. Confused, he read it again, finding it hard to understand what the site suggested.

"Exciting challenges await you as you begin your journey to discover your true destiny. Your past failures will burn up, setting you free to soar beyond the limits of your mind."

He pursed his lips as he closed his laptop. He fell back down in bed and thought some more. Perhaps the dream of the treasure chest meant his dad would finally get rich from all of his long hours of work. Then he might finally relax and even realize that he had a family.

Adam closed his eyes, but instead of falling asleep, wild images from the old diary he had found bounced around inside his mind. Tossing and turning, he felt agitated and alert. He jumped out of bed, grabbed a flashlight from a drawer and rummaged through his backpack on the floor. He pulled out the diary and flipped through the pages to where he had left off reading.

Brilliant orange flames shot into the smoke-filled sky, set against endless, white glaciers. All of our defense weapons were destroyed and our entire fleet of warships sat floating, crippled. Then as quickly as it all began...it ended.

It was pretty obvious that if they really wanted to, these flying machines could have easily sunk every one of our ships. But they only targeted our weapons. Whoever—or whatever—sent these flying machines to greet us must have discovered our secret plans to destroy the entrance to their world.

Then one by one, those flying machines all gathered together perfectly synchronized and zipped away in the direction of the South Pole.

I couldn't resist the urge to jump into the pilot's seat of the plane to follow them. I was just a civilian scientist. And even though I knew how to fly, I was not authorized. Without hesitation I climbed inside and taxied down the runway, barely getting past all the debris on our flight deck. I began traveling in the direction of the flying machines.

I hoped this would not be the biggest mistake of my career, flying without permission, even though getting killed probably should have worried me more.

Adam yawned and couldn't read anymore. So he put the diary down. He flicked off the flashlight, and he climbed back into his comfy bed. He closed his eyes. Then she came into his thoughts again. The beautiful girl from his dream, calling out his name, "Adam...Adam..."

❊ ✳ ❊ ✳ ❊ ✳ ❊

"Adam? Sweetie, wake up, dear."

His mom kissed him on his forehead, trying to wake him. "Good morning, sleepy head," she said, standing over his bed, pushing the hair away from his eyes.

"Mom, it's Saturday," he moaned in a comatose voice, his eyes still closed.

"It's moving day, Adam, and you have to get up and finish your packing."

He remained unresponsive, trying to hang onto his dreams, especially the one about the girl.

"Adam, come on. Get up...now!" She raised her voice, shaking his shoulder.

"I'm so sleepy. What time is it?" he asked, as he opened one eye, only to roll over and sink back into his familiar pillow.

"Adam, it's almost six-thirty in the morning and the moving truck will be here soon. Look at your room. You haven't even finished all of your packing. If you don't get up right away, we'll have to pack your bed into the truck, with you in it."

"But Mom, it's still dark outside!" Adam argued.

"You need to finish your packing and there's no time for sleeping right now. Mark's already up and totally packed."

Adam barely lifted his head to look over to his

brother's side of the room. He dropped his head back down pulling a pillow over his head.

"That's it. I'm getting your dad."

Adam's eyes popped open. "Okay, okay. Chill. I'm up!"

His mom was an attractive woman with reddish hair and dazzling blue eyes that matched Adam's. Suzie generally was a patient lady, but whenever she had too much to deal with, she became quite cranky, too.

Quickly throwing on a pair of his favorite jeans and t-shirt, Adam rubbed the sleep out of the corners of his eyes. Heading to the kitchen, he joined his parents and Mark already seated around their breakfast table.

Adam was used to eating breakfast accompanied by light coming through the windows. Getting up before sunrise was confusing to him as he sat down to a glass of orange juice waiting for him.

"G'morning, son. Lots to do around here," Larry, his dad, said.

"It's so early," Adam complained.

"There's still a lot of stuff to get packed and now is not the time for sleeping in," his dad muttered.

"I'm up now," Adam mumbled, gulping down the glass of juice, followed by a contented burp.

"Excuse me!" his mom said.

You're excused, Adam thought, chuckling to himself.

"And your posture. I swear, you're going to be a hunchback when you grow up," she continued.

"When are the movers getting here, Suzie?" Larry asked, not bothering to peek up from his morning newspaper.

"They scheduled us for eight," she answered, reaching into a partly cleared out kitchen cabinet.

Larry glanced over his reading glasses. "Eight? Can't they get here any earlier? It's a ten-hour drive to Mount Shasta, and we need to get started soon if we're going to get to our new house at a decent time."

"You're welcome to phone them, dear, and see," she said, fumbling with some pots that wouldn't quite fit into the packing box.

Larry ignored her suggestion and said, "Adam, after breakfast I want you to help your mother finish packing whatever is left. Mark, I need you to go through each room to make sure we didn't forget anything. And also label all the moving boxes according to the rooms they came from."

"But Dad," Mark complained, "I told you yesterday I was going to say good-bye to my friends this morning. I promised the guys I would meet them real early down at the track. It won't take long. I promise."

"This isn't the time for that, Mark," his mom said.

"Oh Suzie, let the kid go," Larry intervened. "He

did tell me he was going."

"Don't worry about it, Mom. I'll have the twerp help me finish as soon as I get back," Mark said.

"Dad!" Adam protested. "I'm not even done packing my own stuff yet, and I need to go down to the pet shop to say bye to Nicky and all the animals."

"Oh, I think the animals will forgive you," his dad said sarcastically.

Didn't anyone understand he might also have stuff to do before leaving Beverly Hills? Mark gave his dad one of his 'Adam is so weird' expressions, while his mom studied her to-do list, trying to hold back her laughter.

"Adam, right now it's more important to finish packing all your stuff and getting these boxes labeled so the movers will know where each box goes," his mom said.

"So Mark should stay and help too!" Adam argued.

"Stop fighting and get busy, son," his dad put an end to the conversation.

"I'm gone," Mark blurted and jumped up, grabbed his phone and scooted out of the kitchen door before his father could change his mind. The screen door slammed behind him.

This is not fair, Adam thought. Mark always gets away with everything around here. One day I'll show them. He got up from the table and stormed back to his room.

Leaving his home and school didn't bother Adam at all. What made him sad was saying good-bye forever to all his friends at Nicky's Pet World. There was no way he was going to leave without a final visit. He especially wanted to see that new dog with the freaky eyes one more time. He kicked his bedpost in frustration, only managing to hurt his big toe.

Adam wasn't a bad kid, but once an idea got lodged in his brain, he usually acted on it.

Without thinking, Adam opened his bedroom window just as the sun was lighting up the morning sky.

He decided to copy Mark's unauthorized exits. It seemed simple enough: open the bedroom window and jump out. He knew he might get in big trouble, but right now he really didn't care.

Better to apologize later than beg for permission, he reasoned as he hit the ground, searching around to see if anyone had spotted him. The coast was clear. He ran down the street, heading towards Nicky's place.

Chapter Four –
The Gift

Adam impatiently knocked on the front window, waving his arms in huge gestures and trying to catch Nicky's attention inside the store.

"Why, Adam. What a nice surprise," Nicky greeted him warmly at the door. "We're not used to seeing you here this early! In fact, you're lucky I'm even here."

"Well, I came to say good-bye, Nicky. We're moving today."

Nicky's mouth fell open. "What?"

"I told you almost a month ago, remember?" Adam explained.

"Really? It seems like it was just last week. Now what are all the animals here in the shop going to do without you to cheer them up every day?"

"I guess they'll have to get used to dealing with you." Adam shrugged his shoulders.

"A fate worse than death, eh?" Nicky laughed half-heartedly. "Well, come with me to the backroom quick sticks. I've got a little something special for you as a parting gift."

"Really? What's with quick sticks?"

"It means like right now, pronto!"

Adam followed Nicky towards the back into the dingy storage room which was normally locked. Upon entering the windowless space, Nicky flipped on the overhead fluorescent light. Only one of the two lamps came on, flickering intermittently.

The room was quite a mess. There was a mishmash of papers piled everywhere; bags of animal food and dilapidated cages were scattered about. An out-dated computer and old-fashioned phone sat on the desk. Everything was covered in dust.

Nicky went to the other side of the room and turned on the desk lamp, talking to himself. "Now, which drawer did I put it in? Oh, here it is. Seems like I've been holding onto this forever."

Nicky pulled out a small box from the top drawer. It was wrapped in plain white paper and neatly tied with a brown string. Tearing off the wrapping, he placed a small white jewelry box on the old desk directly in front of the boy.

Adam's eyes opened brightly, excited to get an apparent gift from his good friend.

Nicky talked genuinely, "Son, you really have a special gift. It shows in the deep love you have for animals. That says a lot about a person. And one day soon when you master it with people, you will become a great leader."

Adam rolled his eyes. "Yeah, right, Nicky. Maybe

lead a circus some day."

"Now don't say that! You must always believe in yourself if you want anyone else to," Nicky said.

"And just how do I go about doing that?" Adam asked.

"That is an enormous question, one that people spend an entire lifetime looking for the answer to. Your special gift will help you find your destiny and make a big impression on this planet. But right now I want you to open the box."

After Adam removed the top of the white box, he noticed a square wristwatch attached to a copper band. What caught his attention were the purple numbers tantalizing his eyes. Next to that were tiny green numbers that counted the seconds to the next minute. Just underneath the time was a little sun lit up in bold yellow. Next to that he could barely see a faint moon. On the bottom was written "Telos Watch."

The face had a strange dial and two small buttons on one side. Nicky took the watch out and placed it around Adam's wrist.

Adam's face lit up with excitement. "Whoa! What a nice watch!"

"This isn't an ordinary watch. It's a Telos multi-functional device I have been working on for years that does many cool things. And yes, this is for you, in part as a token of our friendship and also to keep you safe until we meet again. So promise me you will take real good care of it. One day you will be that leader we talked about, and this Telos watch will help you get there," Nicky said.

"Help me? Really? Come on." Adam didn't know if Nicky was being serious or not. He stared intently at the watch, waiting for the punch line. None came. "Are you kidding me?"

"Of course not, Adam."

"How do I use these buttons on the side?" Adam asked.

"Don't worry yourself with what the buttons do right now. Just use the watch to tell the time. Soon you will discover on your own how to use the special powers within the watch." Nicky's voice was serious, without even a hint of a smile.

Adam didn't know what to believe or say. Special powers? What could he be talking about?

"Well, keep in touch. We're sure going to miss you around here."

"I'll miss you too," Adam echoed, "and thanks so much! Um, well, I guess I'll say good-bye to the animals now."

"That's a good idea, son."

Adam cherished his last minutes in the store, making his rounds one by one to all the animals. His last stop was the little brown and white dog that had arrived yesterday. Gypsy's nose was already pushing through the metal bars of her cage. Her tail spun excitedly as Adam approached, sticking his hand through the bars.

Gypsy licked Adam's fingers. Adam instinctively turned away, avoiding direct contact with the dog's eyes. He was afraid of being hypnotized again. He opened the cage and picked up the warm ball of fur. Gypsy snuggled into his arms.

"I'm moving today, Gypsy, so I won't be seeing you again. Take care, little friend," Adam spoke softly.

After cuddling her for a minute, Adam tried to return Gypsy to her cage, but she physically protested. Spreading her legs out and pushing them against the cage, she made it impossible for him to get her back inside. This little dog was not going to make things easy. Gypsy was obviously telling Adam she wanted to go home with him.

Finally, Nicky said, "Here, I'll take her."

Adam was relieved to hand her over. "Hope you find her a good home," Adam said, perplexed by this odd dog, wondering about its unusual eyes.

"Sure there's no way I can convince you to take her?" Nicky pressed, as he coaxed Gypsy back into her cage and secured the latch.

"My dad would flip out. He's not a big dog fan," Adam said, shaking his head.

Checking the time on his special gift, he sighed. "It's way after eight o'clock. I better get home before I get into serious trouble, Nicky!"

Good-byes were usually not a big deal for Adam,

but as they stepped outside the pet shop, a heavy feeling crept inside Adam.

"See ya, kid, and good luck," Nicky said, patting him on his back, sending him on his way.

Adam glanced behind one last time and waved, reluctantly heading homeward, where he was likely to find two angry parents waiting for him with an annoying lecture.

Back in the shop, Gypsy nervously whirled in circles inside her little prison cell. Suddenly a shimmering, bright light engulfed her, and Gypsy was gone.

Chapter Five –
The Big Move

Nearing his home, Adam saw Nathan with a group of kids ahead, hanging out. They apparently noticed him too.

Nathan spoke up, making a funny face, "Hey, lover boy, where's your girlfriend?"

The other kids heckled as their laughter echoed up the block.

Adam searched for an escape route to avoid these jerks. He took a shortcut through an alleyway to get out of sight. About halfway down, he got the fright of his life when, out of nowhere, a bright light burst midair in front of him, spinning into a large black opening. Adam didn't know it at the time, but that was a space portal to the Draconian underworld.

Cautiously approaching to look inside the blackness, he noticed something very odd. He spotted a distant palace situated on a dark mountain. Orange streaks painted the sky above it.

When he put his hand through the hole, the most freaky thing happened. A massive green dragon flew up to the opening of the portal, spitting fire from its mouth towards Adam. Completely panic stricken, he tried ducking away from the hole, but he felt himself being sucked towards the portal. He grabbed onto a nearby trash dumpster, holding on for his dear life.

Adam hadn't realized that Gypsy had followed him into the alleyway. It attempted to scare off the dragon with pathetic, yappy barks. Suddenly, two beams of light shot from the dog's eyes, reaching into the opening, striking the dragon. The large hole instantly shrunk into a tiny, black golf ball, fell to the ground and rolled under the trash dumpster.

Totally clueless as to what was happening, Adam didn't waste any time waiting around to figure things out. Grabbing his bag, he ran away from this strange scene as quickly as he could down the alleyway, never looking back.

Dread replaced his fright just thinking about his parents. They were probably out right now looking for him. He was certainly in deep trouble by now for sneaking away, especially today. What would he tell them? What could he say? He got attacked by a dragon? Not a chance.

Turning the corner to his home he saw Gypsy trailing closely behind him. Adam stopped to pick her up. She licked his nose.

Putting her onto the ground he said, "I can't keep you. Go back to the pet shop," Adam ordered, pointing the opposite direction he was headed.

The little dog sat down and tilted its head to the right, its tail sweeping the sidewalk. He turned away and continued walking. He smiled when he detected that she was following him home.

The moving men were loading furniture into their big truck. Pieces from the dining room and living room were all over the front yard.

Pausing for a moment, Adam removed his watch and placed it in his pocket. He would have enough explaining to do when he got inside without being interrogated where he had gotten this sensational watch.

With his heart racing, Adam rushed to the side entrance, opened the screen door into the kitchen, shooing Gypsy away. He immediately came face to face with his mom.

Uh-oh! he thought.

She carefully wrapped the last piece of her best china in newspaper, placed it into a heavy cardboard box, when she noticed her son.

"Oh, there you are, Adam. Where have you been?" But before he could say anything, she continued, "I need you to take that outside to our van," motioning to the cooler box next to the fridge.

"Sure, sure, Mom," he stammered, as he looked around to see if anyone else had seen his entrance. Luckily, they were alone.

"I've packed the cooler with things for the trip and something to eat when we get to our new home. Have you finished all your packing, dear?"

"Almost done, Mom," said Adam, taking a deep sigh.

"Well, hurry up. We're running out of time."

"Right away," he promised.

Stressed and tired, Suzie was a wreck today. Heading to his room, he could hear her talking to herself in the kitchen, "Every time I think we're done packing, I find more stuff!" Like her husband, she didn't do well under pressure, particularly when things were disorganized.

Unbelievable, Adam thought to himself, heading to his room. It looked as if nobody had realized he had been missing for over an hour.

He told himself he didn't really care, but deep inside he secretly wished they had. This was not one of the scenarios he had anticipated after sneaking off to Nicky's place. After all, he could have been killed there in that alleyway, never to be seen again.

He found his mom's cell phone resting on a box. He decided to quickly call Nicky and tell him his unbelievable tale about the dragon attack, and to let him know that Gypsy was here. He shut his door and tried to steady himself from shaking so hard. He punched in the number and waited four rings…

"Sorry, the number you have called has been disconnected."

Redialing three more times with the same disappointing results, he simply couldn't understand what was going on here. He stared at the phone, thinking maybe he was so stressed out he forgot the number. But it was such an easy number to remember.

He put his mom's cell phone on the box, returning to his room. Deciding what to pack and what to throw out, he continued to mull over the morning events, like an endless recording inside his brain. Finally done packing all the stuff in his room, he dragged out the last box into the hallway for the movers to carry out.

In the kitchen he could hear his mom pleading as one of the movers grabbed her precious box off the kitchen table. "That's my best china set in there. Is there any way you can put that box in a safe place to keep it from getting damaged?"

"We'll do our best, Ma'am, but no promises." He loaded it on a hand cart with other heavy boxes and then headed out the door and down the front steps. Suzie shook her head. The mover's dirty flannel shirt and toothless grin gave her no comfort about the future of her priceless belongings.

"Please, be careful!" she begged in an attempt to console herself.

Adam carried out a black, plastic trash bag filled with the stuff he was planning to toss out. But not before his mom stopped him and began rummaging through it. "Why are you throwing out these old DVDs? They were some of your favorite shows," she complained.

"Mom, I'm thirteen years old and those are little kids' shows."

"So, keep them for your children. These were the

special collector's edition I bought for you. Don't you remember? Oh no, not this! I just got you this camera on your last birthday. Adam, come on."

"Mom, the camera doesn't work anymore."

"See! You always break things. And why are you tossing out these shoes? They're almost brand new."

"Come on, Mom. They hurt my feet."

"So give them away! And look at this! You're incredible, Adam. How could you ever throw this into the garbage! Of all the things, your old year book from the first grade!" His mom's voice became more agitated with each new discovery. "I can't believe you're throwing away all these good things. Don't you have any appreciation for anything?"

Adam was about to say to her, I have really bad memories from that yearbook, besides I looked so dorky.

Not waiting for a response, she put everything back into the plastic bag and walked outside, forcing the bag in between two boxes inside the moving truck.

"Mom, that's why we have so much stuff to move!" he told her upon her returning to the kitchen. Throwing anything away seemed to cause her real pain. That was one thing his parents had in common: two crazy hoarders.

Wondering what the time was, Adam glanced at the clock over the kitchen sink, but it was already packed inside some box. He remembered his gift still in his pocket. Adam pulled out his special watch and realized it was well beyond the eleven o'clock deadline his dad had given the movers.

He looked out the window to see if the dog was still hanging around. He poked his nose out the side door and he grinned seeing Gypsy sitting in a small box next to the side fence. He walked out toward her and got a strange feeling she was telling him to pack her in this box and take her with them.

What a crazy idea, he thought. Ignoring his logic, he ran inside to grab some packing tape, a pen and a sandwich he snatched from the cooler box.

"You sure you want me to pack you in this box?" Adam asked Gypsy.

The dog barked twice.

Adam peeked behind him. The coast seemed clear. He knelt down next to the small box, threw the sandwich inside, petted the dog on her head, and closed the box, sealing it shut. He poked a few air holes with the pen on the sides. He wrote on top "Adam's room."

He walked over to the truck containing the boxes, jumped inside the back and found a secure spot to place the box. "Better not bark, or you'll be kicked off along the way," Adam warned her quietly.

"Come on, guys! Let's go!" Larry roared from the front yard. "Mark and I will be waiting for you guys in the van."

Adam jumped out of the back of the truck and walked over to their van.

"We're going to be driving for a while. Did you use the bathroom?" Suzie asked Adam.

"Yes, Mom."

"Did you wash your hands?"

"Duh," Adam muttered.

"Is that duh, yes, or duh, no?"

"Yeeeeeees!" The word strung out of his mouth.

"Good, then let's get going before your dad has a coronary."

With a sigh, Suzie locked the front door of their home for the past three years, one last time. After walking down the front steps, she climbed into their packed van with Adam.

As they pulled out from their driveway, Adam stared back at his house for the last time. Goodbye Beverly Hills, was all he could think, seeing one of the movers shut the back door of the truck. The driver started the loud diesel engine, sending a black cloud of exhaust smoke into the air.

Adam felt bad for Gypsy being stuck in there for ten long hours. He prayed she could keep her mouth shut on the drive all the way to Mount Shasta.

Adam shifted in his seat in a hopeless attempt to find a comfortable position. His legs were wrapped like a pretzel. He felt squished in the back, sitting next to two suitcases stacked between him and Mark, who really enjoyed annoying him, especially on a long, boring ten-hour trip like this. At least the suitcases kept Mark away from him.

Adam tried not to dwell on the numbness in his legs. Instead, he stared mindlessly out the window at the endless tracks of barren land, occasionally interrupted by a small farm.

On the other side of the highway stretched mountain ranges. Practically hypnotized by the repetition, every now and then Adam's spell would be broken as a general store or gas station would zoom by. But after a while, even this change in the scenery became monotonous. Every small town started looking pretty much like the last one, as Adam dozed off to sleep.

He was abruptly awakened by loud yelling. His dad's aggressive personality really came out in his competitive driving style. Adam kept waking up from the frequent outbursts of frustrated name calling at other drivers and sudden braking. His dad was on a schedule and had little patience for anyone who got in his way. It seemed he was always mad at someone, usually for messing with his perfectly calculated plans.

Adam didn't understand how he could have been born into this hyper-critical, stressed-out family, since he considered himself an easy-going kid.

Maybe he was adopted and they had never told him. His parents also had a thing about germs, and they sometimes freaked out in public places, especially restaurants.

His father was the worst, always insisting the first thing they do at any restaurant was to wash their hands. Leaving the washroom, he was careful to use a paper towel to open the door.

Then his mom would inspect every fork, knife and plate, usually wiping them just to be sure, she would say. Sure of what, she never actually told him. Adam's attitude was if he didn't bother with the germs, they wouldn't bother with him.

It wasn't hard to figure out how his parents ended up together. They had met in college when Larry was working on a doctorate in astrophysics and Suzie was some sort of research assistant. The perfect match—two oddball, clean freaks with a common interest in science.

Larry was impossible to ever please. He accepted nothing less than perfection. Everyone stayed clear of him when he got home. Fortunately, he was gone a lot since he had landed a new assignment for a private research company. His work was secretive, and this move to Mount Shasta, in the northern part of California, apparently had something to do with that.

Adam and Mark were occasionally granted a vague explanation of his research, but never any juicy details. Whenever they asked specific questions, his standard answer was, "If I told you, boys, I'd have to erase your memories." It was one of those things he liked to say over and over again. The boys would usually laugh, but sometimes they wondered if it was really a joke.

Even more secretive than his dad's work were the lodge meetings he frequently attended. Adam would sometimes wake up in the wee hours of the night when he heard his dad shut the front door and head straight to his den. Needless to say, his dad was pre-occupied, if not obsessed, with whatever he was working on.

On the rare occasion when the whole family sat down for dinner, few words beyond "how was your day" were exchanged between his parents. Thinking they were both pretty weird, Adam usually returned to his room after dinner and spent the rest of the night playing video games and watching YouTube clips about obscure and interesting topics he would stumble upon.

Often when Adam heard his family talking about science, politics, aliens, or any words that ended with "ology," he would tune out. It seemed that's all they talked about. Thinking they were nuts, he would slink back to his room because he really could not care less about that stuff. His plan was to graduate from high school and move as far away as possible from his weirdo family.

Adam was anxious to see their new home in Mount Shasta, a much larger house, according to his mom. His family had outgrown their three-bedroom rented home in Beverly Hills, and more space was a welcome change.

This new house was exciting because Adam and Mark would finally get their own rooms. The concept of privacy was exhilarating. It was one of the few positive outcomes of his dad's new research project. The previous week his dad had flown up to sign the real estate papers, to get the keys and to have the electric and water service turned on.

His dad described the new place as a two-story mansion built in the 1920's that had two main staircases and five bedrooms, each with its own bathroom.

Adam had seen a dozen photos that showed the house surrounded by acres of wooded land. Adam knew that there would be plenty of room to keep Gypsy. And besides, a pet wouldn't be such a big deal since he was the one who would feed it every day, right?

With any normal family this wouldn't be such an outrageous thought. He could recite his dad's past responses by memory. "They're dirty. They'll make a mess in the house. A pet is a serious commitment."

Life was so unfair sometimes! This was just another issue he would have to deal with once they got there. Just a few more hours left to go.

Adam envisioned what his new life was going to be like living without neighbors directly across the driveway to overhear his father's outbursts every time something didn't go according to his plan.

That was a plus, but it also meant no more Nicky and all his special pals in the pet shop. He pushed those unpleasant memories out of his mind. He turned his thoughts to the story of the South Pole battle written in the diary inside his backpack that was between his feet. Since nightfall was creeping in, he flicked on the overhead light, took out the diary and began reading where he had left off.

My heart raced as I looked at the fuel gauge. Only half a tank remained! I wasn't sure I could reach my destination, wherever that was. All I could think about as I flew that plane as fast as it could go towards the Pole was, who were the masters of these deadly, flying machines?

Adam paused, thinking that same question, as well as who would write such nonsense. Plus, he still couldn't see how any of this stuff had anything to do with him.

Adam suddenly smelled a stinky odor in the van.

"What's that smell?" Larry said and glanced back.

"Adam, did you let out some gas?" Suzie asked.

"How come I get blamed for everything?"

"Because your farts are silent, but violent," his dad said.

"Look who's talking," Suzie said.

"At least with mine you get a warning," Larry said, chuckling to himself.

"Yep, loud and proud," Suzie joked.

Laughter filled the otherwise pretty boring and serious drive. Adam wished his family shared more silly times like this.

Staring out the window at the monotonous scenery passing by, he nodded back off to sleep.

Ouch! Adam's head banged against the van's window as his father swerved, trying to pass a slow-moving truck on the single-lane highway.

"What the...!" Adam cried, rubbing his head.

He knew better than to say anything else while his father was competing for the highway. Instead he decided to take a closer look at his Telos watch and pulled it out from his pocket.

He couldn't help but admire the intricate design of the watch, unlike anything he had ever seen. He noticed a little moon had replaced the tiny sun on the dial. He was tempted to wear it, but that would definitely lead to endless questions from his parents and Mark that he didn't want to answer, so he put the watch back into his pocket as his special secret.

Keeping secrets was fun sometimes.

Chapter Six –
The Mansion

It was just after ten o'clock at night when Adam was awakened by a spasm in his left leg. He rubbed it until the stiffness eased up. Checking out the window, he noticed a full moon perched on the snow-capped mountain ahead.

"Are we there yet, Mom?" Adam asked.

"Oh, did you have a good sleep? We just got off the Interstate and we're driving up McCloud Avenue. Our new home is just a couple miles ahead."

Adam felt sorry for Gypsy being stuck in the box for this whole time, but shortly he would let her out.

Larry made a sharp, left turn off McCloud and onto a narrow, unmarked gravel road that could easily be missed, especially in the dark.

Adam rolled down his window to get a better look and was taken by surprise. The chill of the outside air blowing against his face almost froze his nose.

"Wow! It's freezing here," Adam said.

"The van's temperature gauge says it's 45 degrees outside," his dad said.

That was about 40 degrees colder than the temperature they had left behind in Los Angeles. Quickly closing his window, Adam suddenly missed the warmth of Southern California.

"There she is, folks!" Larry said with boastfulness in his voice. He smiled, looking around inside the van for the family's approval of the impressive house and grounds, even in the dark. Adam and Mark weren't sure what to say. The first thing they saw was a dim light suspended in the middle of a large archway, framed by a pair of open, iron gates.

As they passed through the gates, the road led to a circular driveway in front of the house. Nestled between stately pine trees, the large estate was set facing a lake that reflected the shimmering moonlight. In the distance beyond the lake was the ever-present Mount Shasta. As their van rolled to a stop, it triggered motion-sensing lights around the property.

In the middle of the courtyard stood a large, brightly lit fountain with a white statue of a young boy pouring water from a pot. To Adam, this place seemed more like a hotel than a home.

It was obvious from the overgrown bushes all around the house that no one had lived here for some time. The building was painted a shade of mountain brown paint with beige trim. Two white Roman style columns stood guard on either side of the home's grand entrance. A rusted light fixture hung on a long chain over the front porch.

Sliding open the van's door, Adam stretched out his cramped legs. Soon everyone extracted themselves from the van, and Larry began assigning duties to each member of the family.

"Mark, take out the suitcases, please. Adam, I want you to take out the air mattresses and blankets and set them up in the living room. We're going to camp out tonight and we'll finish unpacking the van in the morning."

"Where are the movers?" Adam asked.

"They're staying in a nearby hotel and will be here early in the morning," his dad said.

Not believing this bad news, Adam heard his dad with half of his brain and surveyed the property with the rest of it.

"They're only coming in the morning?" Adam asked in a panic, worrying how Gypsy was managing, probably freezing, starving and having to pee by now.

Not paying much attention to all the background chatter, Adam dragged the heavy mattress bag to the front door. Mark took out suitcases from the stuffed van.

Adam paused on the steps approaching the two tall, front doors, each adorned with large brass knockers. They were tarnished, yet still impressive and strangely haunting. He felt totally engrossed by the size of the whole place. Even the smell of the air was different.

On the drive here, Adam's dad had mentioned that the real estate agent's father had known the original owner, a reclusive scientist. Shortly after he had built the house, he mysteriously disappeared back in the 1940s. He was presumed dead. The house had stood vacant ever since.

How freaky, Adam thought. Some reclusive scientist living all alone in this big place…and then vanishing!

The first order of business as soon as they entered the home was to light the fireplace in the living room so they wouldn't freeze to death.

An hour later they had unpacked everything needed to spend their first night sleeping on the polished wood floor in this grand, old home. The fireplace was burning brightly as Larry turned off the ceiling lights and everyone gathered close together in front of the warm flames. The burning logs crackled and cinders popped into the air, creating a light show against the white living room walls.

A vision of that beautiful girl unexpectedly drifted across the shadowy walls. "Adam. Adam. I'm here with you," he could hear her call out to him. Closing his eyes, he drifted off to sleep.

An obnoxious blast from a really loud air horn interrupted another one of Adam's fantastic dreams. The moving van had arrived. Three movers jumped down from the high cab and followed Larry inside. Adam overheard them complaining about driving that big truck down the narrow, gravel road to their home. And they weren't too crazy about the nearly freezing temperature, wrapping their arms around themselves trying to stay warm.

Larry, being the efficiency nut that he was, handed the workers printed directions to the rooms where each box and piece of furniture was to be placed.

"Look, Mr. Mason, we'll try to do our best, but that's it!" the head mover shot back, and with that, he headed out and began unpacking the truck.

Adam jumped into the truck to retrieve his precious box. There it was, in the same spot he had left it. No pee stains anywhere. He hoped that Gypsy had survived the trip. The only thing worse than explaining how a dog got up here in the truck would be explaining how a dead one landed up in there.

He ran into the backyard to open the box and let her out. He ripped open the tape, flipped open the box. Believe it or not, that dog was gone. In complete disbelief, he searched all around him, looking at the box that said, "Adam's room," and he shook his head. His heart pounded. Maybe the movers heard her whining and let her out. But the box was still taped shut.

He walked over to one of the movers and asked, "Is it possible that you opened the back of the truck during the trip?"

"Hey Joey, boy wants to know if we opened the

truck during the night."

"Nope. It gets locked with this key and stays locked until we arrive," the main guy said, pointing to his belt.

Adam's heart ticked away as his mind couldn't understand what had happened to her. This was just dreadful. As each box was opened, Adam hoped that she would surprise him and pop out like a Jack-in-the-Box.

Over the next few hours furniture from the old home filled the many rooms and slowly the place became more familiar. Amidst all the chaos, there was a feeling of tranquility, something Adam hardly expected. Perhaps it was the burning logs peacefully crackling in the fireplace last night.

"Adam, did you hear me?" his dad shouted into his ears. "I said to finish unpacking the van completely. Your room is upstairs at the very end of the hallway."

"Sure. Unpack the van. My room, end of hallway. Got it, Dad!" Adam blurted, snapping out of his daydream.

Two staircases on either side of the foyer curved upward to the hallway on the second floor. Walking up the wide stairs with some of his things, Adam felt like he was on a movie set. The view from the top landing looked out over the foyer. Through the windows above the two tall doors, he could see leafless trees everywhere.

Adam leaned into his bedroom door and was greeted with an annoying squeak from the old brass door hinges. He dropped his stuff onto the wooden floor and noticed two large windows that presented an impressive view of the snow-capped mountain outside. Adam had an eerie feeling as if it was "watching" the house, and maybe its occupants too!

Wow! This bedroom is way bigger than my old room, he thought, breathing a sigh of relief. And best of all...no more Mark. That alone was worth leaving L.A.

Adam got out his laptop, sat cross-legged on the floor in the empty room and hoped for a connection. He loved searching on-line for strange facts, and this house definitely qualified in that category. He launched his web browser and waited. Nothing!

His brain swirled with questions about this mysterious place. He decided that if he couldn't explore on-line, then instead of unpacking his stuff, he would begin exploring the house itself. Downstairs he found his mom alone in the kitchen.

The movers had brought in their old table and most of the boxes marked "kitchen." She was busy searching for things she needed for this morning's breakfast.

"Until we do some grocery shopping, you'll have to be content with cornflakes."

"That's cool, Mom," Adam said.

"So what do you think of this place?" she asked.

"It's way bigger than I thought it would be. My new room has potential. What do you think, Mom?" Adam asked.

"Like you say, it's got potential, but it's going to take a lot of work," she added.

Adam could see something was bothering her. Suddenly she blurted out, "I don't know what your father was thinking by moving everyone to this big house like he's some big shot. It's not as if the place came with servants to do all the housework. I'm not sure how I am going to manage. Look at this!" she said, rolling her finger over a cabinet shelf.

She winced when she saw a thick layer of dust come off. "I can't even unpack until I wipe down all the shelves. This place is going to take me forever to clean up," she moaned, clearly distressed.

"I'll help you," Adam said.

"That's sweet of you, but that's not the point. You know he never talks to us anymore since he started this new assignment! I mean, I'm his wife! Shouldn't he at least spend a little time with me? You know, he didn't even discuss moving here. He just bought this big house and then expects me to manage everything around here."

"You'll do a great job, Mom," Adam finally said.

"I'm glad you think that, but your father always expects perfection. Not all of us can be perfect."

Adam was thinking, Now you know how I feel around here, but he didn't say anything.

"No matter what, I've never complained. Not once. All these years I have always supported whatever he wanted. I keep hoping to find the loving man I once knew in college. But he just keeps drifting away from me," her voice trailed off as she wiped away a tear rolling down her cheek. Nothing was going to change. Both of them knew it.

"You know, Mom, I remember you saying that behind every good man is a great woman, and you're great in my book."

She looked at Adam for a moment. "I changed my mind."

"What do you mean?" Adam said, clearly confused.

"I don't want to be behind him anymore. I want to be out in front of him," she announced. "I've had enough of this 'behind a man' business."

"Either way, Dad is only successful because of you."

"Thanks, sweetie. It would be nice if your dad realized that. Maybe someday when he finds whatever he is looking for."

Adam rarely saw this side of his mom. She hardly ever talked about her feelings, and especially never with him. She usually buried them inside until she couldn't take the pressure anymore. Then she would explode and lose all self-control. She would stomp her feet and behave as if she were the victim of some terrible crime. Then she'd storm out of the room and into her bedroom, usually slamming the door behind her.

In an hour or so she would calmly emerge, her pleasant self, just as if nothing had happened. But lately her outbursts had increased, especially on the weekends when her husband was not home. Adam and Mark had learned to ignore her, knowing this was just her way of dealing with stress.

✿ ✳ ✿ ✳ ✿ ✳ ✿

Larry walked into the kitchen a few minutes later sporting an uncharacteristic smile, with Mark not far behind.

"We finally got the wireless network working. What's for breakfast for two hungry men?" Larry asked Suzie.

"Well, like I told Adam, until we get into town to do some shopping, you'll have to be happy with the cornflakes we took with us."

"Cornflakes?" both Larry and Mark moaned together.

"Well, I'm open to other suggestions," she said. "Tuna?"

"If we had left on time like I planned, we could have done some shopping before the grocery store closed," Larry retorted.

"It wouldn't have mattered," she said. "I can't even cook in this filthy place."

"Don't worry about it," Larry said with slight agitation, sitting down to eat his bowl of cornflakes. He liked eggs with cheese, complete with hash browns, orange juice and freshly brewed coffee.

The tension around the table was hard to ignore. Mark broke in, his mouth stuffed with cornflakes, "So, Dad, what are we supposed to do over our spring break?"

"Well," his dad answered, "I don't think that's going to be a problem. Let's start with the overgrown hedges out front."

"Did you see the dust on every inch of this place?" his mom complained.

"While I'm away this week I expect you boys to help your mom get this house into shape."

"What? Away this week?" Suzie interrupted. "I thought you promised me you were taking the week off so you could help get us settled!"

"Didn't I tell you? Simon rescheduled our field research trip to tomorrow morning."

"Since when is your business partner calling the shots here?"

"I'm sure I mentioned it to you," Larry said.

"I'm sure you didn't say anything about you and your partner going anywhere the day after we arrived, Larry!" she retorted. "So of course now everything is left for me to do, right?"

The boys watched the argument like a ping pong match, waiting to see who got the last volley in the game.

Larry shot back, "You know every time I've tried to plan this trip, there's always an issue. So now is the only time we can go before I start my new job, so cut me some slack. I'm still beat from that ten-hour drive and sleeping on the floor all night. And now cornflakes for breakfast. Anyway, Suzie, you'll have the boys to help you during their spring break. You know, some wives might be grateful to live in such a great place," he said, trying to sound convincing.

She glared at him for a moment before speaking. "Listen, Larry, we'll do our best around here, but it's really unfair to be so inconsiderate and ditch us when we need you the most," she added.

"See? Complain, complain. It's all I get around here!" he shouted across the table, leaping up from his chair. Larry walked towards her, pointing his finger right into her face. "Look, I have a big trip tomorrow to finish planning, and right now getting this house fixed up is your only job!"

"Stop pointing at me!" she shrieked, looking as if she was about to cry. Her voice weakened. "You know, Larry, I actually miss the old days working with you at the institute. At least I knew a little bit about what was going on in your life. Is it too much to ask when you plan to return?"

"I hope by next Monday, but it might take longer," he answered, leaving the kitchen and heading off to his new den.

Breakfast was officially over.

Suzie's eyes became angry; shaking her head she said, "Men!"

"Where's he going?" Mark asked.

"Timbuktu for all I know! Who cares?" she said.

As usual Mark jumped up and left before helping to clear the table.

Adam wasn't sure how to deal with his mom's stress, knowing that eventually she could unload it on him. He was angry with his dad for stressing her out. Adult problems confused him. It was hard to understand how his dad could be so inconsiderate. He often wondered why she had married him in the first place.

Anyway, his mom might be upset that he was leaving, but as far as Adam was concerned, good riddance!

After Adam cleared out what was left in the van, he headed upstairs and saw two moving men leaving his room. His bed, dresser, desk and a bunch of boxes marked "Adam" were all there waiting for him to sort out. He locked the door and dropped down on his sheet-less bed, leaning back against the headboard.

Sitting alone in his quiet room, he thought he heard someone talking. Looking around, Adam noticed a large air vent near the bottom of the wall directly across from him. Jumping out of bed he walked over, got on his knees and put his head against the grill. It was his dad's voice clearly echoing through the air vent.

"Listen Simon, that's the way it's got to be," Larry spoke hurriedly. There was an obvious tension in his voice. There was a pause. Adam realized his dad was talking on the phone.

"...Yeah, I'll have everything ready by tomorrow morning."

Another long pause, "... Look Simon, we already tried many times to get to Telos through the tunnels, but now we need to follow our back-up plan through the South Pole entrance...I got a great deal for the plane and leased it for the week. We'll be fine. Let's just stick to our plans."

Telos? Adam was thinking, wondering where in the world this place might be.

The silence was again broken by his dad's voice.

"Yes. That's why I'm bringing the gun...Yes, I'm sure... What has gotten into you, Simon? Just relax. Get me tomorrow at eight AM sharp. Be on time, okay? Bye."

Adam's head was spinning trying to figure out what these guys might be up to. He couldn't help worrying that they were getting themselves into some real danger. The South Pole? Why in the world would anyone go there? Adam thought. There's nothing but a ton of ice.

His dad's work frequently involved some pretty strange stuff. But this time it sounded as if he was working on his own. And what was Telos? Endless thoughts about his dad's conversation with Simon bounced around Adam's head, and yet he could not make any sense of anything.

Opening his laptop, a smile came across his face as he connected to the Internet and his search page loaded. Unsure of exactly what to research first, he decided to type in "Tellos." The search engine replied, "Do you mean Telos"? Adam quickly clicked on the link.

He found a lot of websites using the name. The first was an electronics company that might be interesting, but probably not related to his dad's trip. Looking down the search list, something caught his eye.

"Inside Mount Shasta's Sacred City of Telos." He clicked on the link, describing someone's trip to the city of Telos. Adam settled in and started reading, but before he got past the introduction, his laptop froze.

He rebooted his computer and quickly searched for "Inside Mount Shasta's Sacred City of Telos." But his computer froze again.

He was about to try one last time when he was jolted out of his thoughts. A hard knock on his door echoed across the room's high ceilings.

"Adam, did you see the box from my office marked 'Field Research'?" his dad shouted through the door.

Closing his laptop, he opened the heavy door and stepped into the hallway. "What's up, Dad?"

"Have you seen a small cardboard box labeled 'Field Research'?" His dad looked panic-stricken. "I can't find it anywhere in the house! You unpacked the van. Where did you put everything?" He glared at his son, waiting impatiently for an answer.

Adam felt trapped again since no matter what he said, he was sure to get yelled at for doing something wrong. He was pretty tired of being treated this way, but what could he say?

"I haven't seen it. Why am I responsible for your stuff?" Adam blurted out, startled to hear his own words.

His dad was taken by surprise. "Excuse me, young man? I asked you to unload the van, you ungrateful little brat!"

"I mean, I unpacked the van like you asked me to. I put everything by the front door. Did you ask Mark if he moved it? You know you have more than one son!"

"All right...forget it. I'll deal with you later."

Adam rushed back into his room and slammed the door. He resented how his dad turned the lost box into his problem. But maybe if he could find that stupid box, his dad might show him a little more respect. And if he did find the box, maybe he could get a peek inside and get some answers about Telos and the South Pole.

Chapter Seven –
The Revenge

A dam searched through most of the house for wherever a box might hide. It was the first time he really got to look around the place. But after nearly a half hour searching, even in the creepy basement, the missing box was nowhere to be found. He decided to search the front lawn thinking maybe someone might have dropped it.

No luck. That only left one place; it had to still be somewhere in their van.

He grabbed his jacket and the van's keys sitting on the small table in the foyer.

Outside, the movers were getting ready to leave on their long trip back to Los Angeles. Adam moved as quickly as he could trying not to freeze between the house and the van. His breath came out like steam into the cold mountain air.

He opened the front passenger door and began looking for the missing box. It wasn't very big; maybe it somehow got pushed under one of the seats. He started to feel around with his hands. Nothing there, or under the driver's seat. Moving to the back, he reached under the seat where Mark had been sitting. His fingers touched something.

"That must be it!" he cried, grabbing whatever

was there.

There it was! The lost box was taped shut and on the top written in large, black print "Research Project." A huge grin covered his face.

"Oh, yeah!" he said with triumph.

Stepping out of the van, he scanned the front yard to see if anyone was watching. He quietly shut the van's door and ran back to the house with box in hand. He walked into his dad's den, but he was not there. Adam ran upstairs thinking his dad might be in the master bedroom. Still no luck finding him. Walking into his room and closing the door, Adam sat on the edge of his bed holding his father's precious little package.

He looked down at the box and the van's keychain dangling around his finger, and he wondered what could possibly be inside that got his dad all crazy. Then another one of Adam's wild impulses came into his mind. Using the edge of the van's key, he ran it across the top cutting through the plastic tape and he opened the box.

His heart beat faster as he reached in, pulled out each item one by one and quickly skimmed through the contents. Inside there was a book titled "Telos," a tattered map called "Inner Earth," countless articles and information about Telos and the South and North Poles and a small plastic case. When he opened it, he saw a steel-blue automatic revolver fitted in foam with two extra ammo clips.

"What the heck!" He dreaded, thinking of his dad using this gun. Adam loved guns in video games, but the thought of actually shooting something real, well, that was completely different. He couldn't believe his dad even owned a gun, let alone might use one.

He listened for any sounds outside his room, especially for his dad. His curiosity quickly turned to fear. If his dad discovered what he had done, man, would he be in trouble. Then he had another great idea. Grabbing his camera he shot a close-up of the old map, the book about Telos and some of the papers. As he snapped away, the thought of getting caught by his dad made his heart race faster. Adam had done a lot of crazy things, but he knew this was really over the top.

After what seemed to take forever, Adam took the last picture and was anxious to start reading. He knew his dad was out there someplace still looking for the missing box. He had to get it back to him and move fast.

Rushing downstairs, he found a roll of packing tape in a kitchen drawer. It was nice to have an organized mom.

Flying back to his room, he returned the stuff into the box. Taping it shut, he did his best to make it look like it had never been opened.

This time he tip-toed downstairs, placed the van keys back on the table and walked into his dad's den. He put the box in the middle of the desk and turned around to leave just as his dad walked in.

"Hey, Dad, guess what I found?" Adam said, smiling.

"So you finally found it," his dad said, almost knocking his son over, rushing to it. "Where was it?"

"Someone shoved that box under Mark's seat. I know I didn't put it there," Adam said.

"I thought I told you to clean out the van completely!"

"Ah—" Adam's smile disappeared.

"You didn't, did you?" his dad ranted. "It was a simple request! Didn't you hear me? Why don't you ever listen to me? You never pay attention. You're such a space cadet."

Adam suddenly realized his dad was right about him being a space cadet, even though he didn't want to be.

"Unbelievable! I wasted all morning looking for that box that I need for my trip tomorrow." His dad was irritated and tired; a dangerous mix.

Some parents are totally clueless how their endless criticism can get to a kid. And then they ask themselves why their kids hate them.

Adam couldn't think of anything to say. Instead he gave his dad a blank stare as a numbing feeling sank through his body.

His father grabbed the box and sat down in his

chair. He quickly ripped through the plastic tape, unaware that just a few minutes ago the box had been opened. He didn't even notice his son walk out the door, heading back to his room.

Adam resented how his dad didn't give him any appreciation for finding the box under Mark's seat. Feeling totally frustrated, he slammed and locked his door. He was tired of being treated like a useless nobody. Now it was his private war—a war between father and son. And it was kind of fun to think about, at least for the moment.

Sitting up on his bed, he turned on his laptop and downloaded the camera files, dying to see them. Excitement replaced his former dread.

Anxiously he opened the first picture, zoomed in and read a page titled "Greetings from Telos." It was an article that talked about an ancient city located beneath Mount Shasta. It was also known as the Crystal City. It stated that the people called Lemurians who live there are a peaceful and super-intelligent race who had fled to Telos to avoid extinction when the whole surface of the earth sank into the ocean. It explained about a great battle between Atlantis and Lemuria that happened many thousands of years ago.

Adam continued reading and learned how the main entrances to this incredible city were actually through very large openings at the South and North Poles.

"No way! What the heck!" Adam could barely contain himself after he finished the article. He remembered the old diary mentioning something about the South Pole. He pulled it out from his backpack and found where he had left off reading.

After flying for over two hours, I was ready to give up finding anything but ice, when I noticed a massive green mountain jutting out of the landscape. As I descended to get a closer look, it felt like my plane was being pulled downward. In contrast to the white wonderland, I saw a green landscape all around me. I panicked when I heard both engines stop. Another force then began steering my plane and it landed me next to one of those flying machines. Where in God's name am I?

Adam put the diary aside and loaded another page from his computer. He was surprised when he read that many scientists had tried to fly into the Telos entrances, but they failed or died in freak accidents. Adam scratched the back of his head when he read that Telos was some sort of space portal to other worlds.

"Space portal?" he blurted out loud.

How could his dad get involved in something this crazy, especially where people got killed? A chill ran through Adam's body and he was suddenly afraid for his dad's life.

Chapter Eight –
The Surprise

As sunset approached, a light rain beat a soft rat-a-tat-tat against Adam's bedroom window. The pitter patter suddenly turned to sheets of rain slamming in waves into the glass. A loud crash of thunder echoed through his room.

Resisting the urge to continue reading, he decided to search out another soul to ride out the storm. He ran down the stairs as if an invisible monster was right behind him. He was relieved to see his mom relaxing on the sofa in the family room next to the warm fireplace.

"What a storm, huh?" she said, seeing Adam walk into the room.

"Yeah! A perfect way to spend the night in this freaky place," he joked, sitting down next to his mom.

He stared at her while she thumbed through some silly women's magazine, sipping her herbal tea. He rarely saw her taking it easy like this. Most of the time she was busy doing one thing or another. Now the stress from the whole trip had passed, even though she was still upset her husband was leaving in the morning.

"What was that?" his mom gave an attentive

glance back and forth.

"What?" Adam asked.

"That sound. There it is again!"

A pitiful, high-pitched whimper came from the direction of the front door. Adam bolted into the foyer, knowing only one thing made that kind of noise; an animal in distress.

Turning on the porch lights and opening the front door, he felt an icy wind blow against him. A wet, shaking little brown and white dog sat there looking at Adam. The pooch scampered right inside past him, dripping water all over the floor.

Adam stared in complete disbelief and breathed a sigh of relief. Gypsy!

It was lucky they had even heard her cries in that loud storm. Adam bent down, cradled her in his arms and kicked the front door closed, heading back to the family room.

"What was—" his mom trailed off as she saw what he was holding. Adam was smiling.

"Absolutely not!" she shrieked. "You're not bringing that wet thing inside this house!"

"Mom, she's already inside," Adam protested with a whine. "It's pouring outside. I can't just throw her out into the freezing rain!"

"It might have all kinds of diseases! Just look at how filthy it is."

"But she has a collar!" Adam said.

The collar had a small golden key with the word

"Gypsy" printed on it. He tried to tell his mom this was no ordinary dog, but she wasn't going to have any part of this business.

"Adam, I already have too much to deal with around this place."

"But Mom, she obviously belongs to somebody. Can't we just keep her until tomorrow when we can try and find out who owns her?" he pleaded, putting on his warmest smile, and a long drawn out "Pleeeeeease."

"I know I'm going to be sorry, and your dad will probably kill me, but I guess it is all right just for one night. I mean, as long as you clean it up and it stays in the kitchen."

"Thanks! Oh man, this is great!" But before Adam could get to the kitchen, his dad appeared.

"What's going on?" When he saw the small, wet dog, his face turned red. "What the heck's this? A filthy rat?" His angry voice shook the room like the thunder outside.

"Larry, honey," she said calmly, "this little dog was in the rain at our front door, so we thought—"

"—that you could keep it?" Larry interrupted. "Not a chance! We are not having any animals in this house...Get it out right now!"

Gypsy seemed to know she had to do something, and quick, if she wanted to stay with Adam. She had to find a way to convince this irate man that she had already gone through a lot to get here, but all she could do was communicate through her dog talk.

At first she tried growling at Larry. But instead of intimidating him, Larry began laughing that this puny, little dog tried to scare him. Realizing she wasn't getting anywhere with this tactic, Gypsy then tried pitiful whining.

Adam tried to quiet the dog to avoid irritating his dad further.

Some strange fate had brought him and this dog together, and now she was about to be snatched away, just like that. Why couldn't his dad be gone already? He looked at his mom with his big, sad eyes. He already knew there was no way she would argue with this irrational person. His heart sank thinking about throwing Gypsy back out into the freezing rain. But to Adam's astonishment, his mom surprised him.

"Come on, Larry. Try not to be such a heartless person. The dog has a collar, so it belongs to someone. It's cold and raining outside. Let's just keep it in the kitchen until tomorrow when we'll find the owner," she said, stroking Gypsy's little head.

Mark heard the loud verbal match that was going on between his parents and came down to see what was going on.

Larry was dead set against the idea of living with any animal, but right now he had a lot more important things on his mind. Tomorrow morning he was leaving on an expedition only he could appreciate.

"Okay, okay. Just for tonight," he said, not wanting to waste any more time on a silly argument about this stupid animal. He had a lot of preparation to do before his long flight.

"Thanks, Dad. You won't be sorry. You're the best," Adam exclaimed.

"Yeah, best sucker," his dad mumbled, walking out of the room back to his den. Mark gave a "whatever" shrug.

Suzie winked at Adam. "It's your responsibility," she warned, pointing a finger.

"I know," Adam promised. "Thanks so much, Mom." His voice trailed off into the kitchen.

Adam filled the big kitchen sink with warm, soapy water and gently placed Gypsy in.

"There you go, little doggy. Doesn't that feel good?"

Gypsy was already so wet and cold she didn't resist as Adam used the sprayer handle to wash the mud and dirt off her coat. Adam tried to imagine what this little dog must have been through getting here all the way from Los Angeles.

As the last trace of dirt ran down the drain, Adam lifted her out of the sink and wrapped the wet dog in a kitchen towel like a mummy.

Once she was dry, Gypsy was really a beautiful creature, sitting on the kitchen counter. Adam examined her closely. She was mostly brown and had the cutest pink stomach and ears that stood straight up. Her white paws looked like she was wearing little white boots. Most noticeably, Gypsy had those weird eyes that seemed to randomly glow.

Adam knew she must be hungry, but there wasn't much to eat except for a little leftover tuna sandwich in the cooler box from their trip. He couldn't help smiling as the dog gobbled it down in a second and looked at Adam in obvious appreciation. He dreaded the thought of giving away Gypsy now that she was in his house.

Back in his room, Adam began to yawn as the exhaustion of the day finally got the better of him. Gypsy curled up next to him on his bed, and they both fell asleep.

It wasn't long before Adam's sleep turned into a nightmare. He saw a frightening picture of his father waving a gun and screaming at Adam to mind his own business.

Then his dad's voice was replaced by a soft voice that called out to Adam, "Tell your father great danger awaits him if he disturbs our peace in Telos."

Adam awoke in a panic. What an awful dream, he thought. His heart pounded with fear and his forehead was covered in sweat beads. Still lying next to him, Gypsy helped calm his nerves. She cuddled closer to Adam's face, licking his cheek as he drifted back to sleep.

Chapter Nine –
Cottage

His mom called, "Adam, Adam, wake up, sweetie," but he ignored her, pretending to be asleep. He was still thinking about the dream and wanted to stay in bed.

"Adam!" Her voice was a little louder. "Dad's leaving. You need to say good-bye."

"Dad's leaving?" he asked in a surprised tone. His eyes popped open. "Now?"

"Yes. Now hurry!" she said anxiously and headed out the door.

Adam sat up a little dazed as Gypsy's cute face came into focus. He patted Gypsy on her head as she yawned, stood and gave a yoga-like stretch.

Adam couldn't believe that his dad was heading off to Telos, especially after reading the stories. Telos, wherever it might be, seemed to be a dangerous destination. As much as Adam didn't want him to go on this trip, he knew there was nothing he could say to change his mind. If he mentioned anything to his dad, he would be in the uncomfortable position of explaining how he even knew about it.

Heading downstairs still dressed in his pajamas, Adam smiled as the little dog ran playfully between his legs. At this moment, Gypsy seemed to be the only living thing in the house that was happy. Halfway downstairs he could see three large aluminum suitcases by the front door. Mark squatted on the bottom steps staring at them like a watchdog.

Larry had just finished his breakfast when Adam walked into the kitchen. He could feel his mom's resentment practically oozing through the air.

"Wow," Adam said. "That's a lot of stuff you're taking. How long are you going for?"

"That's what I keep asking him," his mom quipped.

"Look, dear. I'm really sorry for leaving you like this."

"It's just not right, Larry. We really need your help organizing this place."

"I'm sorry, but this is the way it has to be." Larry couldn't deal with any more disapproval, so he looked at the floor, avoiding eye contact with anyone.

Suzie shook her head in disappointment and crossed her arms.

He took one last sip of coffee and checked his watch. "Simon's ten minutes late," he complained, glancing out the window and shooting a dirty look at Gypsy. In response, she growled at him.

Mark said, "Wish I could go with you." His face was hopeful.

"Sorry, son, but you know better," he said, heading to the front door.

"Don't take it personally, Mark. I'm not invited either," his mom said sarcastically.

Larry really felt guilty leaving, but he had no choice. It was now or never. Every minute was painfully long. Where in the world was Simon? he thought, as he pushed the heavy suitcases out the door and onto the porch.

"Adam, I want you to listen to your mom and Mark, and no funny business. Do you understand?"

How do you answer that? Adam thought, walking outside with Gypsy.

There was a long silence that was interrupted by a welcoming honk coming from the driveway.

Adam was behind Simon's car when he overheard him talking on his phone. The door was open and Simon had one leg hanging out, preparing to exit.

"I'm picking him up now. He doesn't know yet. Larry is a sucker for this stuff. Don't worry. Trust me, I'll—" Simon said smoothly. He suddenly turned his head and noticed Adam standing there, looking at him worried. "Let me call you back."

"What were you just saying about my dad?" Adam asked sternly.

"I wasn't talking about him."

Adam knew he was lying, and Simon could tell. He slammed his car door and nervously inhaled a drag of his cigarette. Simon walked over to Adam and aggressivly smashed the butt into the dirt with the tip of his boot. He arrogantly blew the puff of smoke off to one side.

"Listen, kid. Mind your own business. This has nothing to do with you," Simon said in an angry whisper as he went past Adam toward the house.

Adam ran back inside, thinking he should tell his dad to watch his back since Simon was planning on being a backstabbing, no-good slime ball, as far as he could tell.

"Simon's here," Larry announced excitedly, walking past Adam down the steps.

"Couldn't help being late, Larry. I missed your turnoff and got lost," Simon said in an annoyed tone.

"The street is a bit hard to see. At least you're here now. Everything ready?" Larry asked.

"Yep. You sure have a nice place," Simon said, buttering Larry up and looking around the property.

"Thanks," Larry said, putting the suitcases into the trunk of Simon's car. He walked back up the steps and grabbed his carry-on bag. "Good-bye boys," he said and shook both of his sons' hands, smiling. He turned to Suzie and saw her cold stare. For some reason he felt compelled to give her a hug, even though he knew the act would not be returned.

While Suzie avoided his attempt to hug her, Larry still managed a quick peck on her cheek. As he walked away, Adam couldn't help but notice how ticked off she looked.

"Honey, take care of the farm." It was the

best he could think of at the moment, trying to be lighthearted.

"Please call us," she replied back. Everyone followed Larry to the car.

Getting in, he rolled down the window and looked at Adam, "Make sure that the dog is gone when I get back."

With those parting words, Simon and Larry sped away under the arched gates, and in a moment they were off.

For the first time since arriving, Adam had no idea what he wanted to do next. He followed his mom into the living room, and he watched her sink into the sofa, kicking off her shoes.

"I expect you to start looking for the dog's owner today," his mom reminded him.

Gypsy barked as if to say she didn't approve.

They both laughed.

"Sure, Mom," Adam promised, and at the same time he tried to think of a plan that would make it possible for the dog to stay.

The rest of the day it poured with rain.

Adam and Mark helped wipe down the counters and flat spaces that had accumulated quite a thick layer of dust over the years, while Suzie unpacked as much as she could. She made pretty good progress, as a pile of empty boxes accumulated on the side of their house.

❁ ✳ ❁ ✳ ❁ ✳ ❁

The next morning the rain cleared and the sun beamed brightly, peeking behind some scattered clouds.

Just after breakfast, Gypsy sniffed and romped around every inch and crevice of the house until she found a worn-out tennis ball in one of the boxes. She wanted to tell Adam she needed to play, so she began tearing through the house, nearly tripping his mom a few times. Adam worried that she would regret letting the hyper dog stay. He decided to take Gypsy outside.

Adam grabbed his coat, opened the door and motioned for the dog to follow.

"Come here, Gypsy. Let's go!"

He threw the ball to the edge of the driveway. As if on cue, Gypsy tore across the property and retrieved the ball with incredible speed, ready to repeat this fun activity.

Throwing it again even farther and standing there waiting for Gypsy to return, Adam was startled when Mark tapped him on the shoulder from behind and said, "Hey!"

"What?" Adam asked, surprised to see Mark.

"Well, I was thinking of having a look around the property and thought you might want to come along."

Adam was shocked. This wasn't the Mark he

knew. His brother never did anything with him. Mark must be bored without his old friends from school. That was it.

Being alone was normal for Adam, but Mark wasn't used to it. Now he didn't know what to do with himself.

"Sure," Adam said. "Where do you want to go first?"

They explored the entire front yard. Hidden in the overgrown grass was an assortment of odds and ends that only boys could appreciate. For over an hour they acted like close brothers who had always been best friends.

The sunshine lit up their faces as they wrestled on the grass and joked around with each other. Gypsy jumped into their game and little by little won over Mark. She was now officially a part of their new pact.

After coming in for a brief snack and unloading onto the kitchen table all sorts of strange rocks and weird stuff they had found, they headed out again to conquer the backyard. It wasn't long before they came across a small cottage near the lake that was partially hidden by trees.

"Awesome!" Mark exclaimed. He took a few steps toward it and glanced over his shoulder at Adam. "Are you coming?"

"Yeah," Adam said hurriedly, looking down to avoid tripping on Gypsy. The dog was running closely around his legs, jumping with delight.

Next to the front door, the old cottage only had one small, round window covered in sticky cobwebs, making it hard for the boys to see in. Even after they wiped off the dirty glass, the dust on the inside of the window prevented a clear view.

Mark cupped his hands around his eyes and peered into the desolate room. "It looks like one big space."

"It would be perfect for a clubhouse," Adam said, struggling to see in.

"Except you don't have any friends to be in your club," Mark teased and swiped at Adam's head.

"We have three already." Adam gestured to himself, his brother and Gypsy. "That's all we need to get started."

"Nah," Mark laughed. "The rat doesn't count. She's leaving, remember?"

Gypsy growled in protest.

Adam frowned, remembering that she had to leave soon. He didn't want to think about that. He had already bonded with Gypsy, and that was that.

"I'm sure you'll meet some kids in school who will love this place," Mark said, trying not to ruin their good time.

"Let's see if we can get in," Adam suggested.

Gypsy began scratching to the right of the cottage door, whining for their attention.

Pushing and kicking on the door didn't work. It

was locked and the window was bolted shut. They decided maybe they could use some tools to pry their way in.

Adam quickly raced to the house, scrounged around and ran back to the cottage with a screwdriver and a hammer. Mark, being good with his hands, tried to use the screwdriver to unlock the door. The lock made clicking sounds. The knob turned, but the door still wouldn't budge.

"I think it's sealed shut," Mark said.

They tried to smash the window with the hammer, but surprisingly, it didn't even crack.

Mark finally gave up. "I'm going back to the house."

"What about our clubhouse?" Adam said. He wasn't ready to quit yet. Gypsy kept scratching at the cottage, whining and barking as if she was trying to tell them something about this mysterious place.

"Whatever," Mark said. "You can stay if you want. I'm outta here."

Chapter Ten –
The Carpet

Adam's determination to get inside quickly turned into an obsession. It was like the cottage was calling, inviting him to come in. He turned the knob.

It felt unlocked, but the door would not move. Something must be stopping it from opening, but what? He pounded and kicked on the door a few more times. He pushed even harder with his shoulder. It would not budge. With all the power he could muster, Adam gave one final kick, but the door still wouldn't open.

Gypsy barked and scratched with her front paws at a small panel next to the door a couple of feet from the ground.

That's strange, Adam thought.

He hadn't observed it before. He opened the little panel's door and in the middle he saw what looked like a small glass window. Adam was surprised when Gypsy stood on her hind legs in front of the panel and a beam of light from her eyes flashed on the glass window. A moment later, to Adam's amazement, the door cracked open!

His eyes widened, giving out a big "Yes! How did you do that?"

Gypsy barked with excitement and without any hesitation slipped through the opening, her tail wagging wildly.

Adam pushed the door open a bit more and peeked inside. A moldy smell permeated the dimly lit cottage. All the windows were boarded shut and the only source of light came from that small, oval window. When he pushed the door completely open and stepped inside, the floorboards beneath his feet creaked.

Squinting his eyes to scan around, he saw one big room filled with a zillion dust particles floating slowly around. It looked as if no one had been inside this place for ages.

He was disappointed that the room was totally empty, except for the dust. Gypsy began barking. Turning around, Adam spotted an odd-looking, black walking stick leaning against the wall by the door. Lying next to it on the floor was a small wooden box that resembled a miniature version of the treasure chest from his dreams. Adam's heart began to race with a new sense of adventure.

He walked over to the stick, picked it up and saw on the side engraved in gold letters "Throw me on the floor. Move aside. Wait for more."

That's odd, he thought.

Adam did as it directed. He threw the stick on the floor and stepped aside. It began shaking and spinning. Startled, Adam grabbed Gypsy and stepped back, wanting to get out of the way of whatever was going to happen.

The stick began to get longer until it grew to twice its size. Then a stranger thing happened. What looked like a carpet slowly rolled out from the stick until it reached about six feet long. The small box hopped into the middle.

"You've got to be kidding me!" Adam cried, stunned.

He stepped onto the carpet to reach for the box when a radiant sparkle flashed under his feet. He glanced around and realized that his footsteps were leaving imprints on the carpet that lit up and then slowly faded after a moment.

What is that? he thought.

Tiny semi-precious crystals of different colors lined the entire carpet's border. Turquoise and ruby red squares blended into its beige background.

Adam's face beamed, now turning his attention to the wooden box, hoping to find a treasure inside, just like in his dreams. He sat down Indian style and tried to open it. To his immense disappointment, the box was locked. Of course, right? He wondered where in the world the key could be? This was indeed another mystery that needed to be solved. He couldn't wait to tell his mom and Mark.

Grabbing Gypsy, he headed out the door. Adam raced back to the house, finding his mom in the living room absorbed in unpacking boxes.

"Mom, you gotta see this! You won't believe what I found in the little cottage down by the lake. Come see it!"

"A cottage by the lake?" she stated, barely paying attention to him. She envisioned something else to clean.

"Yeah, by the lake, Mom."

"Oh, not now, sweetie. I'm busy. I'll come as soon as I'm done here."

"You gotta come now. It must be magic!" Adam could not contain himself. He jumped and waved his arms so that his mother had no choice but to pay attention.

Moved by his persistence, she reluctantly agreed to go see what had gotten her son so excited. The disorganization in the house was killing her, but a little break might be just what she needed.

Adam led his mom down to the old cottage. When she stepped inside and saw the carpet, her face lit up.

"Wow, I bet it's really expensive. Who would store it in this disgusting place?" she said. "It will be gorgeous once it's cleaned," she continued and crouched down to inspect the masterpiece with admiration.

"Called it! I want it for my room," Adam said excitedly.

"We'll have to get this professionally cleaned before we move it anywhere near the house. I didn't even know this cottage was here. Did Dad mention anything about it?"

"Nope." Adam took several steps onto the carpet. "Look how it glows when I walk on it!" he said, barely containing himself.

Gypsy walked to the edge, sniffing every corner and then plopped herself down right in the middle. A glow of light surrounded her.

"That's just incredible," his mom said. "It's truly magnificent. Where's that light coming from?"

"Beats me," Adam said. He didn't want to mention anything about the stick trick, or else she'd freak out and not let him bring it in to his room.

"Maybe it's static electricity," she said. "Anyway, come on. Let's get some lunch and I'll call the carpet cleaners." She put her arm around Adam and together they walked back to the house. Gypsy followed closely behind, checking out a few bushes along the way.

His mom called a carpet cleaner and also contacted the local dog pound. If someone were missing their pet, they would be the first to know. Adam spent the rest of the afternoon with Gypsy on his bed in his cluttered room. Boxes were randomly placed in different areas. He was quite proud of his new room, despite the chaos and plain, white walls that were just a bit too dull for him. The brightly colored carpet would definitely liven up the bedroom. He couldn't wait to move it in.

His room had a big, walk-in closet and bathroom, which made him feel special. Back in their old house he had to share a bathroom with Mark and that caused many of their fights. Mark was quite tidy and Adam couldn't care less where his clothes fell once they left his body. Toothpaste would somehow get smeared all over the bathroom and Mark's toothbrush and things were often missing in action. Adam just couldn't understand why Mark got so upset over such insignificant things. Thankfully, that was all in the past.

He rested on his bed, looking at the ceiling. A small shelf ran all the way around near the top on the wall. It was a perfect place for him to put some of the new rocks he had collected today. He daydreamed about opening the treasure chest and flying away on the carpet to Telos.

In Beverly Hills, hardly anything fun ever happened. Here, so much was going on already, and it was only the second day since they moved. Adam suspected there was more to come.

He impulsively wanted to call his dad just to tell him about the cottage by the lake and to warn him about Simon. He dialed his number. Disappointment replaced his excitement when it rang twice and went straight to voice mail. "Oh, never mind," he said, dropping his cell phone on his bed.

❊ ✳ ❊ ✳ ❊ ✳ ❊

Adam simply couldn't wait until the carpet cleaners got there. He had a great idea. After dinner he decided to return to the cottage to shake off any dust that might be on the carpet before bringing it into his room. Besides, how dirty could this thing be since it actually popped out of a stick?

He snuck out the back door with Gypsy close by. The sun had disappeared into a beautiful, pink sky.

Inside the cottage, he tried to pull the carpet, but it was heavier than he had realized. Struggling, he managed to drag it outside and tried to shake it until it was clean enough to bring into the house.

Returning to the cottage to get the wooden box, he observed a small door that was built into the floor that had been hidden under the carpet. Pulling hard, he tried to open it, but of course, it was locked solid.

Where does the door go? he thought.

Adam grabbed the box and placed it in the middle of the carpet. Dragging the carpet while walking backwards, he tried not to trip on Gypsy who was right under his feet. He struggled to drag it across the yard, into the back door and up a stairway, leading next to his room. His mother would have surely killed him had she seen the mess it made as it left a trail of mud behind.

Once in his room, Adam stuffed the carpet into his walk-in closet and put the box on his bed. Gypsy barked a few times and began tugging at the carpet, uselessly attempting to pull it from the closet. She obviously wanted the carpet spread out on the floor. There wasn't enough room for the entire carpet to be laid out flat because of the boxes, so Adam moved some of them out of the way. Gypsy jumped on the bed and sat next to the chest, resting her chin on it.

It had been a strange day.

That night, Gypsy slept on the carpet. Adam collapsed onto his bed with a long exhale. He was sure the carpet would haunt his mind and prevent him from falling asleep, but he was wrong. Within a moment, he was out like a light.

Adam had a vivid dream that played out all the events surrounding Gypsy's arrival on that rainy day. In his mind he heard the pounding rainfall and crashing thunder echoing around his house. He saw himself getting Gypsy and wrapping her in a towel. He showed his mom the collar. Immediately, his dream zoomed in and focused on the small golden key attached to Gypsy's collar.

Adam awoke, sitting straight up in bed with a bolt of excitement screaming, "Yes, that's it!" He bounced like a kangaroo out of bed and rushed to Gypsy's side. Examining the key on the collar, he quickly unhooked the key and brought it to the wooden box.

"This can't be. Too weird!" he exclaimed. "If this key fits that lock, something very strange is going on here."

He held his breath, inserted the key into the lock and turned it to the right. Click. It popped open. Adam's chest swelled and a rush ran through his body. Eagerly, he peeked inside. The box contained a quartz crystal wand, about five inches long. He also saw inside a small, blue box and several rolled parchment papers.

Adam got the crystal wand and examined it. A warm energy radiated into his hand, moving through his arm and then spreading throughout his body. He sensed a strange tickle in his head. His eyes slowly shut and he felt as if he were floating. Without moving an inch, he sat for a while almost in a trance, relishing this supernatural experience.

Knock, Knock, Knock.

Adam opened his eyes, feeling hypnotized and lightheaded. He jumped out of bed and threw his blanket over the carpet in an attempt to hide it. He partially opened the door and popped his head out, finding his mom standing there.

"Goodnight, Adam. I'm going to bed. Sweet dreams."

"You too," he said, quickly shutting the door and locking it.

Little did he realize that this would be the last time he would see her for quite some time.

Gently placing the crystal into the box, he unrolled the yellow-aged parchment. It snapped closed. Again, he patiently unrolled it. The first few pages were written in a strange language he couldn't read. Flipping through them, he was relieved to find the last one handwritten in English.

He narrowed his eyes and slowly began to read, pulling Gypsy close to him.

This mystical carpet is part of an old legend. The stories have been told for countless generations about its real nature, and now it is in your possession. Treat it with care.

Adam's heart beat faster.

Unbelievable. So many strange events, Adam thought. Gypsy mysteriously arrives at my front door and happens to have the key to a chest.

He reasoned with himself. Not likely. And what about moving into a house with all these things? Impossible. Trying to control his excitement, Adam read on intently.

The carpet does not run on magic. The creators used quantum technology and gravitational force to lift and maneuver it. The race that made this carpet was highly intelligent, even more than the scientists of your modern day. This civilization disappeared, never to be seen again, leaving only a few carpets behind. The fight for ownership was bloody, and the very people who wished to possess them destroyed most of them. This carpet is relatively new. It was made only two centuries ago by the people of Telos, who live inside the earth.

Isn't there hot lava inside of the earth? Adam thought.

Each carpet works differently. The one in your possession is programmed to travel to nine space portals. Telos is one of them. The other eight locations are entrances into other ancient cities.

To activate the carpet, you must place the pointed end of the Lemurian Seed Crystal on the carpet in the direction you wish to go. Remove the Telos watch from the blue box and place it on your left wrist. Simply press the green button on the side of the watch to activate the carpet.

"What? A Telos watch!" He grabbed the blue box and opened it.

Empty!

"This definitely is no coincidence." He stood and took the Telos watch out of his pocket and stared at it in disbelief. It had to be the same watch that he had gotten from Nicky as a gift.

How did Nicky know about this? Adam wondered and rushed to read on.

When the carpet is activated, make sure you

are seated in the center. Each colored patch on the carpet can become a handle when pulled out. While seated, state your destination out loud clearly three times. The carpet should levitate immediately. After that, it steers itself and travels at incredible speed.

Everything kept getting more amazing. What was next? Now there was no doubt in his mind that all this was very real, and he desperately wanted to prove that it was.

Chapter 11 –
Trip to Never-Never Land

Adam was dying to see if the carpet worked, but he was chicken to try it alone. It was almost midnight and his brother was usually awake until late. Adam knocked softly on Mark's door and peeked in.

"Yeah?" his brother said, looking over his laptop as Adam stepped in. "What do you want this late? Milk and cookies?"

"I need you to come to my room for a minute," Adam replied, sounding as serious as he could, not wanting him to think this was just one of his late-night stories.

"What for?" Mark clearly didn't want to be bothered.

"There's something important you gotta see," Adam said impatiently. "You're not going to believe this."

"Show me tomorrow," Mark said and returned his eyes to the screen.

"No!" Adam shouted. "You need to come now."

Mark sighed irritably, but put his laptop aside and stood up. "This better be good."

"Oh, it will be," Adam assured him and led Mark

back to his room.

Mark shook his head looking at everything in disarray on Adam's floor. "What is all this mess?"

"That's not important," Adam said. "I have something to show you, but I need to start from the beginning."

"Stop stalling and just tell me," Mark snapped.

"Okay. So yesterday I overheard Dad talking on the phone with Simon ..."

Adam told Mark about their dad's plan to go to Telos, about finding the box in the van, and what he discovered inside. When he began to explain where Telos was, Mark tried to interrupt, but Adam shushed him.

He told him how Gypsy was the same dog from the pet shop and how the key on Gypsy's collar opened the chest. Nothing was left out, not even Nicky's gift of the Telos watch and the directions on the parchment explaining how to use the fantastic carpet. He even mentioned the stick trick. When Adam finished his strange story, Mark had a wide grin on his face.

"What's so funny?" Adam asked. "Don't you see what's going on? Somehow I'm involved in some weird plan that has to do with this place called Telos."

Adam's excitement turned to disappointment when he saw Mark's mocking expression. He was sure his brother would definitely find this interesting, at least as good as some of the UFO stories they had exchanged.

"I don't believe any of this. You don't really buy into this garbage, do you?" Mark asked, pulling the parchment out of Adam's hand.

"It fits like a puzzle. I just don't have all the pieces," Adam argued.

Mark glanced down at the parchment. "I might be willing to believe Dad took a trip to find this Telos place. It sounds like something he would do, but the wild carpet thing? I can't believe you're taking that seriously."

"Here, read this."

Adam showed him the Telos article on his laptop, hoping this might change his brother's mind. "It can't be just a coincidence," Adam insisted.

Mark read through some of the articles and then looked at Adam. "So, I'm guessing you want to fly off to Telos on this carpet."

"Well," Adam said, "I was kinda hoping you'd try it with me."

"Me?" Mark laughed. "I'm not making a fool of myself, but if you want, I'll watch you."

Adam finally resigned himself to the fact his brother would not be a part of his adventure. "I'm trying it," Adam announced, shrugging off his fears. He glanced over to Gypsy for approval, her tail wagging in apparent agreement. "Plus, I have to warn Dad."

"Why?" Mark asked skeptically.

"Because Dad took a gun with him. If they see he's armed, they might kill him. I gotta at least try and change Dad's mind about exposing their hidden city to the world. That's just wrong. Plus, Simon's going to try to screw him when they get to wherever they are going."

"How do you know?"

"I know these things," Adam said.

"Dad's a big boy. You worry too much." Mark sat down on Adam's bed. "Ten bucks says the carpet won't work."

"Ten bucks says it will. Deal," Adam agreed.

"Go ahead. I'm watching."

"Not here," whispered Adam. "We have to go back to the cottage."

"What for? Can't you embarrass yourself here?" Mark asked sarcastically. "Does it have to be in a filthy room in the middle of the night where all sorts of big spiders and flying bugs are hiding out?"

"You don't have to come," Adam said, trying to sound convincing. "I just thought you'd want to."

Mark sensed his brother's resolve and courage.

"Okay. I wouldn't miss this for anything," Mark said, with a new sense of adventure. "After all, it's not every day that I get to watch my little brother go nuts and try to fly off to never-never land."

It took them a few minutes to put their coats on and get everything down to the cottage. Adam was happy to have Mark around, even if he was only there to ridicule him. It was better than being alone with only a Yorkshire terrier as a guard dog.

Once everything was in the cottage, Mark leaned against a wall and shined the flashlight toward Adam.

"Are you going to do this hocus pocus stuff or not?" Mark asked with a grin.

He handed Mark the crystal rod. "Here. Hold this." Adam paused a moment, then asked, "Do you feel anything?"

"What? Are you nuts? What in the world are you talking about?"

"Just wait. I felt this amazing energy coming from it before. You don't feel anything?"

"No!" Mark laughed. "Come on. What's happened to you?"

Ignoring Mark's concerns, Adam snatched the crystal out of Mark's hand and placed it on the carpet. He figured that if his dad were going to Telos through the South Pole, he should point the crystal south.

When everything was in place, he removed his coat, put on the Telos watch, sat down in the center of the carpet and put Gypsy between his legs.

Mark curiously tilted his head, walking closer to Adam. "You don't want to know how stupid you look."

"Quiet!" Adam shouted, trying to push Mark's teasing out of his mind. He pressed the green button on the watch and was startled as two handles emerged on each side of the carpet. The large crystal started to glow, pulsating on and off. Gypsy's ears went up.

"Telos," clearly and distinctively Adam commanded. "Telos, Telos."

Tiny crystals bordering the carpet turned on like little lights, while Adam and the rug rose a few feet in the air.

"Holy %@!!" Mark used a word that would get him grounded if his mom had heard him use that language, but he didn't care. His jaw dropped in utter disbelief, staring at Adam sitting on the floating carpet.

Mark cursed again. "Adam," he begged, "get off!" He sounded worried.

Gypsy curled up into a ball in Adam's lap so only her nose poked out. After Mark's warning, Adam wanted to jump off the carpet, but he was terrified and couldn't move. He closed his eyes tightly.

Mark screamed as the hidden door under the carpet opened, revealing a bottomless, dark hole.

"Adam! Adam, get off now!"

But he couldn't hear him because the sound of

loud, whirling winds came from the hole. It was like being in a hurricane. And even if Adam could have heard him, he couldn't move. Fear had frozen him.

Adam, Gypsy and the carpet sped downward into the hole followed by a swirl of color. The door in the floor slammed shut behind them.

Then silence.

Mark stared at the floor, mouth agape and eyes unbelieving. Adam, the dog and the carpet were gone. Mark bent down to touch the floor. It was hot.

He cursed for the third time from pure shock, "Holy %@!!"

Adam saw nothing but white light engulf himself, and he felt his body trailing a few feet behind. He passed out from sheer overload to his system, traveling at incredible speed of light downward toward Telos.

Chapter 12 –
The Flight to Telos

We should see something soon," Larry shouted over the plane's loud jet engines, glancing across to his partner sitting next to him.

Adjusting his binoculars, Simon nodded. "I still can't see anything but ice," he moaned. "Are you sure we're in the right area?"

"According to the aircraft's GPS compass, we should be right over the South Pole's entrance," Larry assured him. "Keep looking."

After hours of searching, their nerves were frazzled and their bodies stiff and cold. But there was no way they could turn back now. They were determined to carry on since the moment they had been waiting for so long might be just ahead.

The two men had driven to Redding Airport near Mount Shasta and taken a commercial flight to Los Angeles. Simon had begun keeping a log of their journey when they had arrived in Los Angeles on the first leg of their trip.

Day 1: Los Angeles to Punta Arenas, Chile. Our long 14-hour first-class flight gave us a chance to go over our plans one last time. We finally arrived in

Punta Arenas where we spent the night in a hotel and double checked our equipment and supplies for the final leg of our journey.

Day 2: Punta Arenas to Base Camp. In the morning, Larry flew our leased twin-engine aircraft to base camp 600 miles from the South Pole. The six-hour journey to the Antarctic interior crossed endless stretches of windswept snow before arriving that night at base camp at the foot of the Ellsworth Mountains.

Day 3: Base Camp to South Pole. In the morning we made one final check to make sure nothing had been forgotten and readied for departure. At 66 degrees latitude we crossed the Antarctic Circle where the sun rises and sets only once a year.

Continuing south we saw icebergs, some the size of a small country. We landed on a runway of blue ice over 3,000 feet above sea level. We arrived at our Antarctica base camp where we settled down to a welcoming meal.

Day 4: The South Pole. In the morning, we refueled and made a final weather check. We taxied off the blue ice on the six-hour flight headed as far south in the world as possible. At the half-way point between base camp and the Polar ice cap, we made one final stop to refuel at Thiel Mountains.

After three hours flying we neared the final leg of our flight south, catching sight of the American research base. A century ago this trip took years, but today only six hours later we found ourselves nearing the South Pole. We became a part of a select group of people who could journey this far south on our planet. We congratulated ourselves for making it this far!

"I see something over there!" Simon cried excitedly, pointing to a distant black spot. "Can you take her any lower?"

"I'll try." Larry pushed the plane into a gentle dive.

At 2,500 feet everything was stable at first, but as they dropped lower, the instruments in the plane began going haywire, then just stopped working altogether.

"We must be close," Larry said, biting his lower lip. "Better get the Magna Force ready and pray it works."

Simon put down his binoculars and fumbled to attach a round metal disk to what looked like a shiny rifle stock with a trigger and a long cable that attached to a battery pack. They had built it together and crossed their fingers it would penetrate the energy field that prevented anything from flying into the area.

"That's it," Simon shouted. "Look there."

"Hey, now I see it directly ahead," Larry said, taking a deep breath. "Looks like the energy dome we had expected. Must be at least a mile high."

Both their hands were sweaty, despite the cold temperatures. An unexpected adrenalin rush hit both men at the same time; success was close at hand, finally!

As they approached their target ahead, Simon took aim and fired the Magna Force. A blue beam passed right through the cockpit window, hitting one side of the energy dome. He tightened his grip on the device as the plane started shaking, while trying to keep it pointed toward the window. The beam instantly created a circular opening just big enough for their plane to pass through.

"Well, here goes nothing," Larry screamed. Entering the hole, the two men felt as if they were being sucked through a huge vacuum.

"It worked! We're through!" shouted Simon, slapping Larry a high-five.

Their heads stretched against the cockpit windows like turtles, trying to get a better look at whatever might be below.

Instead of the white scenery they had watched for hours, a green hilly terrain now greeted them. A waterfall cascaded down a tall mountain, crashing into a river of blue, shimmery water.

Larry grabbed the binoculars with one hand while trying to control the plane with the other.

"Wow! Take some video, fast," Larry said with a tense voice, trying to get his composure.

Simon grabbed his camcorder, but before he

could do anything, their plane flew into a large black cloud.

Splat! Splat! Splat!

Black goo covered every inch of the plane's windows, making it impossible to see anything.

"Quick! Get the Magna Force!" Larry snapped as his body arched in fear. "I don't know what that black stuff is, but I'm not sticking round to find out. Let's get outta here!"

Simon stared at Larry.

"What about Telos?" Simon said stubbornly. He had come a long way and wasn't ready to give in so quickly.

"You idiot!" Larry screamed. "We won't find Telos if we're dead! I can't see anything. We got to get out of here."

Making a sharp turn back, the plane shook from side to side. Simon fired the Magna Force again. A moment later they were on the outside of the energy dome, leaving behind the black cloud.

Larry struggled to see through the black patches on the window.

"What the heck was that?" Simon said, wiping his forehead.

"I don't know," Larry said, noticeably shaken from the ordeal as he throttled back the engines and relaxed his grip on the wheel. "Once we land we can examine whatever that stuff was. We'll try again tomorrow. At least we know that the Magna Force works."

"Did you get any video footage?" Larry eagerly asked.

Simon shook his head from side to side. "No! I don't believe this. Probably the greatest find in the world, and we don't have even one pathetic shot."

"Damn it!" Larry banged his fist on the seat and winced.

"We didn't get any proof," Simon said, agitated.

"We'll get some tomorrow. Don't worry," Larry said encouragingly, trying to keep their spirits high. "At least now we know the place really exists."

"True," Simon agreed. "I was pretty sure all along, but it's still hard to believe we actually found it."

❀ ✳ ❀ ✳ ❀ ✳ ❀

There was no conversation. Both men were lost in their own thoughts while flying back to base camp.

Larry thought about Admiral Byrd's many failed attempts back in 1947 before finally getting through the Pole's entrance. His personal diary talked about when he had met the inhabitants of Telos, they warned him about the danger his world faced with their new-found power: the atomic bomb.

Admiral Byrd had learned from the Lemurians living in Telos that they had long ago destroyed the entire surface world using those same devastating atomic weapons.

It was hard to believe, but Larry knew that there were all kinds of crazy things he couldn't explain. His own grandfather had vanished years ago searching for the same mysterious hidden city. His disappearance in 1947 occurred while on the Antarctic mission "Operation High Jump" with Admiral Richard B. Byrd in command.

Larry and Simon had met many years back while learning to fly a twin-engine jet when they discovered they had a similar interest in finding Telos. From that moment forward, they were unofficial partners on a secret expedition only they could appreciate.

They had suspected that the Lemurians lived for hundreds of years, disease free. The two men's goal was to get a single strand of Lemurian hair containing the DNA they needed to unlock the aging code. Maybe it would explain how these beings lived so long. Then Larry and Simon would create an anti-aging serum that everyone would want, and they would be rich and famous in no time.

Throughout their years of research together they had investigated many UFO sightings and eventually realized that at least some of these actually had come from inside the earth. The Lemurians living in Telos couldn't be dangerous since any civilization that could create such advanced technology would certainly be able to destroy surface life, if they so wished.

Whoever these beings were, they had repeatedly attempted to communicate with us, but their messages had been intentionally prevented from reaching the general public.

Once they landed back at home base, Larry inspected the remains of the black crud on the plane's windows. The stuff was everywhere. It wasn't a cloud that had surrounded them. Rather, it was thousands and thousands of locusts, giant grasshoppers about three inches long.

"So that's the reason we decided to quit," Simon snickered and flicked a piece of bug off the glass.

"Well, it'll make an interesting story one day," Larry said, scraping off a few of the dead insects from the plane. He placed a few samples in a small plastic bag he would examine later. At least there would be one less surprise. Their plane was washed, refueled, and prepared for the next day's attempt.

The two men headed to their hotel.

When Larry got into his room, he fell back onto the couch, exhausted. It had been a grueling day and he just wanted to relax and get some sleep. The roar of the engines was still ringing in his ears. His mouth was parched, and both feet were frozen into his boots.

He reached for his cell phone on the table next to him.

It registered forty-three missed calls, mostly from home. Someone needed him. He didn't bother listening to any of the messages, but immediately called home. Every second the phone rang felt like an eternity. Something was clearly wrong.

"Hello?" his wife answered. Her voice sounded anxious.

"Hi, Suzie? What's going on?"

There was silence, then he heard her burst into tears. "Oh, Larry!"

"Suzie, what's wrong?" A cold sweat broke over Larry's face. "What happened?"

Suzie was overwhelmed and could barely talk. "It's Adam. He-he's gone!"

"Gone?" Larry repeated the news slowly as his brain tried to comprehend the news. "What do you mean, gone? Where did he go?"

"I'm not sure. Mark said he took off to find you!" Suzie wailed. Nothing could be understood as her sobs changed to hard gasps and nose blowing. Finally, she caught her breath. "I tried to call you all day. I don't know what's going on. Mark saw the whole thing. I'm going to call the police back. They said to call again in twenty-four hours for an update. I was waiting to talk to you first. Like he can't be in danger in less time? Something horrible could happen in five minutes. And you're gone...and

I'm all alone. I don't know what to do...ohmigod. Oohhhhh."

"Suzie!" he interrupted. "Try to control yourself." She was a mess, and right now he needed some straight answers. "Calm down. Get a grip on yourself! I'm here now."

"I'm sorry. Okay," she quivered.

"Suzie, let me talk to Mark."

"Hi, Dad." Mark was hesitant because he knew his dad would not believe what had happened. Even he didn't know what to think, and he had been right there! Should he tell the truth? Heck. What was the truth?

"Son, what happened?" his dad screamed. Someone had to have answers as to why Adam was missing.

Mark tried to slowly explain every detail, but the whole story ran out of his mouth faster than he wanted. "Adam found this old carpet in the cottage down by the lake. The carpet had written instructions that said it could take you to other places."

"Mark, what does any of this have to do with Adam's disappearance?" his dad screamed even louder. "Get to the point!"

"Well, the stupid kid went and tried it out. And well, Adam knew you were going to Telos. And, uh, he wanted to go find you...he just vanished on that carpet with that yappy dog. I was right there."

"What do you mean, just vanished?" he snapped,

apparently missing Mark's reference to Telos. He couldn't hold his frustration in any longer. "He can't just disappear!"

How could something like this happen right in the middle of his incredible Antarctic flight? This was too much to absorb for one day. Bad luck had struck twice.

Mark tried to reason with his dad and calm him down. "I watched it happen right in front of my eyes. He was sitting there in the cottage on that dirty carpet with that mutt in his lap. Next thing...he's gone, totally vanished in a blinding light. That's all I can tell you. I know it's hard to believe, Dad."

"Come on, son, you're not trying to cover for your brother with that ridiculous story, are you?" his dad demanded. "Just tell me the truth. We have to get to the bottom of this. Your brother's life may be in danger, for Pete's sake."

"Dad," Mark responded with certainty, "could I make this up?"

That somehow rang true, and Larry thought about it for a moment. He never knew Mark to make things up. And talk about crazy. Imagine how insane his own story would sound to anyone except to Simon and him. Sometimes strange things did happen in this world. Telos was proof of that. So why couldn't this carpet story be true?

"Wait a minute," Larry stopped in his tracks. "He was going to where, did you say?"

"Telos," Mark responded

"Telos?!" his dad yelled.

"Telos, yeah, that's right." Mark repeated it to make sure his dad was clear. "He said you were going there too."

"What! Ohmigod!" Larry was almost speechless. "What in the world is going on back there? I hope you didn't tell the cops about Telos."

"No, Dad. I'm not that dumb."

"Oh, good. Put your mom back on the phone." Waiting, he nervously tapped his foot.

Suzie was still crying. "Yes? she said, as she sniffled.

"Don't call the cops again!" Like a military sergeant, Larry barked out his orders, hoping his resolve would help calm her. He hated weepy females.

"Why not?" She couldn't believe he had said that.

"Don't ask me why," he said, feeling frustrated and helpless. "Just listen. We need to think this through before we do anything else. Don't tell a soul about this for now. I'll call you back soon." He felt in charge, at least for that moment.

"But Larry," she protested with a plea. Her voice dropped into a slow whine. "What if he's hurt?"

"The kid's fine. He probably just ran away and will come back home as soon as he's tired and hungry," Larry lied. "If the cops call, tell them

Adam's fine, okay? I've got to go. Bye."

Larry terminated the call and sat perfectly still in total shock. He was relieved that he had at least called Suzie before she had called the cops again. What if they had found out about his trip to Telos?

Larry shivered at the thought of how much trouble he would be in if any of this story got out to the people he worked for. To make matters worse, what about his son? Where was he?

Acting fast, he went over to Simon in the next room and told him what was going on. To his surprise, Simon was quicker to buy the story than he was.

Tomorrow they would make another attempt to enter Telos and look for Adam. There were too many unknowns to figure out a sure-fire plan. Now they were flying by the seat of their pants.

"Great, just great!" Larry's frustration with the whole ordeal was showing. "We head out on an expedition and it turns into a rescue mission...for my own son!"

Chapter 13 –
Welcome to Telos

The fantastic carpet ride ended with an abrupt halt.

Adam cautiously opened his eyes and sat up. It took a minute for things to slide into focus. Confused as to what had happened, he felt completely nauseated and dizzy. He remembered taking off on the carpet, but after that, it was all a blur.

Gypsy jumped all about, trying to nudge him out of his stupor.

Scanning his surroundings, the first thing that caught Adam's attention was baby blue waves gently cascading onto a light purple shoreline in front of him. He twisted his direction to get a better view of his surroundings. Not far behind was an assortment of trees popping out of the lush vegetation growing on a nearby hill.

Delicate butterflies fluttered a welcoming dance in front of him. The sheer beauty was overwhelming. Adam took in the land with a big breath and sighed. He wanted to lie down on the carpet and rest, but Gypsy's sharp bark dragged him into the reality that he was, in fact, utterly lost, somewhere.

Gypsy frolicked down the deserted beach, kicking

purple specks all over Adam and the carpet. At first he thought she was scared, but she wasn't. Gypsy was thrilled and happier than ever. Seeing her jump, run in circles and seeming right at home comforted Adam somewhat.

His eyes darted across the coastline that stretched endlessly in both directions in search of anyone who might be there.

Where in the world am I? he thought.

He knew he had to be somewhere in Telos, but how big was this place? He could be in the middle of nowhere and never find a living soul in this wonderland.

The mesmerizing journey on the carpet felt almost instantaneous, but the time on his watch said it was just after twelve o'clock, the same time he had left Mount Shasta. Both the moon and the sun on the dial were gone, confusing him even more. The sun was shining brightly above, so he figured it must be the afternoon. He had left somewhere around midnight, and if the Telos watch was accurate, he had been traveling for twelve hours.

What? That's impossible, thinking that it seemed just like a few minutes.

He reached down and dug his hands into the candy-colored sand again. Just like the large crystal had done, he felt the same soothing sensation that had penetrated his body and calmed his nerves. Now feeling focused, he straightened himself up.

Hanging around and worrying wouldn't get him anywhere. He had to search for help. His concern turned to fear when he looked for Gypsy and realized that his travel companion was nowhere in sight.

"Gypsy? Gypsy, come here, girl," he called out, panic stricken. There was nothing but silence.

He whistled. There was no answer.

"Gyp...sy!" he shouted with all his might. He walked along the shoreline, but there was no Gypsy to be found.

How could he have been so stupid to just fly off into la-la-land without any clue where to go when he got here? But even worse, how to get back home? He was in big trouble this time, and he had no idea how to get himself out.

Why had he been so determined to meddle with his dad's stupid plans? Why did he have to find this strange carpet to bring him to this place stranded, alone and maybe to die? He was really angry with himself. There was no one else to blame. Not Mark, not his mom and not his dad.

He walked back to the carpet and sat down, crossing his arms over his knees and burying his face between them. He couldn't think of anything else to do.

He was overwhelmed with exhaustion and just needed to sleep. He thought taking a little nap would be helpful before continuing on with his adventure. He hoped that while he was resting, Gypsy would return. At least with Gypsy by his side, he felt a little safer. Now she was gone and he wanted to cry, but he was even too tired for that.

Chapter 14 –
A New Friend

A voice called from behind. "Hi, Adam. Don't be alarmed."

"What the—" Adam jumped up and stumbled on the carpet, seeing a tall man in a long white robe standing before him. Silvery white hair fell to his shoulders and he had light honey-colored eyes. Strangely enough, his presence was comforting to Adam.

"I think that you are looking for something," the man said solemnly with confidence. Adam felt he was in the company of some great leader. As the man lifted one of his arms, Adam spotted Gypsy snuggled inside his white robe.

"Gypsy!" Adam shouted with relief. The tiny dog sprung out of the man's arms and ran to Adam. He scooped her up and looked at the man's beaming face before him.

"Welcome to Telos, Adam. I'm Charlie," the man said, opening his arms in a welcoming gesture.

"How do you know my name?" Adam said in amazement and widened his eyes. "And is this really Telos?"

"Yes," Charlie replied.

"I can't believe it. I just can't believe it. Then

how did I get down here? Why—"

Holding up his hand, Charlie gestured for Adam to stop talking. "I'm sure you have many questions." His voice became deeper. "I have been sent to assist you while you are here."

Adam opened his mouth to ask another question, but he was once again silenced.

"Yes, this is Telos. Why are you so surprised? Isn't that where you asked the carpet to bring you?"

Adam looked completely stunned. "I didn't think it really worked."

"Yes, obviously the carpet does work. There are few of them left, not that it matters with the more advanced technology we have today. It certainly is exciting to travel in such a fairytale manner. I enjoyed it immensely during my time in your world."

Adam listened intently.

"By the way, we know about your dad and his partner. Don't worry about them. They are fine for now, but they are fools for trying to find Telos."

Adam stared at him totally dumbfounded. He rubbed his eyes thinking he must be dreaming again. To his surprise, Charlie was still there.

Really spooky. This guy knows my thoughts.

"I know what you are thinking. It may seem like I can read your mind," Charlie said, grinning. "But I am actually reading your aura. That gives you away."

Adam stared at him blankly.

Charlie motioned with his right hand. "Follow me." It wasn't a command but rather a beckoning gesture.

There was nowhere else he could go, so why not? Before he walked off, Adam tried to get the carpet.

Charlie said, "Oh, don't worry about that." He clapped his hands three times and said, "Retract."

As the carpet rolled up into the stick with a quick whip, the crystal rod fell onto the sand. "Take that, Adam, because we will need it later."

Adam grabbed the crystal and shoved it into his back pants pocket.

"Follow me."

Adam paused a moment, uncertain as to whether he should listen or not.

"Well, aren't you coming?" There was a little more strength in this request, as Charlie began to take his next step, looking behind.

"I don't know you," Adam said warily. Then something made him more direct. "I don't know where I am or what's going on, and you haven't really answered any of my questions. Why should I trust you?" Immediately he felt embarrassed by his honest words.

"Oh, I forget. You come from a world where people don't trust each other," Charlie said kindly. "Don't worry, my son."

Peering over Adam's shoulder, Charlie smiled at another person walking towards them.

"Perfect timing." Excitement broke into his voice. "Good to see you, Nicky."

Turning around, Adam stared totally flabbergasted to see his favorite person in the world. Nicky, from the pet shop, was walking down the mountain right toward them.

"Nicky? Is that you?" Adam asked. Could this be his best friend and the person he felt the closest to down here in Telos? This has to be a dream!

"Who else?" Nicky boomed with his usual cheerfulness.

"Wait. What are you doing here, Nicky?"

"Same thing you are, my friend," Nicky said with a grin, the wrinkles in his face showing. "Looking for truth." Seeing the confusion on Adam's face, he went on. "It's a long story, Adam. It's too involved to discuss here. We have to get you ready for something very special. We must move quickly."

Of course Adam trusted this gentle soul with whom he had spent the greatest of times. Passing a glance from his good friend and then to Charlie, it wasn't long before he was nodding in agreement. He looked around for Gypsy who had jumped from his grasp and scurried off to sniff some interesting red berries.

"You have yourself a smart dog," Nicky said and walked ahead with Charlie.

"But..." Adam said, trailing closely behind them. His head was spinning with a gazillion questions.

❀ ✳ ❀ ✳ ❀ ✳ ❀

Adam followed the two men through a narrow wooded path that ended at a small lagoon. Colorful bushes reflected into the green, glassy water. In the center was a large fountain. In the distance a white, powdery mist followed a waterfall that fell from a high cliff.

"Nicky, I don't understand what is going on here."

"We will tell you everything as soon as we get to Charlie's place. Before we go, you must bathe in there," Nicky said, motioning to the water.

It didn't sound like Adam had an option.

"Bathe like a bath?" This was certainly an odd request in the middle of a walk.

"Yes." Nicky did not smile. Instead, he pointed past Adam. "In there."

It seemed strange to him to bathe in this place, but everything else about today was weird.

"But I had a shower last night," Adam said with hesitation. He wasn't interested in getting wet right now.

"It is not to clean your body, but to clean your soul. Only pure souls can come here, so you need to move quickly or you can't stay," Charlie said in a convincing tone.

"Take off everything including your Telos

watch," Charlie instructed, pointing to a small hut by the edge of the water. "Once you get in, dunk yourself completely under the water three times. When you are done, do not put on your old clothes." He handed Adam a robe similar to his own, except it was light brown instead of white. "Put this on when you get out and put your clothes in this basket."

With a nod Adam headed to the hut, leaving Nicky and Charlie behind.

"And remember," Nicky called, "it is deeper than it looks. Hurry, you have only a few moments left."

Gypsy ran to the edge of the lagoon and barked.

After tearing off all of his clothes as quickly as he could, Adam darted toward the water. This was really embarrassing, but it was also exciting. Adam first stuck his toes in to test the temperature. It was perfect, so he just jumped in. He held his breath, slowly slipping under.

To his surprise, the water had a pulse, as if it were alive. Even stranger, the bottom of the lagoon suddenly vanished. He lost his balance and sank into the deep fathoms of the water like he was being sucked downward. He frantically tried to swim back to the top and gasped for air.

When he bobbed his head up, he saw Nicky and Charlie laughing.

"Very funny," Adam mumbled, coughing. He swam around for a bit and dunked himself under two more times.

As he emerged, he covered himself with his hands and scurried toward the hut. Adam put on the robe made of a foreign material; not silk or cotton, but somewhere in between. It slid over his body like satin. Clothed in the loose-fitting robe, he put his sneakers back on, placed his clothes in the basket and joined them.

He was happy and full of positive energy. His body actually seemed lighter, as if a great weight had rolled off his shoulders.

"Well, you certainly took your time," Nicky joked.

"It was great, except that I almost drowned. I don't know what just happened, but I feel so light."

"Glad you liked it," Nicky said. Excitement beamed on everyone's faces.

"You just washed away all the dirt from your old life." Seeing Adam's puzzled expression, Nicky continued, "Think of it as leaving your old life behind and being reborn here in Telos."

"Well, okay. Weird, but cool," Adam said.

"Now you are officially welcome to stay. Oh, and now you just added about five years to your youth," Nicky said nonchalantly, as if it were no big deal.

"What?" Adam almost choked.

"Have you ever heard of the Fountain of Youth?" asked Nicky.

"Well, yeah, but," Adam stuttered, "I want to look older; not younger! Can you reverse this?"

It seemed absurd to contemplate the fact that he would stay young for another five years.

"And no offense," Adam blurted out, "you both look pretty old."

"It doesn't make you younger. It keeps you the age you are until you wish to get older or die," Charlie explained.

"Who would want to die?" Adam asked, raising an eyebrow.

"You'd be surprised at the number of people who lose hope and miss the lessons they need in order to get the blessings to fulfill their purpose in life," Charlie said in a serious tone.

Adam wasn't sure he had heard correctly.

"Blessings? Hope of getting what blessings?" Adam asked skeptically.

"Nicky and I are trying to help people figure out special lessons. Once they learn them, they will receive certain blessings. Eventually, all of this will bring peace to mankind." Charlie said simply.

"Amen," Nicky chimed in.

Adam looked at them, clearly perplexed.

They walked through a rocky path dotted with dainty yellow and orange flowers, before coming to an opening that cut into the mountain. The entrance was framed by two gigantic, golden gates with a stiff guard standing on either side, each holding a fiery sword. A sign above the gate stated: City of Luz. Only the pure may enter.

Gypsy led the way.

Nicky walked ahead to the amazing gates to talk to the two guards, while Adam and Charlie waited. Adam thought they looked human, until he spotted delicate feathers behind one of the guard's shoulders. He had wings.

"Charlie?" In a fit of nervous jitters Adam blurted out, "Why do the guards have—"

"—wings?" Charlie interrupted him.

Adam nodded.

"They're angels," Charlie said, sounding as though this were perfectly normal.

Blinking a few times in confusion, Adam said nothing. He stared at them wide-eyed, thinking that somehow they didn't look like angels. They looked disciplined and stiff.

"Where's the halo? Yes, that's what's missing," he finally figured it out.

Charlie laughed. "Angels don't really need wings or halos. That's what people on the surface world think because angels fly around. Plenty of folks down here are angels but they don't wear wings. Those who do are showing authority. It's like wearing a badge of honor. The angels don't need them to get around. In fact, Nicky says he doesn't like wearing them because they slow him down."

"What are you saying? Nicky's an angel?" Adam asked.

"Of course," Charlie confirmed, folding his arms. "How else would he have gotten you down here?" This time he winked at Adam, as if he was sharing a great secret.

"He what?" Adam shrieked.

"Who gave you the Telos watch?" Charlie said, as if he were beginning a logical argument, and he pointed to Adam's left wrist.

"Nicky," Adam answered, feeling quite odd.

"That's right. He gave me one too. See," Charlie said and showed Adam his identical watch.

Adam leaned over to examine it. He didn't know what to say.

"Nicky did a lot more than that for you, but we'll get to that later once we get past the gates. Nicky's done. Here he comes. Let's go now."

What is going on here? Adam thought.

Just as Nicky returned, the angel guards extinguished the fire on their swords and opened the gates.

"We're good now," Nicky said. "Come."

As they walked through the gates, a soft white fog completely engulfed the path and Adam's shoes. It was like they were walking on a cloud. He saw hundreds of little huts built into gigantic trees that seemed way too small to hold more than one person. Each hut had a narrow door and a round glassless window in the front.

"What's the sign above the doors?" Adam asked.

"Each person picks the quality that he or she admires the most and writes it above their door so they don't forget," Charlie answered.

Charlie led them to a house with a sign that said "Humility."

"What's your sign mean?" Adam asked.

"It's a reminder not to let my ego get in my way," Charlie said humbly.

Chapter 15 –
Facts of Life

Gypsy had run ahead and eagerly waited for them to come. Charlie opened the door and gestured for Adam to go in first.

Ducking his head, Adam felt foolish entering something so small. But to his surprise, once inside the hut, it was almost the size of his mansion back in Mount Shasta.

How could this be? he thought. This was another wonder.

Gypsy plopped down in the middle of a giant pillow. With a deep sigh, she had found her peace for the afternoon.

By far, the most stunning part of the hut was the ceiling. The sun beamed through a kaleidoscope of colored jewels that looked like a stained-glass window. The first room had a large window offering a breathtaking view of high trees bearing an abundance of fruit.

There were couches and chairs arranged all around, and a gentle breeze swept through with a scent of sweet jasmine. Huge crystal clusters were placed everywhere, giving off an aura of tranquility.

"Please have a seat, Adam," Charlie said, motioning his hand towards a chair.

Adam sat in a white stone chair in front of a table decorated with a vase of flowers. "It's so beautiful here," he said.

"I agree. I love it," Charlie replied enthusiastically. "You must be thirsty."

Adam's mouth was terribly dry. He took the glass that Charlie handed to him and gulped down the liquid.

"That was good," Adam said, smacking his lips and licking them from side to side. "What is it?"

"It's called Calaberry juice," Charlie proudly announced. "You'll only find it down here. One day I stepped on something that squished under my foot and discovered a whole patch of little red berries. I ate a few, and there you go, Calaberry juice was born."

"Sorta tastes like sweet lemonade with a strawberry aftertaste. Yum."

"Want more?"

"Thanks, but I'm good."

On the table in front of Adam, Charlie placed what looked like a plate of red goo with a side dish of small pink bread rolls. Staring down at that, Adam made a face.

"I know it looks gross," Charlie said, chuckling, "but you'll see. It actually tastes like whatever you want. Just close your eyes and imagine anything you're in the mood for. Think of something and hold it in your mind for a moment."

Adam played along. "Anything? I love chocolate cake," he joked.

"So imagine that it's chocolate cake, and it will taste just like that. It's one hundred percent nutritious and will help you live a long, healthy life."

Adam gave a quizzical look like, Are you serious?

"Go ahead. Try it." Charlie's palm motioned toward the goo, as if he were the headwaiter at a five-star restaurant.

Adam dipped his finger into the stuff. Out of habit, he smelled it. Wrinkling his nose and squinting his eyes, he took a taste.

"Oh, wow! You're right. It does taste just like chocolate cake." With a spoon in hand, Adam dug in. When he finished everything, he pushed the plate away. He was tempted to burp, but nothing came up. "That was delicious. Thanks. What kind of rolls were they?"

"These rolls grow in our garden from that bread tree right there," Nicky said, pointing out the window to a tree indeed filled with pink rolls.

"I never heard of bread growing on trees," Adam wasn't shy to comment.

"They only grow down here," Nicky said, "but soon they will grow on the surface too."

Adam blinked quickly a few times, not quite sure how to respond to that information.

Now that Adam was full and refreshed, Charlie

and Nicky needed to explain what this incredible adventure was all about.

Adam looked expectantly at Nicky and Charlie.

"Adam," asked Nicky, "do you know why you are here?"

"Because my dad was coming," he said, shrugging, and he gestured with his hand, "and I found a magic carpet, so I figured I would see if I could get it to bring me here, and it worked, and here I am."

As he finished, he realized this story sounded quite unbelievable, even though it was totally true.

"Do you think this was all by chance?" Nicky probed further, placing his elbows on the table, interlocking his fingers. "What are the chances that you would have been given the kind of watch you needed to make the carpet work? Coincidence?"

"Well, no," Adam admitted in a low whisper, "I don't think so. So why did you give me the watch in the first place?" Then he thought of something he hadn't considered before. "What if I had never gone to the pet shop that day?"

Nicky leaned towards Adam. "I hoped that you would say good-bye to the animals, if not to me." He spoke with deep understanding. "But even if you hadn't come to the store, I would have made sure that you got the watch. There was no doubt it was to be yours."

"Wouldn't it have been easier to just leave it

in the blue box inside the wooden chest with the directions?" Adam asked. This seemed much simpler to him.

"Actually, that was the original plan, but once I realized you were on your way to say good-bye, I teleported myself to the cottage in Mount Shasta and removed the watch from the box and returned back to the pet store."

"Teleported!" Adam interrupted.

"It's another way we get around. I didn't have time to change the directions, but I knew you would figure it all out. You're a smart boy. Plus, it was easier for Gypsy to find you. We could've shown her the picture she took of you with her eyes, but it was simpler to just say, 'Find Adam who wears the watch.'"

"She took a picture of me?" Adam asked.

"Yes, she did," Nicky said.

"How did Gypsy do that?" Adam exclaimed.

"I told you she is a special dog, right?"

"Okay, but that's just really weird," Adam said.

Nicky continued, "The watch possesses special technology that activates the carpet. It has a tracking device, so I was able to monitor your exact whereabouts without me traveling all over to find you. That's about it."

Frowning, Adam felt let down. "So it wasn't me who did all that stuff? I was set up?"

"Not set up, no, no, no," Charlie exclaimed, as

he shook his head. "You possess all the qualities needed to get down here, but they are hidden within you. Your self-confidence has been shattered and your spirit crushed. It's there, but needs to be strengthened. The Telos watch works with the Law of Attraction."

Adam stared at Charlie, waiting for more information. "What's that?"

"The Law of Attraction teaches us that what you think will attract the same energy to you. Imagine the entire universe as one big mirror that reflects back to you whatever your thoughts are," Charlie explained.

"Really?" Adam said. "I never noticed myself in the universe."

"Very funny, kid," Nicky said, laughing.

"If you complain a lot, the universe gives you more to complain about," Charlie said. "If you have a positive outlook, greatness will naturally be attracted to you."

"Okay," Adam said. "So?"

Charlie continued, "Before you got the watch, your lack of self-confidence was attracting negative energy. The watch helps to block your negative thought patterns. But you must practice positive thinking within yourself."

"I don't know what you're talking about, plus you didn't answer the most important question," Adam said, thinking to himself, Grownups never want to give you the whole story. "Why did you want me all the way down here to begin with?"

He had just asked the million-dollar question.

There was a long moment of silence while Adam waited for the answer to his question.

Nicky finally spoke up. "The surface world is running out of time."

He picked up a light blue crystal wand and waved it at the table in a circular motion. A hologram of the world emerged with huge chunks of land missing from most of the continents.

"See all these missing sections?"

Adam nodded with a blank stare.

Nicky continued, "Evil is outweighing good. The earth is sick, causing parts of the land to disappear. The world is on the brink of annihilation and the end is near. This planet is facing its greatest challenge since it was created."

"But why?" Adam asked simply. "I never heard of land missing."

"Oh, you won't hear about it on your nightly news," Nicky said. "We have been trying to warn the surface world for centuries. They do not want to listen, and instead try to settle their problems without looking within their hearts. Peace must start inside each person.

"The heart is one thousand times more powerful than the mind in terms of bringing peace to the world. The mind analyzes everything, but the heart is what connects people together through the collective consciousness.

"We were about to give up trying to help until we realized something. Adults are set in their ways, while young people are still open-minded. They are filled with natural kindness, and most importantly, the belief that anything is possible."

Adam nodded and listened to Nicky intently.

"For a long time we searched for a young person just like you. We wanted someone who could jumpstart a movement to stop this destructive cycle and start a chain reaction of love and peace. Once it is set in motion it will continue."

Should I be taking notes? Adam wondered to himself.

"The problem is that young children are completely pure until about eight years old, but they are not mature enough to take charge. And most teenagers have already lost the qualities we need. They are skeptical, self-conscious and often self-centered.

"Usually, they are heavily influenced by the media and their friends, whose morals lead them off the right path. Peer pressure. It is awful." Nicky paused to make sure Adam was following him. "Then I met you. You have the kindness and compassion that we were looking for in a person.

"I can tell by the way you treat animals. The other qualities have to be tested by the leader of Telos, but I know he will agree with me. Plus, once you learn how to channel all that extra energy you have, it will come in handy to help you with your mission."

Nicky smiled warmly at Adam when he finished his talk. Adam stared back at him.

"Well," Charlie broke in with a clap of the hands, "now that we got that out of the way, let me show you around."

"Hold on a minute. Got what out of the way?" Adam blurted. "You want me to start this peace-loving, oh, let's save the world, crazy mission?"

"Something like that," Nicky said. He put down the crystal wand and the hologram disappeared.

"Yeah, right. And just how am I supposed to do that?" Adam exclaimed. "I don't even have peace in my own family. We sorta hate each other. How can I possibly bring peace to the world?"

"Of course you would feel that way," Nicky said in a calming voice. "Do not worry. We do not expect you to just return to the surface world and bring peace. We have a strategic plan and everybody will pitch in to help. We will prepare you. I am not saying it is going to be easy."

Adam couldn't comprehend how they thought that he could save the world. He was just this meek kid that everyone ignored. Yeah, world peace would be nice, but to think that he could help bring it? Not even a chance. He couldn't bear to see everyone laughing at him when he failed.

Maybe I should give it a try, a little voice whispered in Adam's head. After all, it's better to try and fail than to have never tried at all.

"Well, I suppose I can give it a try," Adam said hesitantly.

"That is all we expect you to do," Nicky assured him.

"What if I fail?" His mood turned somber.

"Stop! You are forgetting the first Universal Law, the Law of Attraction. Remember, positive thoughts attract positive results," Nicky said.

"Let's get one thing straight," Charlie chimed in with a forceful tone. "The words 'can't' and 'fail' are no longer a part of your vocabulary. Are we clear?"

Adam nodded. "Well, okay. But what if the world is destroyed before I succeed?" Adam asked, bending down to pull Gypsy onto his lap.

"If you think you can't, then surely you won't. You will fulfill your own belief," Charlie said firmly. "You must think positively."

Nothing they said made sense to Adam. His brain was whirling with erratic thoughts and confusion.

"Come. Let us show you around," Charlie said.

Walking out the door, Charlie beckoned the other two to follow him.

❂ ✳ ❂ ✳ ❂ ✳ ❂

As they headed outside, Nicky said, "I see you're in good hands with Charlie. I have to go. I will be back soon. Don't worry."

Nicky winked at Adam and suddenly faded out of sight.

"Whoa, where did he go?" Adam gasped.

"It's okay. He had to return to the surface world to take care of an emergency," Charlie said.

How can he leave me now? Adam thought.

Charlie showed him around the gardens. They were beautiful, blissful and serene.

"I see why my dad wanted to come to Telos," Adam said with inspired awe. "Who wouldn't want to visit here?"

"Oh, this isn't Telos," Charlie said. "We're in the city of Luz."

"What?" Stopping in his tracks, Adam was stunned again. "Where's Telos, then?"

"There are three cities in our inner world," Charlie continued. He snatched a long stick from the ground and drew three circles in the dirt. "We are in Luz, the angel city." Charlie gestured toward the right. "Then there are the Lemurians in Telos. They are a mix between humans and angels. For instance, they cannot fly and exist mostly in the fifth dimension."

"But you're not an angel, right?" Adam asked.

"I am just a humble human like you." Charlie tried to keep the story as simple as possible.

"So the Lemurians live in Telos?" Adam said, trying to get the facts straight.

"Right. Our neighbors, the Lemurians, live in Telos. That is where your father wants to go. They are the geniuses behind all our sophisticated technology. They fled down here to escape the fate of their ancestors who destroyed the surface world many centuries ago. A nuclear war between the Lemurians and the Atlanteans from Atlantis caused most of the land masses to sink into the ocean."

"Atlantis, as in Atlantis under the sea?" Adam asked.

"Yes," Charlie said. "They knew it was happening, so they prepared the inner world before they came down here."

Adam listened with awe.

"When man was created, he was initially made within the fifth dimension. Man quickly made the same mistakes as the previous civilizations from the lost world. Man was quickly downgraded to the third dimension, which looks more physical, as if we have spiritual blinders on.

"We are returning to the fifth dimension as time is speeding up. Soon all the blinders are going to be removed from all humanity and the truth revealed. People will see that many things they believed to be important in this physical world were, in fact, just an illusion. That painful realization is true hell on earth."

"You said that there are three cities." Not wanting to miss anything, Adam reminded Charlie to finish that part of the story.

"Ah," putting his finger to his head as if it would jog his memory, Charlie said, "there is also dreaded Draconia. That place lies over that mountain range to the west." He pointed towards a distant mountain. "That place is occupied by the world's fiercest and most cunning demons. As you can imagine, it's not a real fun place."

"Demons are down here?" Adam didn't believe in them to begin with. He never thought in all his life he would learn where they actually lived. He was intrigued, but also frightened at the idea of meeting one in person.

"Fortunately, we are not worried about them down here because they go from Draconia to the surface world and back again, never entering Telos or Luz."

"What do they want?"

"Oh, they look at humans like cattle, just waiting for the opportunity to suck out their vital life forces and piggyback on them to gain access to the surface world," Charlie explained.

Adam looked worried.

"The real problem with them is that their power

has grown out of control within the last hundred years over the surface world."

"How did they get so powerful?" Adam asked.

"They get their power from people like you, such as when you make the wrong choices. They are always searching for an entrance into your mind. They wait for just the right moment, initially without you realizing. Then they offer you information making you seem so smart. Or they give you some power that feeds your ego. Or they allow you to tap into some energy that makes you feel fantastic. Then they ask for your permission to take over your body, telling you this will give you even more power.

"What actually happens is you give up your free will and then you belong to them. That is a high price to pay. Now they have easy access to the surface world via that poor person."

"Why would someone let that happen to them?" Adam asked.

"It's a wonderful question, Adam. Many times an unsuspecting person gets confused and doesn't realize the choices he is making are bad."

Adam thought about it for a minute. "That's pretty freaky knowing that making wrong decisions can have such an effect on you."

"Don't worry. Remember, demons are actually quite weak unless you give them power over you. If you feel them trying to bother you, just say 'You have no power over me.' Then busy yourself doing an act of kindness for someone else, like being charitable, sharing a kind word or even just a smile. It's a tricky battle that we are fighting. That is why Nicky and I came together," Charlie said. "Of course, the Telos watch helps too."

Chapter 16 –
The Mission

Charlie and Adam walked along the edge of a mountaintop that cradled a small valley. Pointing to a stunning stone building that stood proudly in the center, Charlie announced, "That is the Third Temple. It is being built as we speak by all the angels down here."

The building emanated a light that blended upward toward the sky.

"Third Temple? What's that?" Adam asked, staring at the building with awe.

"It's a special place that the Creator of the universe chose to make home on the surface world so we can feel His intense presence and know He exists."

"I don't know why, but somehow this Third Temple sounds familiar."

Charlie paused. "Does King David ring a bell?"

Adam studied Charlie's face, searching for an answer. "King David? No. Why?"

"Don't worry about it. It's not really important at this point."

"But what is that Temple doing down here and not up there?" Adam said, pointing towards the sky.

"Well, that's part of our job. Once we have

completed our work, hopefully the world will deserve to have the Third Temple. Then we will bring it to the surface."

"Finish our work? I don't really understand how I can help." Adam was now frustrated with all these crazy ideas.

Adam listened cautiously. "My dad says only fools believe in a god."

"Well, kid, only fools don't."

"How do you really know there's a Creator of the universe? I mean, you know." Adam gave a puzzled look.

"You think this complex world just evolved over time as science suggests? Who created you?" Charlie asked.

"I really don't know," Adam responded. "My mother?"

"Well, that's true. But who is the ultimate Creator of all?"

"God?"

"Right. Just ask Nicky. He has met Him."

Adam stared at Charlie with a stunned expression. "Really? Did he say what He looks like? Or is It a she?"

"Whether It's a he or a she, God is indescribable. To the believer, no words are necessary. For the non-believer, no words are enough. But according to Nicky, He's pure love and light. Where do you think humans came from?"

"Monkeys? I mean, that's a good question I have thought about. I know something must have made us. I mean, there is no real proof there is a god, is there?"

Charlie became animated, explaining, "Who else could have made faces, fingerprints and DNA all unique to the billions of people on this earth? Even your voice has its own unique sound. Do you think He went to all that trouble for no good reason, for no purpose whatsoever? Plus, you have your own special soul that only belongs to you. It craves to connect with Him as the ultimate pleasure. Everything else is a counterfeit feeling. The body, mind and soul eventually get bored and experience deep feelings of emptiness." Charlie paused and waited for Adam to comment.

"I see your point. I have thought about it, but I just don't know," Adam said.

"Imagine finding your Telos watch buried in your backyard. Would you think it just evolved from the dirt? Or would you assume that someone with intelligence had made it?"

"Of course someone made it. That's so obvious," Adam answered.

"The world is so much more complicated than this watch. So obviously, there was a Creator, right?" Charlie argued.

"Well, yeah," Adam reluctantly agreed. He gave Charlie a look indicating he didn't entirely understand what he was saying.

"Don't worry, son. You can't understand algebra until you've learned the times tables, can you? You will see. Be patient, Adam."

❁ ✳ ❁ ✳ ❁ ✳ ❁

Turning in another direction, Charlie led Adam down a grassy path surrounded by white flowers that led to a massive tree. Strong green branches overflowed with large golden berries. Thousands of them glistened on the floor. Adam picked one up to examine it.

Charlie was quick to stop him. "Put that down now. You don't want to touch that or you might die."

Adam threw down the fruit as instructed. "Why? Is it poisonous?"

"It's the Tree of Wisdom. Within this small fruit contains all the knowledge in the world a human can learn."

"You mean if I eat it, I don't have to go to school anymore?"

"If you eat it, you won't have to go to school anymore because you will be dead. Humans aren't allowed to eat it."

Adam thought about learning everything there is to know about the world simply by eating a golden fruit. How tempting it would be to just try a small bite.

Adam stared up, looking at the magnificent tree.

"Come, let's go, Adam, before you get any funny ideas in your head," Charlie said, motioning with his hand.

Gypsy followed closely behind them.

"What's the point? I don't get what that's doing here if no one can benefit from it. Actually, why are you here?" Adam asked. "If you're a human, why did you come down here?" He raised his eyebrow.

"Well, I was a close friend of Nicky's. When my life was in danger, Nicky arranged for me to escape down here, and I was allowed to stay in Luz," Charlie explained. "You see, I was a scientist who lived in your house in Mount Shasta."

Adam's jaw dropped in surprise.

"I hid for years in the mansion you now call home, until I realized I couldn't hide like a coward and do nothing."

"Really?"

"I was doing research on super important scientific breakthroughs that could have brought enlightenment and peace to the world. However, a powerful group of people didn't want the masses to know about that. I actually knew too much, and they wanted me dead.

"In fact, they had attempted to kill me years earlier in a fire. When the Navy offered me a consulting job in the South Pole, I felt I would be safe for a while, since the whole trip was top secret. After I got down here, I wrote the old diary you found in your locker."

"You wrote that?" Adam said, clearly shocked. He couldn't get over the fact that this was the same reclusive scientist he had heard about from his dad. Wow! "But how did you get that diary into my locker?"

"Nicky took care of that," Charlie said simply and smiled.

"Nicky?" Adam repeated.

"Who else? The one and only. When I didn't return from the South Pole during my trip, nobody suspected that I was alive. They knew that anyone who tried to enter the middle of the world through either side of the Poles would most likely never make it back. Now they think I am out of the way, I have nothing to fear if I return to the surface. They are not looking for me."

Adam stared at Charlie in utter disbelief. "What a story," he said.

"I waited until Nicky found somebody to help us finish our work. Thank heavens you are here."

Adam had no idea what Charlie was talking about.

"I just can't imagine how you guys picked me," Adam asked, as panic replaced his intense interest. "I don't know the first thing about all of this, and for sure no one is going to believe anything I say."

"That is your distorted perception of yourself. I know it doesn't make any sense now, but there is a calculated plan."

As they came to the end of the path, Charlie pointed to the horizon just beyond the highest hill.

"There it is. That is Telos."

Out in the distance Adam noticed dozens of towering skyscrapers shooting into the sky. In Luz everything was natural, but Telos looked totally man made.

"Wow! That's awesome," was all he could say.

"Yes, it is truly amazing."

"How are the Lemurians living there connected to world peace?" Adam wanted to know.

"They have sent what you know as flying saucers to try to warn the surface world of what is going to happen, but they have been repeatedly fired upon. The Lemurians have attempted to contact individuals, but the stories had gotten played down as laughable figments of people's imaginations."

"Who's covering this all up?"

"The ones trying to take over the planet and our consciousness, that is who!" Charlie's voice trembled with aggravation. "They know the world is evolving too quickly. Their solution is to cause so much distraction that we don't notice the change.

You will come to understand a lot in your short stay before your dad arrives."

"When is my dad coming?" Adam asked anxiously.

"Soon," Charlie said. "He will understand it all once he gets here."

"You know, I'm so tired. I really gotta go to sleep. My brain can't take anymore right now," Adam said.

"We will start tomorrow. You have had an overwhelming day, and the next few will be even more so. Let's retire to my humble abode so you can rest."

Adam followed Charlie to his home.

When they returned to Charlie's place, Adam was brought to a small room with a cozy bed. It looked welcoming.

Sleep finally, Adam thought, while his brain ached with exhaustion. He sat on the bed. Gypsy plopped down next to him and pushed her nose into his side.

Charlie closed the window blinds to darken the room. The stained-glass ceiling above looked like a multi-colored nightlight.

"Have a good rest. I will be right out here if you need anything," Charlie said, shutting the door behind him.

Initially, Adam couldn't fall asleep even though the bed was soft and comfortable and the gentle light soothed his mind. He couldn't turn off his racing thoughts. He struggled to sort out all the information he had heard today. There was too much to understand. Just then, a question popped into his mind.

Wait! How did Gypsy fit into this whole picture? But before he could think of a possible answer, his brain surrendered to sleep.

Chapter 17 –
The Flight Back to Telos

Taking off from base camp for the second time, neither Larry nor Simon were much in the mood to talk. Larry worried about his son's disappearance, unable to understand what possibly could have happened to him.

Adam could never have found his way to Telos, Larry reassured himself. He just wasn't smart enough to do something that difficult. More likely he was pulling some prank to get attention. But how in the world did the boy even know about Telos in the first place?

This is totally ridiculous, he thought, shaking his head. But then again, what if Adam had stumbled onto something? As far as taking off on some carpet? Well, what nonsense, he scoffed to himself.

Larry had discovered that Mount Shasta had tunnels going all the way down to Telos and other unknown places. Before taking this difficult Antarctic route he had repeatedly tried to get into the mountain and find the tunnels, but without any success. So there's no way Adam could have gotten into them. Besides, even if he had, it would have taken him weeks to travel all the way to Telos, many miles below.

The more Larry thought about it, the more agitated and helpless he became about the situation. What would he do if he actually found Adam in Telos?

Sensing Larry's mood, Simon remained quiet while gazing out at the white glaciers and snow-covered mountains passing by. Looking at the plane's chronometer, Simon noted that almost four hours had passed since leaving their base camp for the second time.

"According to the GPS compass, we should be real close to that energy dome again," Simon announced. He glanced out the window of the plane. "There it is over to your left! Begin our descent to 2,500 feet."

"Here goes." Larry pushed the plane into a gentle dive. Everything was stable at first, but as they dropped lower, the plane's instruments suddenly went haywire, then stopped working, just like on yesterday's failed attempt.

Fortunately, Simon had the Magna Force all ready to go. He took aim and fired. The blue beam passed right through the cockpit window, instantly hitting the energy dome in front of them.

Their plane shook violently as a large, circular hole opened up where the beam hit. Larry steered the plane into the opening and once more, they were sucked inside. An instant later they were flying normally.

"It worked!" Simon shouted. "Take her lower."

With a restored confidence, Larry guided the plane downwards.

"There she is. Look at those green mountains," Simon exclaimed, scrambling to shoot video of the scenes below them.

Larry gave a thumbs-up sign when he noticed the camera pointing towards him.

Their excitement instantly turned to panic when the plane's engines died with no warning and refused to restart. The plane rolled violently from side to side, quickly losing altitude.

"What the—" Larry shouted in surprise.

"Look at that!" Simon yelled, indicating out the front window.

Neither man could believe what he saw. The plane seemed to be surrounded by a glowing bubble similar to the energy dome. It came at them from somewhere below and felt as if it was pulling the plane down to the ground.

"Oh no!" Simon screamed. "We've got to get out of the plane before we crash!"

Both men leaped out of their seats and quickly strapped on their emergency parachutes. They had no choice but to bail out.

Larry forced the plane's door open and climbed out onto the wing struts. Simon was right behind him. Both men leaped into the bucking air, and a few moments later their orange nylon parachutes opened, and they soared through the sky.

They watched helplessly as their plane went into a spin dive down to the ground. All they could do was to wait for it to crash. Oddly, it didn't.

The same glowing bubble that had surrounded their plane and disabled their engines reached out from the ground and caught the plane seconds before it hit the ground, causing minor damage to one of the wings.

The men looked at each other stone-faced.

As they descended from their terrifying heights, the updraft hit their parachutes and stopped their fall for a moment, then whipping them around.

Before they knew what was happening, the updraft blew Simon away from his partner.

"Simon!" Larry bellowed. "Don't worry! You're headed east towards Telos."

"What?" Simon yelled, as the wind whistled around his ears.

"You're going to Telos," Larry's voice trailed off into nothingness.

At first Larry thought he would simply join Simon in Telos once he landed. However, he was drifting west, farther away from Simon. The wind picked up and heaved him and his chute around like a ragdoll.

"Oh no!" Larry groaned. He was jerked around again.

If his memory of the map was correct, he was headed straight for Draconia. From what little he knew, it was a dark place where evil resided and the last place he wanted to go. A numbing dread filled his gut. He began to sweat as the air around him got hotter by the second. As he glanced down, he saw it; the pit of hell itself.

Chapter 18 –
Father Connection

A dam slept soundly for a few hours. When he awoke, he stared at the colorful ceiling for a moment and decided he had slept enough. Under normal circumstances, he would have stayed in bed for as long as possible, but this situation was anything but normal. He could not imagine what he might encounter today. He felt a rush of pure energy flowing through his mind.

He petted Gypsy and ruffled her ears. She responded by licking his face. As Adam jumped from the bed, he noticed a large glass basin filled with water beside him. When he washed his face, the water reminded him of the lagoon he had bathed in the day before.

Another folded robe rested at the foot of his bed. He wasn't used to this type of treatment. When he was refreshed and dressed, he opened the door. He found Charlie sitting on the floor with tears streaming down his cheeks. Adam stood silently, unsure of what to do. He was embarrassed to see a man in this sad state.

Why is Charlie crying? he wondered.

With his eyes filled with tears, Charlie looked at the boy and motioned him over. "Adam, come here."

Adam crouched down beside him. "Why are you crying?" he asked, thinking all sorts of uncomfortable things.

"Because I'm overwhelmed with emotions. I am not sad. They are happy tears," Charlie said.

"Oh, well, I'm glad to hear that. Wow. I'd hate to see what you do when you're sad."

Grinning at the boy for his humor, Charlie said, "I'm not joking, Adam." Choking through his tears, he said in a serious tone, "I am extremely happy right now."

"Really? What are you so happy about that would make you cry?"

To Adam, crying meant deep sorrow or pain, but certainly not happiness.

"Well, it's more like gratitude. I am grateful that you actually made it down here. Now all of my hard work will pay off. I just got emotional when I started thinking about everything."

"What do you mean?"

This didn't make any sense to Adam. He wasn't sure what to think, let alone what to say to a grown man crying in front of him. He had never felt so awkward in his life.

As Charlie talked, tears continued down his face. He sniffled between the words. "Adam, crying is a great thing. It helps release your angry and sad emotions."

Adam confided, "I almost never cry. I just don't

feel sad enough."

"It's really good to cry once in a while. I was so upset, I couldn't even cry when my wife and son were killed in a fire. I was totally numb for years from the grief I was going through. I switched off all my emotions. I realized I was full of so much anger and hurt. I was mad at myself for getting involved in something that ruined me.

"I was so angry that no one seemed to listen to me. No one cared about all the poverty, violence and hatred in the world. Even among families, they destroy each other with hurtful words and stupid fights caused by inflated egos. It is a cycle of life that doesn't have to be, but because people choose a certain path, it creates a lot of unnecessary pain."

Adam nodded his head to indicate he kind of understood.

"Anyway, it wasn't until I came down here and felt all the love that everyone has that I started feeling again. Once I learned to forgive myself for the way my life turned out, I was able to feel good emotions again. Forgiving myself allowed me to cry. The more I cried, the more layers of pain fell away, and the more I felt love towards myself and the world. And so it goes."

Charlie's words struck true in Adam's mind. "I kind of see what you are saying. But I can't stand my family. My father doesn't seem to care about me. And my brother, let's just say he thinks I'm an idiot.

They make me feel so unloved. I wish I had never been born into that family. So what? How does that change anything?"

"Well, that is one of the reasons why you are here. Most people like to try to change the world before they change themselves, but that never works. It seems easier, right?"

Adam nodded, but he wasn't sure how he could use this knowledge. "I guess so," he said, glancing at Charlie with a blank look.

"Come. Let's get you something to eat before we begin with your first lesson."

Charlie and Adam finished eating breakfast, and Adam's stomach felt quite full from that red goo. He was still baffled how such a gross glob of guck could taste just how he imagined it. Adam gave Gypsy a spoonful, imagining what she was thinking. Maybe a turkey leg.

"I need to take you on a little journey," Charlie said. "We will go back in time before the day of the fire in my home. Just stay with me. Let's sync our Telos watches to March 1, 1943 at 2:35 p.m. In case you get lost, just remember to push that little red button. That is the return button. It will bring you to where we are at this very moment. It also works as a walkie-talkie so we can always communicate with each other anywhere in the world at any point in time."

With a playful gesture, Adam looked at Charlie. "Are you kidding me? We're going back in time?"

"Yes. It is important that you know some things before we begin. Basically, you see… well… "

Adam was totally unprepared for the bomb that Charlie was about to drop on him.

"You see," Charlie paused and began crying again, as he tried to continue. "You were my son who died in that fire. I missed you so much. It hurt too much." Charlie grabbed Adam and hugged him tightly.

Uncomfortable with this emotional outpouring and strange story, Adam backed away. Here was a crying man hugging him and claiming that he was his father from a previous life. Was he supposed to say, "Great. Nice to see you again, Dad"?

"Charlie, no offense, but that sounds nuts. I only have one father. His name is Larry."

Charlie wiped his eyes on his sleeve and composed himself. "Once we go back in time, you will see. You have the same blue eyes and even that little mole on the side of your cheek. When we get there, look closely at yourself. You will see that it is you. I am going to close my eyes and concentrate for a minute. I need you to just think of nothing until I say, 'Push the green button.' Then push the button on the watch and within a second or so we should be there."

Adam gave a doubtful grin.

"Very important," Charlie warned. "You can't say a word while we are there because our words affect the vibrational energy of our world. This has consequences that will change the course of history, which has already happened. So just observe what is going on there. When we are done, I will motion for you to push the red button and we will return here. Do you understand?"

"Yeah, I think so," Adam said. "Press the green button to go back in time. Don't say a word. Press the red button when it's time to leave, right?"

"You got it, kid," Charlie said, moving around so he was facing Adam. "Ready? I am going to concentrate on where we are going, so please be quiet. Hold onto my hand so you don't get lost somewhere along the way."

Charlie closed his eyes and focused.

"Okay. Push the green button!" Charlie commanded.

Adam pressed the button, while holding Charlie's hand. A moment later they disappeared in a flash of light.

They instantly appeared in the living room of someone's home. There was a fire burning brightly in the fireplace, and a dog was curled up next to it on the floor. This dog looked just like Gypsy! Sitting at a desk, a younger version of Charlie was reading a book. He apparently couldn't see them, even though they were standing right in front of him. The younger Charlie had black, curly hair and a look of concentration on his face. He was engrossed in a four-inch book titled Quantum Physics. A half-drunk cup of black coffee rested next to the book on the desk.

Adam glanced over to the older Charlie and noticed how he had aged and become worn out through the years. Even so, it was definitely the same person. A series of questions flooded Adam's mind, but he restrained himself from asking because he remembered he couldn't talk right now.

Adam looked around and saw a boy on the floor reading a comic book. He walked toward the boy and stared at him. The boy on the floor had blue eyes and a mole on his cheek.

Ohmigod! That's me! Adam thought, putting his hand over his mouth, afraid he would scream.

The boy on the floor walked over to his father sitting at the desk. "Are you done yet, Dad?"

"Sorry, Peter, but we're just not going to make it today. I have to finish this."

Peter? Wow! Adam thought as he listened to this conversation.

Peter's eyes grew sad, then angry. "You never

have any time for me! You're always involved in your projects. I hate you! You promised me that today would be our day. Now our plans are ruined. Why did you even have a kid if you don't have any time to spend with him?"

Adam noticed the painfully familiar look of a passively rejected child.

Tears formed in Peter's eyes as he ran into his room and slammed the door.

His dad clenched his fist, banged it down on the desk and let out a frustrated grunt. He had been sitting there for hours, undisturbed in his work. He checked his watch and couldn't believe it was so late already. He needed to take a break anyway. He went to knock on his son's door and was greeted with, "Leave me alone!"

"Come on, Peter. Let's take Gypsy out for a walk."

No response.

What? Gypsy! Adam almost blurted out.

Charlie put his finger to his lips.

Adam signaled to Charlie he understood.

Charlie motioned to Adam to hit the red button, and in the next second, they were gone from there.

Gypsy barked at their sudden reappearance back home.

"I feel like I'm going to faint. Ohmigod!" Adam

wailed with excitement, sitting down as he tried to collect his thoughts. "Wow! That was unbelievable. It was really me! I can't believe this. I don't understand what happened back there."

"There were people who wanted me dead. They sent some hit men to my home to set it on fire, mistakenly thinking I was inside. But a few minutes before they arrived, I took Gypsy for a walk out the back door."

"And what happened to me?" Adam needed to know.

"You died in that fire. I watched everything from behind a tree near the front of my house." Charlie looked down. "That was the worst day of my life. Standing there hiding and afraid for my life, I realized that I had practically ignored my entire family for the sake of my research. I justified everything I did to my family by thinking that my work was so important. See, that's my ego getting in the way!"

Adam's eyes widened with a look of horror. "So you mean I was burned to death in a fire?"

"Afraid so, kid."

"You know, I'm scared of fire. That's so weird," Adam said. "So if I died, then how did I get to be me now and how did you find me?"

"Well, I had another son named George who was away in boarding school at the time. He went on to marry your grandmother and she gave birth to your dad."

Adam looked at Charlie utterly perplexed. "Hang on. Say that again."

"Basically, my older son, George, went on to marry Linda. They had a son named Larry, your dad. He married your mom, who gave birth to you."

"Really? So you were my dad and my grandfather?"

"Great-grandfather, that's right."

"How can that be?" Adam said with shock.

"It's called the cycle of life. You had a special mission that you needed to accomplish. Since your life was cut short, you were given another opportunity to fulfill that. When I learned you had been born again into the world, I found out where you were living. I have been tracking you from here with Nicky's help ever since."

"So why did you come here?" Adam asked excitedly.

"During my darkest times when I was on the run for my life and I didn't think I could carry on any longer, Nicky came and offered me the chance to come down here to finish my research. I wasn't sure how I would get here, but as you can see, things have a way of working out for the good."

As Charlie was speaking to him, Adam glanced out the glassless window and around the small, beautifully decorated room.

"We even worked it out so your dad's job

transferred him to Mount Shasta. We made sure he found out about my home being for sale."

"You mean the one we just moved into?" Adam asked.

"Yes. It was pretty funny how Nicky managed to scare away the other buyers at the home auction. Your dad was the only bidder, since Nicky had started a rumor that the house was haunted."

"And how did Nicky get down here?" Adam couldn't help asking.

"While Nicky was alive, his name was Nikola Tesla. Born over one hundred years ago, he was one of the greatest scientists that the world had ever known."

"How come I never heard of him?"

"Nicky was extremely modest," Charlie said, "and he didn't believe in taking credit for his inventions. That's why he was virtually unknown outside of the scientific world.

"Imagine, he created hundreds of inventions that everyone tried to steal from him. His ideas could have brought world peace, but the people who stole them had a different idea of how the world should be. He was a brilliant scientist, but a terrible businessman."

Adam could tell by Charlie's tone that Nicky was somewhat of a hero to him. "Hundreds of inventions?" Adam said with enthusiasm. "Anything I might have heard of?"

"Only all the electricity that flows throughout your house and all the motors that power things like air conditioning, elevators and anything electrical that moves. I mean, the list goes on and on! He knew that his talents and brilliant mind were a gift from a higher power. So he avoided publicity."

"I just can't believe Nicky's an angel," Adam said, trying to make sense of the information. After all, he had spent months with him cleaning out rabbit cages and petting hamsters. Adam shook his head in disbelief. Gypsy jumped onto his lap and rolled into a small ball.

"Animals sure are special. Maybe that's why Nicky loved the pet shop so much," Adam said.

"Actually," Charlie said, grinning, "I think that's where he was the happiest. Nicky preferred a simple life, especially with creatures that truly loved him and didn't have an agenda."

"Agenda?"

"Yeah. It's the real reason why people do things for other people. What's in it for them and always with conditions. You know how people always want something for themselves. I will do this for you if…. I will help you if…. I will love you if…"

"Talking about what people will do, what do you need from me exactly?" Adam asked with anticipation.

"I promise, before you go back home, you will understand everything. There is much to learn, but

I don't want to overwhelm you with too much at once," Charlie said.

"I think it's too late for that," Adam said with a chuckle.

Adam shook his head. He still didn't understand. "But wait! So how does this time travel work exactly?" Adam wanted all the answers now.

"Well, Adam, each second has a numbered vibration that is unique to itself, just like snowflakes and fingerprints."

"What do you mean by vibration?" Adam asked.

"Vibration means the total energy it takes to make that second. There are 189,216 million seconds allotted for this time dimension as you know it. Time is really just a combination of energy and light. Once a second has passed, you can't access it again unless you know how to tap into the Timekeeper."

"That doesn't seem like very many seconds from the beginning of time," Adam said, trying to understand this complex science. "So what happens when time runs out?" Adam realized that this conversation had become quite interesting.

Charlie noticed his excitement and continued with his explanation. "Time resets itself, and the cycle is restarted unless we self-destruct before it ends. It has happened many times already. That is why scientists claim the world is millions of years old. That's because it is!

"There were civilizations, like the Lemurians from Telos, who were one of the many races from the previous time dimension.

"Every few thousand years when the world is overtaken by evil, it is destroyed either by nature or by man. This is not a bad thing, but rather it is the Creator's way of allowing cosmic forces to take their natural path. Then everything is remade. Unfortunately, because of the sad state of our world, the end is coming sooner than planned."

Adam thought deeply for a moment and asked, "If everything gets destroyed at the end of this time dimension and we seem to be losing, why not just let it end early? I mean, I don't want to die or anything, but if this cycle isn't going so well, why fight so hard to save it?"

Charlie looked at Adam and grinned, proud of the insight this question demonstrated. "Well, Adam, we can do something about it. It's our choice to prevent the entire destruction or we can just sit and watch the world be destroyed sooner, which won't be pretty. Billions will die."

"You're just freaking me out. What can we do to stop this?" Adam asked.

"There's one thing we can do. The world can unite together and in so doing, stop this. Each person is actually responsible for the fate of our future. Think of it like this: We are all on a giant ship and one fool decides to drill a small hole in the corner of his cabin. It is just a pinhole, he figures. It's his room and no one will notice. Sure enough, the water starts to seep in slowly drip by drip. Eventually, that boat will sink because of this one person's stupid actions."

Charlie continued, "The Lemurians in Telos will give you a great history lesson later today that will help it make more sense. They invited us over for dinner."

"Telos? Really? No way!"

"Yes way!"

"Come," Charlie continued. "It is time for us to meet the king of Telos. You're going to love him."

"We're going to Telos now?" Adam asked.

"Yes," Charlie replied and grabbed his walking stick.

Closing the door behind them, Charlie, Adam and Gypsy headed out the gates of Luz and down a tall, grassy hill toward the lake.

Nicky greeted them at the edge of the shimmering water by a small boat.

"Hi, Adam. How are you doing?" he said, smiling.

"Hi. I'm great," Adam said enthusiastically. "I'm so glad to see you again. We're going to Telos. Are you coming with us?"

"No, sorry. I am going to look after Gypsy while

you are there with Charlie."

"What?" Adam said with surprise. "Why can't you both come?"

"Leave her here with me," Nicky said. "You will have to do this part without us."

Adam hugged Gypsy and reluctantly handed her over to Nicky.

"Good luck. See you soon, kid," Nicky said encouragingly. He and Gypsy walked off out of sight.

Chapter 19 –
Bad Luck

Larry pulled his legs back as if he could avoid dropping into this cursed place. His feet landed on the black, charred ground that stretched for miles, his parachute draped over him.

He scrambled to find his way out of the tangled mess of his parachute. After he freed himself, he looked around for a place to hide, but all he could find were a few demolished huts. The air was dry and hot, making it hard to breathe. This horrific place looked like the aftermath of a battlefield set against a red sky. Without a doubt, Larry knew he had entered Draconia.

A swishing sound came from above him. He instinctively crouched down and put his hands over his face. When he found the courage to peek out between his fingers, he wished he had kept his eyes closed. He noticed gray shadows dancing everywhere. They circled him like demonic vultures.

Larry's mind raced while confusion gripped his being and filled his chest with panic. He had nowhere to run, but he ran anyway straight into a soft wall. Bouncing off, he hit the ground and looked up.

The wall was a creature about eight feet tall dressed in a long, black cloak. Its face was scaly and dark green with a slimy texture. The face was horrifyingly mutated; part human and part reptile. Larry searched the creature, hoping to find something familiar in this very uncomfortable predicament. There was a permanent grimace stretching over what looked like a mouth. So it must eat, Larry thought, but what?

Even with that thought lingering, nothing was worse than its large, hypnotic emerald eyes, with a yellow streak down the middle. They were hideous and stunning all at once. They held Larry's gaze.

Out from the cloak came a pair of bony, webbed wings.

Just confronting this creature by itself would have been terrible enough, but Larry realized that this thing was not alone. There were two others standing ominously next to it. Larry's heart stopped and he waited motionless.

"Hithesss Nukeresss Ssionee?" The middle creature hissed words that sounded like a question. It had a split tongue just like a serpent's. A long thick tail slowly wagged from its backside.

"I don't understand what you are saying," Larry said worriedly.

The creatures mumbled to each other in a huddle, and then burst into what sounded like a poor imitation of laughter. The middle creature spoke in perfect English. "You are from the surface world."

"Yes," Larry sighed with relief. Maybe he wasn't going to be eaten after all. He knew the residents here were just as advanced and intelligent as the Lemurians in Telos. Perhaps he could reason with them.

"Why have you come here?" it asked.

"For my son," he lied. He figured this answer was safer and more direct. "My son came down here somewhere, and I have to find him."

"Oh, do you? Are you sure?"

Larry felt the creature penetrate his mind. Maybe I should have just told the truth, Larry thought, instead of getting Adam involved.

"Why do you not say that out loud?" it chuckled, looking from side to side for the others to chime in.

"What?" Larry asked, shocked to hear such an answer from this monster.

"Did you not wish us to know your true reason for coming to our world?" it asked with a slight smile.

Larry did not know what to say. He felt trapped. He scanned through the massive bodies and wings for an escape. There was none.

"If so," it advised, "you should lower the volume of your thoughts. Why hide your true intentions, unless you know they are wrong?"

Larry hadn't thought about his intentions like that.

The creature's eyes became more like slits,

focusing in on Larry. The wings of all three surrounded him, closing off all possible exits.

"Ah, so you do think like one of us."

Larry shook his head to protest, but it didn't matter.

"Welcome." It ignored him.

Then suddenly something absolutely amazing happened. The creature transformed itself into the most beautiful woman Larry had ever set his eyes on. She was now his height, slender with long, flowing, black hair that curled around her shoulders and framed her cream white face. Her eyes, though, didn't change. She still had those same piercing green eyes that held him spellbound.

❀ ✳ ❀ ✳ ❀ ✳ ❀

"Hello," she said in a penetrating voice. "My name is Lillith, but you can call me Lily. I am the princess of Draconia, and I welcome you to our fantastic world. What is your name?" As she spoke, she moved closer to Larry, placing a hand on her bony hip.

"Larry." He cleared his throat and loosened his collar nervously.

"Hello, Larry." Lillith smiled again, beckoning him with her charm. "Do not mind these two," indicating the creatures behind her. "They are just my guards. Now, let us sit so we can talk. I am quite sure you have a lot of questions. There is much to discuss."

She clapped her thin hands together, and two chairs and a small table instantly appeared. Lillith sat down and gestured for him to do the same.

"Would you like something to drink?" she inquired sweetly, leaning toward him.

"Sure. Why not?" Larry said. His throat was parched from the hot air.

She snapped her fingers, and suddenly Larry was holding a goblet in his hand. He looked suspiciously into the cup, filled with a bubbling, green liquid.

"It's Draconian ale," she said.

He stared at Lillith and searched her face. "Actually, I would love some water, if you have any," he said hesitantly.

Lillith narrowed her eyes, but kept her wide smile in place. "Of course." She immediately catered to his wish by snapping her fingers, and the liquid turned clear. He cautiously sniffed the cup and froze, not sure of what to do. After all, this was Draconia.

"Are you not going to drink?" she asked.

He gazed into her sultry face. She was beautiful, but there was no mistaking the venom in her voice or the evil barely noticed behind those lovely eyes. He had to remind himself that this beautiful woman just a moment ago was a frightful image.

"I'm fine for now," he lied, placed the cup on the table and tried desperately to ignore his burning throat.

"Well," she said, fluttering her eyelashes, "you should save it in case you get thirsty later. We have a water shortage here."

Larry nodded. "Listen," he said abruptly and stood, "I would love to stay here and chat, but I really do need to get to Telos. Would you mind giving me directions? After that, I will just be on my way."

Larry wished beyond hope that she would let him go.

"Oh, yes," Lillith said. "You need to find your son, not to mention all the other reasons you came, right? We shouldn't stand in your way." Larry blushed with this reminder. "But before you leave, we need to talk."

Larry tried to look away from her uncomfortable glare. "What do you want to talk about?" he asked.

"How did your son get down here to begin with?" she asked with one eyebrow raised.

"I actually don't know," he said, since it was the truth. "I received a call from my wife that he was missing and headed to Telos. So I decided to come down and check to—"

"Since you were coming here anyway," she cut him off. "That makes perfect sense, but why would your son want to come down here in the first place? How did he even know that Telos existed?" she interrogated him like a drill sergeant.

Her guards straightened their backs and their tails began to swish around while waiting for Larry's response.

"I don't know. Really! I don't know," he said. His voice trailed off and his heart began pounding. His mouth felt full of cotton and he could hardly make a sound.

"You don't think he was in contact with the Lemurians, do you?" Lillith asked.

"No," Larry said with conviction, wiping off beads of sweat. "Why would you think that?"

"The Lemurians have always tried to recruit humans for their ghastly projects. And if your son were involved in such a thing, we wouldn't be able to let you go." Lillith looked at him in a stubborn manner.

"Why's that?" He folded his arms as he spoke.

"Well, we are not really at war with the Lemurians, but they do try to destroy what we have accomplished on the surface world. As you can imagine, that doesn't please us very much." Lillith grinned sweetly, trying to hide her displeasure. "They really have no business there. It is not their job. Anyway, if we know their plans, we stand a better chance of protecting ourselves. Bait is always a great thing to have in these situations."

"You want to use me as bait?" Larry didn't know what to make of this.

"Not necessarily," she said with another sugary

smile. "But if your son is working for the Lemurians or the angels in Luz, we have a serious issue."

"My son?" Larry said, giving a phony laugh. "You're kidding, right? He is just a child. He's not working for anyone."

"Well, that is easily checked," she said and leaned back in her chair. She snapped her fingers, and a glowing crystal ball appeared in her left hand. She peered into it eagerly.

"Aha. See here, Larry." She drew her face close to the crystal, her green eyes widening. "Here is your son. He seems like he is walking in Luz with someone... Just as I thought."

"Adam's in Luz?" Larry protested. "Impossible!" He looked into the crystal ball in disbelief.

"Do I have the wrong kid?" Lillith said, one eyebrow raised.

Larry's shock was hard to hide.

"I didn't think so. Nothing is impossible down here. Now, you have a choice. You could help us since we see you are a reasonable man, or I can let my guards deal with you. They haven't eaten in days."

She gestured with her hand to either side of her chair where the winged creatures sneered. Their scaly arms and green claws shot out in unison as if to grab Larry. Their lips formed into horrible grins that showcased their yellow, pointy teeth.

He would rather eat live worms than have his

fate rest in their evil grips, but he also knew that Lillith was bad news too. And if he helped her, what would that make him?

A look of conflict spread over his face. "I can't help you," he said finally with all the courage he had left.

Lillith stood, staring into Larry's eyes and approached him. "Larry," she whispered, taking his hands, "we know you are a brilliant man."

Her magic enveloped his body, and he felt his knees go weak.

He knew she was using some sort of spell. Whether it was magic or just the pure evil of temptation, she was getting under his skin. He couldn't look away. He felt some kind of obsessive attraction for her, covering the disgust he otherwise felt. He tried to think of his wife and family, but he drew a blank. Slowly his will was being broken down.

"I'm a married man," he interjected warily.

"Oh, and what does being married have to do with this?"

She's right, Larry began thinking.

"Such a brilliant and handsome man. I admire your mind," she cooed. "And your body's so strong. Imagine how much power we could have together."

She steadily locked eyes with him and gently stroked his hand until every last bit of his willpower vanished.

"Okay. All right, I'll do it," he sighed

Lillith dropped her hands and grinned. She was satisfied with her work.

"Good. That's good. I knew you were a smart man," she said. Taking a few steps back, she turned around and beckoned for him to follow. "I would love for you to meet my family. Come this way."

He had just met pure evil disguised as a beautiful, sultry woman that he couldn't resist. Larry felt like a puppet. She pulled his invisible strings, and he followed her. He had no idea what he was getting into. There was no way he could pull himself out of this mess. No science or logic could save him now.

Chapter 20 –
Off To Telos

Charlie gestured for Adam to climb onto a small wooden boat tied to a dock.

"Isn't there some cooler way to get there? Can't we fly?" Adam asked. "This place is so advanced. Do we really need to take a boat?"

The truth was Adam got seasick quite easily, but the protest fell on deaf ears. Charlie had another plan in mind.

"Humility, Adam," Charlie reminded him, untying the line to the boat. "Humility is the key to reaching your potential."

Adam remained silent as Charlie began rowing.

"When you give it all of your effort," Charlie said, "that's when you are working toward your highest potential."

"What do you mean by potential?" Adam asked.

"You know, potential is kind of like a pot of dirt. It is just sitting there waiting for you to plant a seed. Otherwise, only weeds will grow."

All of these talks made Adam think about his life in a whole new way. Working on his potential didn't seem like any fun, though.

The rippling waves from the lake gently splashed against the oars. The water blended into a mixture of aqua blue and pink swirls. It seemed alive as if calling out to Adam to jump in. He looked into the colorful water in hopes of relieving his queasiness. While this strategy failed to cure Adam of his nausea, the current strengthened, provoking his stomach even further.

Charlie rowed the boat into a winding channel bursting with overgrown greenery. They meandered their way between two huge boulders that sat on the sandbars.

They reached open water where Adam could see the cityscape of Telos in the distance. He felt a rush of anticipation, and his eyes widened with delight. If Charlie was right, this was where all the pieces of the puzzle would fit together. Then he would finally understand what this was all about.

Tall buildings towered into the cloudless white sky. They shimmered like colorful glass and the reflections bounced off the water, almost blinding Adam. He closed his eyes. He felt the warmth of the sun beaming on his head. It all seemed surreal, like a fantasy painting by Monet. A vortex of tranquility filled his body. He just wanted to absorb everything. It was truly magnificent.

"You know, I haven't seen it get dark yet," Adam said, breaking the silence.

"You didn't realize that daytime never ends here?" Charlie laughed and motioned overhead. "If you can even call it daytime."

Adam looked at the sky. He hadn't actually noticed. His head had been too busy processing so much new information.

"So there is never night here?" Adam asked.

"No. The light just stays in one spot. Our sun is the center of our world. We have no moon or stars down here either," Charlie answered.

Adam thought about Telos, returning his gaze to the glimmering water. "What if the Lemurians don't like me?" A stressed expression filled his face as he bit a fingernail.

Charlie looked at him. "Don't worry. They will love you."

What's to love about me? Adam thought. "Well, that's not really what I'm worried about," he said hesitantly.

"So what is it?" Charlie asked.

"I don't know. I have this weird feeling like something is about to happen."

"Well," Charlie said, "it's called change, and it can be a good thing." Charlie tried to lighten the mood. "You know, the king in Telos is wise and patient. He has searched for years for someone like you to assist him. He can't wait to meet you, so relax."

Relax? How am I supposed to relax exactly?

Adam thought. He stared ahead in awe while they gradually approached Telos.

"Un-freakin' believable!" were the only words that Adam could say as they pulled into an aged, wooden dock. Small boats rested at the jetties, and a few submarines floated nearby. He noticed several silver spacecraft parked along the perimeter of the city.

Charlie tied a bowline making a temporary loop in the end of the rope to secure the boat to the dock.

Adam, feeling that Charlie had everything under control, curiously looked around. The place looked like a futurist space city. "Look at those UFOs!" he cried.

"They're incredible to ride in," Charlie said, extending his hand toward Adam to help him out of the boat as it rocked from side to side.

"It's so colorful here."

"See why they call it the Crystal City?"

"What's with all the crystals down here?" Adam asked, clearly mesmerized.

"Besides their natural beauty, crystals have a power to improve emotions and health."

"Really?" Adam said.

"Yes. You have heard of a quartz watch, right?"

"No," Adam answered.

"Oh, this is amazing. Many watches have a tiny quartz crystal inside. The quartz is infused with the vibration of time, which keeps a watch in sync with the fourth dimension called time."

"Cool."

"In Telos, crystals generate electricity to power up their city and their UFOs."

"I didn't know crystals can do all that!" Adam said enthusiastically.

"I didn't either until I came down here. Crystals absorb light energy, kind of like a battery. Then that power gets transferred to people and things."

Adam admired Charlie for his knowledge. He had never realized there was so much to know about nature, both obvious and hidden. He was learning a lot from these talks.

❁ ✳ ❁ ✳ ❁ ✳ ❁

After a few minutes of walking along a wide brick road, Adam noticed hundreds of modest houses all arranged in neat circles. Perfectly groomed trees with dainty leaves decorated the landscape. Everything on this part of town was orderly and peaceful like a quaint city.

A large white iridescent building stood out boldly on a humble hill ahead. Its roof was the shape of a pyramid. Hundreds of enormous buildings were clustered together on the other side of the hill. Adam felt as if he was in a fairytale dream.

"We're headed to the palace," Charlie said, pointing ahead.

The two walked in silence, passing thousands of very tall people on the streets, attending to everyday matters. They casually glanced and smiled at Adam and Charlie as they passed by. They walked amongst these celestial beings, some young and some old.

They were similarly dressed in pastel robes that skimmed the ground. Their pale faces were unique. Most had golden hair tied back in ponytails or buns. Beautiful headbands rested atop the women's heads to differentiate them from the men. Crystal necklaces were draped around their necks.

Even though Adam stood out like a sore thumb because of his brown hair and sneakers, he thought the inhabitants looked even more misplaced than he did.

They neared the palace. Just as they approached the front gates, Adam panicked for a moment, noticing an enormous white tiger sitting next to a hulky guard who stopped them. He, like the other inhabitants, had pale skin, but he wore a distinctive robe of deep blue. He seemed much more serious than any other pedestrian, nodding slightly when he noticed Charlie.

"Greetings, Kozbi. This is Adam," Charlie said.

The guard's eyes flew to Adam and inspected him curiously.

"Him?" he asked Charlie.

"Yes," Charlie confirmed.

Adam felt really awkward, like being on display.

"Welcome, Adoom. The king awaits for you a long time," the guard said in a stern tone. Between his strange accent and broken English, the man was virtually impossible to understand. Kozbi petted the tiger, took one step back and looked at Adam doubtfully before saying, "Me Kozbi. You follow."

Adam nodded uncomfortably, thinking he couldn't possibly be talking about waiting for him.

The guard left the oversized cat behind and led them into the palace toward what resembled a turbo lift door. He gestured for them to enter into a small square shaft that had silver chairs with seatbelts attached to the wall.

Charlie and Adam sat down and fastened themselves in, but Kozbi stood. He pressed four buttons quickly, and they blinked in rhythm. Adam felt the turbo lift jerk as it started moving upward, faster than anything he had ever ridden in. As it jolted to an abrupt halt, he checked the number on the top of the door. They were on the ninety-second floor.

Imagine, he was about to meet a king. All the while he felt excited and curious, but mostly nervous. Remembering they had a special mission for him made butterflies flutter in his stomach. Adam worried he could not do whatever it was that they needed from him. It was obvious from Kozbi's expression that he doubted his abilities too.

The door glided silently open. They walked down a wide hall until Kozbi brought them to a stop. They stood there, staring at each other until Kozbi opened a wooden door to reveal a room.

The trio stepped forward and the door closed behind them automatically. As Adam's eyes darted around at his surroundings, he found himself in a huge room lavishly decorated. The room twinkled with candles, the stone floor sparkled with all its might and the windows glistened even more so with prisms of light.

"Your majesty," Kozbi said, bowing his head, "Charlie and the boy, Adoom."

Chapter 21 –
The Girl

Adam's face filled with amazement, glancing to the far end of the huge dining area. Lemurian committee members, both men and women, sat in big, comfortable chairs next to tables filled with bowls of fruit.

Charlie hurried forward with Adam close behind until they came to a stop by a table.

"Hello, King Demetrius," Charlie said to the royal figure.

"A pleasure to welcome you both to Telos," the king said with a strong accent. He was more understandable than the guard, but his voice came across the hall as if through an echo. "Hello, my dear friend, Charlie. So, this is our Adam who has joined us from afar?"

"Yes." Charlie looked to Adam.

Some of the committee members sitting around the table broke out into foreign whispers.

"Let us rejoice at this moment," said the king, raising his gold goblet towards them.

Demetrius was nothing like Adam had expected. In his mind kings wore crowns and had beards. This beardless wonder hardly looked twenty-five. He had a solemn face and shoulder-length, white-blond hair tied back in a ponytail. Except for a large ring with a crimson stone, he was dressed quite plainly in a simple, golden robe.

"Adam, this is my dear wife Queen Adina," the king said, indicating the lady to his right.

Adam looked at an elegantly dressed woman. Her hair was tied in a bun, surrounded by jewels, and she wore a long-flowing, deep purple robe with gold trim. She smiled warmly and gave a welcoming gesture to the two guests.

"And our lovely princess, Lena," the queen said, putting her arm around her pretty daughter. "So, tell me child, how do you find our city so far?"

Immediately after he saw the princess, chills ran down Adam's arms. She was about his age and had lovely green eyes. Her long, blonde hair fell past her waist in a single braid. Like the others, her skin was the same pale color. Upon her head was a delicate crown with crystals that dangled onto her forehead. He saw her silver sandals barely visible under her long white dress. The strangest part was that she looked really familiar.

Then a bolt of déjà vu hit him as they went to take their seats at the dinner table. Adam sat, but he couldn't take his eyes off Lena. He realized she was the girl who had approached him at school and the girl from his dreams. She was real. Not only real, but she was the princess of Telos. For some reason, this seemed more impossible to believe than anything else he had experienced down here.

Charlie nudged Adam.

"What?" Adam's body jolted in alarm.

"The queen just asked you what you think of this city," Charlie asked.

Adam blushed with embarrassment. "Oh," he stuttered, "yeah, Telos…" As he tore his eyes off Lena, he could hardly speak. "The city is unbelievable. It's so beautiful!"

"We are glad it finds favor in your eyes," King Demetrius said pleasantly. "But please, dear child, do calm down. Your stress is disturbing the light."

Adam looked around and noticed that the light in the room had indeed dimmed.

"I'm sorry," he said, kicking himself under the table. He tried to steady his breathing by inhaling deeply.

"Perhaps a drink to refresh yourself?" a waiter offered Adam.

"Um, water, please."

He still could hardly talk. No sooner had he said the words, a goblet of water appeared in front of him. In his haste he knocked over the glass.

"I'm so sorry!" he cried. His cheeks turned red and he tried to wipe away the water on the table with his napkin.

"Not to worry, darling. The spilling of water brings good luck," Queen Adina said in a gentle manner.

"Lena, why don't you help our guest relax?" the king whispered to his daughter.

Lena nodded, and with a peaceful gesture she raised her hands toward Adam. After a few seconds, he felt warm energy flowing through his body and he instantly calmed down.

A bell rang and everyone rose. Adam quickly jumped to his feet and strained his neck to see what was going on. The centers of the tables opened up while waiters carried platters filled with a variety of foods. Adam watched intently as they placed the elaborate dishes on the elongated tables.

The king served himself first, then the queen. Afterwards, everyone else chose what they wanted to eat from the buffet. Hesitant to move in fear of doing the wrong thing, Adam just stood there.

"Help yourself," Charlie nudged. "You must be hungry."

Nothing on the table resembled anything Adam recognized except for some large grapes.

"Oh, everything looks so interesting," he lied, speaking to Charlie. "May I ask what this is?"

"It is a tasty mixture of vegetables and spices," the queen answered politely, overhearing his question.

Adam's expression was hard to hide. He really

hated vegetables.

"What would be your pleasure? I will request that my chef prepare it for you," the queen offered.

"Oh, that's okay," he replied.

"Oh, speak up. Don't be shy," the queen said.

"Pizza, chicken, hamburgers, you know, the basics, but don't worry. It's really okay."

"Oh, a thousand apologies, lad, but we are vegetarians. Charlie might have skipped over that detail," the queen explained with a grin in Charlie's direction.

Charlie gave a guilty shrug. "I became so used to it, that it seemed obvious."

Adam couldn't have felt more awkward. He knew he should have just eaten the food and kept quiet.

"Well, I'll just have some fruit." Picking a cluster of grapes from the fruit platter, he noticed how large each one was. "These are the biggest grapes I've ever seen," he said and sat down.

"Please note, Adam, that we grow everything we need on just ten acres of land; enough to feed our million and a half people down here," the king announced proudly.

"And there are no poisons," the queen chimed in. "We do not comprehend why people spray poison on fruits and vegetables."

Adam looked at her confused.

Charlie added, "Plus it's all free. Every morning you just come and take whatever you need. What a great idea, huh, Adam? They don't use money down here. Each person has a job that is for the benefit of the whole community, so everyone looks after each other."

"Socialism at its finest," the king said proudly. "You see, money was created to control people. We just want to love everybody," the king said and began eating.

"Neat!" Adam wasn't sure what to think of a system like that.

As they ate, two musicians entertained the guests. A young lady played a harp-like instrument. Her fingers gracefully danced across the strings. Another lady created musical vibrations by circling her hands around various sized crystal bowls, making the atmosphere feel dreamlike.

As the meal ended, Adam sensed that something important was about to happen.

Chapter 22 –
The King Speaks

King Demetrius cleared his throat and declared, "We hope you have satisfied yourselves, and now we believe the time has come to discuss the business at hand."

Silence filled the room.

"Adam, have you been informed as to why you were selected to join us here?"

"A little," Adam said timidly. He realized that all eyes were on him, and the dignified people at the table probably expected a more eloquent answer. He lowered his head in disgrace. "To be honest, I'm not really sure what this has to do with me."

"Charlie?" Demetrius asked, leaning on one elbow and gesturing for an answer.

"He knows he has been chosen for a mission," Charlie said with authority. "He knows it involves bettering the surface world, but he does not know what this mission will entail. I have left that for you to explain."

"How kind of you. Very well," the king said, and he motioned to a man standing behind him.

On the table a waiter placed a solid white pyramid about a foot high, which had a tiny pyramid etched onto one side. Demetrius stood and inserted a small, gold pyramid-shaped key into the etched section. The top of the white pyramid popped open like a jewelry box, revealing its contents.

Demetrius reached inside and removed a folded sheet of paper and a few bracelets made of white, pink and black crystals. He walked over to Adam and placed them on the table before him.

"These bracelets are called Telos bands, and they possess a great influence over the surface world," Demetrius announced. "We made them for your young people who hold the keys to peace."

"A Telos band?" Adam asked, holding back his uncertainty.

"My son, we are all composed of crystalline elements from the earth, as are all crystals and gemstones. Their purpose is to guide and protect us. This black gemstone, for example," the king said, pointing, "is tourmaline, and it repels negative thoughts from your mind. The crystal rose quartz helps to unblock your heart, revealing feelings of gratefulness. They, like us, all have their own special purposes."

The king looked at Adam to see if he understood his explanation so far.

"This white one is a Lemurian Seed Crystal that we infused with the imprint of love and peace. The power of these bracelets is the special bridge that connects us with each other through love. They transfer that goodness to whoever wears one."

"Interesting," Adam said, examining one bracelet carefully. He unfolded the paper the king had removed from the pyramid, revealing a blank sheet. He flipped it over to check the other side and looked over to Charlie. "There's nothing on here."

"Don't worry about that right now," Charlie whispered under his breath to Adam.

The king continued, "Also, the Telos band is infused with what is called quantum energy. It allows you to tap into the hidden knowledge of the global consciousness of goodness. It helps to remove the blinders of the physical world that restrict your perception of reality.

"Our goal is to get as many kids as possible to come together to bring balance and harmony to themselves and the world. They will become a part of a global movement to alter the cosmic forces at hand."

The people sitting around the table all nodded their heads in agreement and smiled at their wonderful king.

Demetrius could tell by Adam's face that he didn't completely understand what he was hearing. "Do not underestimate the power of this Telos band, my child."

"So the Telos bands are supposed to bring world peace?" Adam asked, raising his eyebrows.

"No," Demetrius said laughing. "These bands cannot bring peace by themselves. They are only the tools to help. It would be one hundred times harder to accomplish peace without the assistance of them. The first step to peace is ridding your mind of negative emotions that prevent you from tapping into the light.

"The second step is to fill your heart with love and focus on the goodness of the world. The crystals help with both things. All you have to do is give them to kids who want to make a difference in your world. It's that simple. Then get other kids to show their friends how they can help until we have our army for peace."

"Why don't you just go there and hand the crystal bands out to everyone yourself?" Adam asked in a curious tone. "Why do you need me?"

"We have tried. Believe me," Demetrius said and waved a bracelet in the air. "The queen and I have secretly gone all around the world trying to accomplish this goal. But we were always rejected."

"Why? It seems like such a simple thing," Adam said.

"People are afraid of what they do not understand, especially adults, as we have discovered," Demetrius said with a sad face. "When we had tried this with adults, they deemed us insane and paid us no heed. The few that believed in our goals were unable to convince others. They simply lacked the vision."

"If you couldn't do it—and you are pretty extraordinary," Adam argued, "—how am I supposed to make any kind of difference?"

The king had a great answer. "The youth are naturally more open to new ideas. They are filled with enthusiasm and curiosity without putting up roadblocks to great solutions. It's just a matter of whether they choose to become a part of the movement, with you to lead them," he said, pointing to Adam.

Adam felt stuck. Yes, he wanted to make a difference in the world, but this project was way out of his league from the sound of things.

"I don't know," Adam said hesitantly, examining the bracelet again. "You had to use pink stones?" He couldn't see himself wearing one, let alone giving them out to other boys.

Demetrius didn't flinch. "My son, that pink crystal helps you feel less judgmental towards yourself and others, which is an important element in your mission."

Adam thought to himself, No way. I'm not wearing one of those. "Okay, and so what's this?" he said, looking at the folded sheet of paper.

"This paper becomes a map when activated that shows where we are storing all the Telos bands," the king said. "We have been carefully planning this for many centuries. Thousands of years ago, our ancestors planted millions of Telos bracelets under various ancient ruins, waiting for the right time to give them out. We knew that one day we would find the right youngster to help us," the king said encouragingly. "Thank goodness you are here now."

Adam looked hopelessly at Charlie and noticed everyone looking at him waiting for his comments. He felt his mind muddled with uncertainty.

"Well, if you're thinking of me, you really must be confused," Adam said. He had a hard time accepting any of this so-called plan. It was way too crazy.

Charlie closed his eyes and lowered his head with disappointment.

"Of course you would feel that way," Demetrius sympathized. "But Charlie and Nicky both believe that you possess the right heart for this mission."

Heart? Adam thought. What do internal organs got to do with it? He let his eyes wander to Lena. She beamed encouragingly back at him.

He quickly looked away and said, "So you want me to go to the surface world and convince a bunch of kids that we can get rid of war and violence if we just wear some Telos crystals around our wrist?"

The committee members at the table, having heard this talk before, lost interest and started talking quietly amongst themselves.

"That is part of it," the king said simply.

Adam stared at him and said, "I'm supposed to

ask them to love one another and come together for world peace? Plus, ask them to tell their friends as well?" Adam asked, recounting the king's idea. It sounded even more absurd to him when he repeated it in his own words.

"It requires a bit more than that," Demetrius said, laughing. "Although, I am glad you have mastered the basic concept."

"I'm really sorry," Adam said. "No one can do that alone."

"Adam!" Charlie exclaimed with alarm. His plan was not going well.

Demetrius said, "You surely cannot if you refuse to even try. Please know that you will be given thousands of youngsters all around the world to help you known as Star Children. Within this group of youngsters are Indigo, Crystal and Rainbow Children. They will know who they are when you call them to action."

Adam looked unimpressed and sighed.

Charlie chimed in, "Gypsy has agreed to help you too."

"Oh, how encouraging to know I have a dog to help me and some Star Kids?" Adam said sarcastically. "No one is going to listen to me."

The king looked humbly at Adam and replied, "My son, once you are born into this grand world, in reality you have little say-so over most of your lot in life. You have no control whether you are born a boy or girl, smart or dumb, rich or poor. For that matter, if you are healthy or sick, pretty or ugly, a slave or free man, blessed with a long life or destined to die young. Would you not agree, son?"

Adam nodded as his brain processed that whole long list of adjectives. "Sure."

"The only say-so you have in your life is how you react to all those predetermined things imposed upon you by your Creator. Wouldn't you want to use your God-given gifts to make your world a better place? Only you can make that choice."

Adam considered that. Although the king had made a good point, Adam felt awkward around people. It didn't matter how many assistants he had. If he couldn't get people to believe in what he had to say, this wasn't going to work.

❀ ✳ ❀ ✳ ❀ ✳ ❀

Adam's head snapped up suddenly. Lena! She was able to place feelings of confidence in people. He had felt it firsthand. Having this beautiful princess next to him would make him feel self-assured and he might have a chance at success.

He looked at Demetrius and realized that he was waiting for a reply.

"Okay. I'll try to do it!" Adam said with some conviction.

Charlie and the king smiled at each other with

pleasant surprise.

"But on one condition." Adam tried to keep himself from turning red again.

Silence filled the air.

"And what, my child, is this condition?" Demetrius asked, as his eyes crinkled slightly in amusement.

"I want Lena to come up to help me as my assistant," he announced with his arms folded. What a brilliant idea, he thought to himself.

All traces of amusement left the king's face and impatience crept across his eyes. "Absolutely not!" Demetrius exclaimed. Controlling his outrage took every ounce of strength he had. "How could you suggest such an idea!"

On second thought, really bad idea, Adam realized.

Charlie quickly spoke, "Maybe we should give the boy a chance to explain himself."

"There is nothing to explain," the king muttered. "I can't let my precious daughter be contaminated by the surface world. Find someone else, Charlie. We need a child with courage and integrity; someone who will melt cold hearts to truth, and not hide behind our princess!"

With every word the king spoke, Adam slid lower into his chair, wishing the sides would fold over and cover him. He had not expected this response. His heart sank into darkness and his blood ran cold. How could the king of Telos be so completely misunderstanding?

"Father," Lena whispered softly in her father's ear and placed her small hand over his. "Please, let me speak to Adam."

"Why?" Demetrius responded.

"Father, please. Listen with your heart and not your mind," she pleaded. "Let me talk with him to see if I can figure this out."

How could he refuse his beloved daughter? The committee of people returned their attention to their agitated king.

"Very well," Demetrius said in a slightly calmer voice. "You may speak with the boy. I need to consult with Charlie and the committee members now, anyway."

Lena stood and walked toward the door, accustomed to people's attentive looks. Turning around to Adam she said, "Are you coming?"

"Oh, yeah," he said, stumbling in haste to follow her out of the room. Adam's feet felt heavy, and he wasn't used to the long robe he was wearing. This whole adventure was turning into a bit of a nightmare.

Demetrius waited to speak to Charlie until the door was closed behind Adam and Lena.

"Charlie, this is the boy you bring me?" he asked warily.

"Trust me, trust me, old friend," Charlie said. "This boy has the suitable qualities we need to save the surface world."

"I am not so sure that is sufficient," Demetrius retorted. "We need a leader, not a wounded soldier who is ready to go home before the battle has even begun."

"Are you going to judge this boy's courage by only one meeting?" Charlie debated. "After all, he has been raised by a typical surface family, being put down and told he is worth nothing. How can you expect him to have any self-respect?"

Demetrius was quiet, trying to process what Charlie was saying.

Charlie continued, "He was taken from his home and brought to our strange, new world, and so much is being demanded from him. You must give him a chance. You should not crush his spirit. I see Adam's powerful potential. After all, he had the courage to speak to you. He didn't actually turn you down. Remember, this is not a small thing that you ask."

"You do speak the truth, my friend," Demetrius said. "But are you not somewhat biased? Wasn't he your son?" the king asked, clearing his throat uncomfortably. He raised his eyebrows in a questioning look.

"My affection for Adam is biased," Charlie agreed, holding his chin high with dignity, "but I would never let that interfere with the future of the world."

"I do not doubt you," Demetrius said quickly. "But from what I have seen so far, Adam is not qualified. I cannot work with negativity. He will endanger the success of the entire mission."

Charlie raised his finger and said, "Remember: Adam possesses the soul of Absalom, son of the ancient King David. Absalom was never allowed to finish his work and they killed him before he could bring world peace."

"Yes, you are right, because Absalom misused his power and wasted his potential. Does Adam understand his past life history?" the king asked.

"It was confusing enough explaining to him that I was related to him in another lifetime. I thought that if I had told him he possessed a soul of ancient royalty, it was far too much for him to handle in one discussion. He does, undoubtedly, have the potential for greatness."

"Charlie, we all possess the potential for greatness, but if we do not know that it exists and we do not use it, it cannot help anyone, can it?" the king said.

"Test him," Charlie said simply. "Let him realize his own greatness."

Demetrius paused in thought for a moment.

"Okay, then, three tests," he said, holding three fingers in the air.

"You will not be disappointed," Charlie said, relieved that he had not been rejected outright by the king.

"I certainly hope you are correct," Demetrius quipped.

Charlie was quick with his reply. "You will not be sorry."

Chapter 23 –
The Pep Talk

Adam followed Lena onto a balcony overlooking the mystical city. Kozbi was several steps behind. Adam avoided any eye contact with her. He realized he had embarrassed himself in front of the king and somehow let her down, which gave a terrible first impression.

Lena and Adam faced each other awkwardly.

"Will you please give us some privacy?" Lena asked Kozbi.

"No," Kozbi said sharply. "Your father...not alone with him!"

"My father would want what is best for everyone," Lena retorted kindly. Kozbi stared at her for a moment, and she returned his glare with a sweet smile.

"Fine," he said. "You talk. I watch."

"Thank you," she said.

Kozbi stood a few feet away, never taking his eyes off them.

"So—" Adam said, shifting his weight and trying to avoid her incredibly beautiful eyes. His knees felt shaky.

"Why do you want me to accompany you on this mission? You can do this yourself," she said.

Lena's straightforward nature surprised Adam.

"I can't do this without your help," he said lamely. "Because you've seen how I act. I am such a klutz. I can be strong if I feel I'm right, but if someone yells at me, I turn into a wimp. Who's going to listen to me if I act like that?"

"How can I help you?" she pushed.

Adam looked down and kicked at the floor. "My mom once told me that behind every good man is a great woman—or is it in front of a man? Well, either way, I really need your help." He couldn't believe he actually admitted that.

Lena shook her head. "You must not mention that to my father. You need to find the greatness in yourself. I would be honored to help you. You just have to convince my father."

"He made himself very clear the answer is no," Adam said. His aggravation was showing. "I thought you people here were supposed to be loving and not so judgmental. How could he embarrass me like that in front of everyone?"

"Being loving doesn't mean we do not feel emotions. Think about it from my father's perspective. He has waited for years for Charlie to bring down a special boy from the surface world. And then this boy, who has not in any way earned my father's trust, asks to take his only daughter to the surface world, which he has always known to be filled with danger. Just think about being in his shoes for a second."

Adam stood quietly. "Okay," he finally said. "I think I see your point. I guess I should apologize and try to express myself better to your father."

"The mission might seem hard, but you will succeed. You'll see."

"How do you know? Whenever I try something, I never succeed. And then everyone thinks I'm a failure, so I just stop trying. I don't want anyone depending on me. I can't accomplish anything by myself. If I didn't have Gypsy with me, I doubt that I would have even made it here."

"That's not true. Where did you get that idea?"

"My dad, my brother and kids at school. Things are never right no matter how hard I work at it," he said with frustration.

Lena's hands flew to her mouth. "Oh, I'm sorry."

"Don't be," he said.

"It's so sad. It sounds as if you believe you are defective, but you're not."

"It's how I've lived my whole life, people telling me I can't do anything right. I got used to it."

"Prove them wrong, Adam," she encouraged. "Show them you can do it. You're really amazing, but you have to believe in yourself if you want others to believe in you."

He looked at her pleading, gentle eyes. He wasn't sure what to say.

"We should get back," she said.

"One more thing," he stopped her. "I've seen you before."

"What?" she asked, delighted. "You have?"

"I've seen you before I came to Telos," he said. "I … I saw you in my dream and at my school."

He waited for her reaction. Saying all this was certainly awkward for him, but Lena wasn't remotely astounded, not in the least.

"Oh, great!" she exclaimed. "Then you are the right one. I sent images of myself to the boy who was destined to help the surface world, but it is hard to do. I was not sure it worked. But it did!" She was overly excited. "Perfect! Just wait until I tell my father. How were they? The images, I mean? Were they clear?"

"Yes," he said, still perplexed with her reaction. "But it wasn't only a picture of you."

"No?" Lena asked. "What else was it?"

"You came to me, but before I could understand what you were talking about, you disappeared," he explained. "I thought you were in some kind of real danger."

"Oh, you don't need to worry about something like that," she said joyfully. "It was probably a mistake on my part. I told you it is quite complicated to send images to people, and I am not very good at it."

They walked back into the palace, Kozbi following closely behind. It was time for round two with the king.

Lena, Adam and Kozbi walked into the dining hall and without hesitation took their seats. Adam glanced at Charlie to see his expression. Charlie gave him an encouraging smile and a thumbs-up that all was well. Adam looked relieved even though his chest was weighed down with heaviness.

Lena whispered into her father's ear, "He is the one! He got my images."

"Adam. Come forward," Demetrius instructed.

"Yes, sir," Adam said, approaching the king, bowing his head slightly.

"I apologize for my hurtful words," the king began. "You must know that Lena means more to me than anything, and worry leads me to act in ways you would not expect from us."

"I understand now, King," Adam tried to speak from his heart, even though it was pounding so hard. Controlling his nerves was even tougher. "You act out of love for your daughter."

"Thank you for understanding," Demetrius said, noticeably calmed down.

"But I would like you to hear me out," Adam said, feeling confident.

"Go ahead." Demetrius gestured for him to continue.

"I think that I can do this mission and convince other kids to help bring peace," Adam paused, "but only if they are willing to listen. Many won't and may even laugh at me. I just thought I would have a better chance at success with Lena's help. People will see her beauty and charm and naturally want to join us. I see now it was a bad idea."

Adam sat down and stared at Charlie.

The king's face was expressionless. He sighed deeply and spoke. "Adam, I see your perspective, and what you say may seem reasonable to you, but know that we couldn't let Lena go to the surface with you. I am truly sorry."

"I understand," Adam said, disappointed.

"This meeting is adjourned," the king announced, facing the people. "Thank you, my dear friends, for joining us."

On that note, the men and women of the committee began chatting in their native tongue as they exited the dining hall.

"You did well," Charlie whispered in Adam's ear.

"I did horribly. It didn't work, and I don't know how I can ever accomplish this mission without her," Adam said.

"Initially, it may seem that way," Charlie said with encouragement. "You spoke your mind, which counts for something. Let's get back to Luz. We will return here first thing tomorrow for another meeting."

"Another one!" Adam asked with dread.

As they began walking toward the door, Queen Adina stopped them. "It was our most honorable pleasure to meet you," she said.

"You too," Adam replied.

"We'll see you tomorrow," Charlie chimed in.

"Oh, why leave just to return again tomorrow?" the queen stated. "Please stay with us. This palace has more than enough rooms for you and Adam. You must. We insist."

"Thank you so much for the offer, but we wouldn't take advantage of your hospitality."

"It was not an offer," Queen Adina insisted. "It is an order from the queen. You can hardly refuse that, can you?" She smiled sweetly, started to walk away and then turned around. "Take the turbo lift to the guest quarters on the fourth floor."

Charlie chuckled. "What a great woman. It's not every day we get to stay at the king's palace. Let's go to our rooms as the queen commands."

"Adam!" A voice called from behind. He turned around and saw Lena hurrying toward him.

"Did I hear you're staying over?" she asked with delight.

"Yes, it looks like I am," Adam answered, holding back his excitement.

"Do you want me to show you around Telos?" Lena asked.

"Sure!" Adam turned to Charlie. "Is that okay?"

"Most definitely," Charlie said.

Adam followed Lena to the turbo lift, smiling with genuine happiness.

"So there! He accepted the mission," Charlie said to Demetrius.

They were sitting in the empty dining hall, drinking some herbal tea.

"In a roundabout way, I suppose he did. Do not think he is off the hook," Demetrius warned. "I still plan to test him. Three tests, and he must pass them all."

"I don't think you will be disappointed," Charlie encouraged.

"Before testing him, though, there's a slight problem that you need to be informed of," Demetrius said.

"What's that?" Charlie asked, putting his cup of tea down.

"I need you to meet someone. His name is Simon, and my guard says he is Adam's father's partner from the surface world."

Chapter 24 –
The Magical Ride

What a feeling to be walking out of the palace with the princess by his side. Adam peeked over his shoulder to see if anyone was around. Unfortunately, Kozbi was walking directly behind them.

People stared at Lena, who was obviously well known, while they walked down a grand street. Tall, colorful skyscrapers reflected the sun above. In mid-air, a silent train raced around the city.

"So where are we going?" Adam asked.

"The beach," she replied playfully.

"Cool!" Adam had already been to the beach in Luz, but he didn't mind going again, especially with her.

When they arrived, Lena told Adam to take off his shoes.

"Why?"

"You'll see," she said grinning, removing her sandals.

They looked cute strolling barefoot on the soft sand together, creating two pairs of footprints as they walked down the shoreline for a while. They talked about the differences between growing up in Telos and the surface world.

"Wow, this is heaven!" he exclaimed. "There's so much light here."

"You like light. Watch this." She cupped her two hands together in front of her and stared intently straight ahead for a moment. A small ball of light hovered just above her hands and radiated onto her face.

Adam stared in amazement. "That's awesome. What is it?"

"It is called Vril energy. This is the force the entire world is made of. When you know how to control it, you can do really incredible things. I use it for fun and enjoy watching the ball of light roll up and down my hands." She closed one hand over the other and extinguished it.

"That's so cool."

"Want to see something even cooler? Follow me."

Lena led Adam to meet to her favorite friend, Shanendeau, who lived in the wooden stables situated next to the palace.

"Is that a Pegasus?" Adam exclaimed.

Lena nodded.

"Of course, only down here," Adam said, cautiously petting Shanendeau's white mane. Large wings protruded from her neck and colorful ribbons streamed from her tail. The striking creature stood proudly with her head high like a great ruler. Her pale blue eyes mirrored the sky. "He's beautiful."

"He's a she," Lena said, giggling.

"This is definitely the highlight of my trip, except for meeting you," he said enthusiastically

Lena smiled brightly. "This is where I love to spend most of my time when I want to be alone."

She plucked an apple-like fruit from a nearby tree. She grabbed Shanendeau's strong, silvery mane with one hand and fed her the fruit with the other.

She lifted her long robe just above her knees and swung one leg over the Pegasus' bare back. He couldn't help but notice her long legs protruding from her robe. Lena looked so regal. Adam walked closely to her as they strolled along the beach.

"Want to join me up here?" she asked sweetly.

He would be an idiot to refuse such an offer. "Sure."

Lena extended a hand down. Adam reached up to grab it, noticing it was soft and warm. She tugged him upwards while he lifted a leg up and over the Pegasus, landing directly behind her. His legs dangled awkwardly. He tried to balance himself, pressing his thighs into Shanendeau's sides. He bent his knees forward, searching for a spot to rest them. The natural spot was just inches behind Lena's knees. He wasn't sure what to do next. He was fearful of doing something wrong.

She gathered her hair out of Adam's face and draped it down her chest.

"Let's go for a real ride. Hang on," she told him, smiling with delight.

Lena scooted back closer to Adam, almost touching her back to his chest. He tried to hold on with his thighs, but that clearly wasn't going to work. He would surely fall right off, especially since he had never ridden a Pegasus before, or even a horse, for that matter. Shanendeau began trotting.

"Hold on to my waist," she suggested.

Her waist? How could he refuse? He raised his arms from his sides and awkwardly grabbed onto her hips. She guided his hands off her hips, pulled him closer and leaned back, nestling into his chest. He wrapped his arms around her waist, completely embracing her.

Adam inhaled, deeply intoxicated by her scent. He had never been so close to a girl. As awkward as this position was, he had to admit it was amazing. He felt a wave of love percolate all over his body.

Lena directed Shanendeau to trot alongside the glistening shoreline for a few minutes, gaining speed. When she spread her wings like a butterfly, they began ascending into the sky.

Adam held on to Lena for dear life. He closed his eyes briefly trying to fully enjoy this seemingly impossible moment. The warm wind brushed against his face and ruffled his hair. Adam grinned widely. Strands of Lena's golden hair escaped from her braid and flew in his face. She looked over her shoulder and smiled.

"See? I don't even have to guide her," she demonstrated. "Shanendeau will go wherever we want without reins or whips; just a request."

Shanendeau began to descend, ending with a running gallop. Adam wished this moment could last forever. Even though Lena was from another world, she seemed so similar to him, even loving animals too. Of course, being so beautiful and graceful was a plus, but best of all, she seemed to really like him. Now that he had her in his arms, how could he ever let go? He knew that his arms weren't all that were wrapped around this exotic girl. His heart was wrapped around hers.

Just as soon as that thought entered his mind, to his incredible disappointment, he saw Kozbi riding his horse, looking through his binoculars, not far behind.

"Stop at once! Return to the castle!" Kozbi shouted.

Shanendeau stopped.

An emptiness crept inside of Adam, and he dropped his hands to his sides.

"I'm just showing Adam around Telos," Lena said.

"Princess, your father won't be happy," Kozbi said, glaring at Adam.

"With what?" she asked innocently.

"You too close," he accused.

"Relax, Kozbi. We were just going for a ride. Adam had to hold onto me or he would have fallen off. You're ruining all our fun," she protested.

"Too much fun!"

Lena directed the Pegasus to return to the castle. Adam knew that his joyride would shortly end, but meanwhile, he had a good excuse to hold on to her for one last time.

Once they arrived at the stables, Adam slid off first and offered his hand up to Lena to help her off. She took his hand and fell right into his arms, taking full advantage of their last moment alone together. Lena wanted to give him lots of motivation to do the mission. She was succeeding admirably.

Then reality sank into the moment as Kozbi approached them. Adam broke his embrace and placed his arms behind him, looking as if he had gotten caught with his hand in a cookie jar.

"Princess! Your father not be happy," Kozbi said in an annoyed voice.

"I am just trying to make him more comfortable. He is so nervous."

"Not with boy," Kozbi warned. "A human boy. Poor judgment. Not good, Princess. Get upstairs."

Adam realized that he had gotten Lena into trouble. He could have just blown his chances of gaining the king's trust.

Wow! I know what I was feeling, but geez, what was I thinking, he thought in bewilderment, following her into the castle and feeling, ironically, on top of the world.

Little did Adam realize at his young age that love always conquers logic.

Chapter 25 –
Reality Check

Adam stopped dead in his tracks once he and Lena returned inside the palace to the guest quarters.

"Simon!" he cried with surprise, entering a large room.

Demetrius and Charlie stood in the room with a guard next to Simon, who looked very nervous.

"Welcome back, Adam," Demetrius said. "I see you know each other."

"Yes!" Adam exclaimed. "This is my dad's partner. You guys made it down here. Where's my dad?"

Simon stared blankly at him, not sure what to say.

"Is he here?"

"No, Adam," Charlie said. He put his hands on the boy's shoulders. "Your father's not here."

"Well then, where is he?" Adam pushed.

"Not sure. We got separated from each other." Simon spoke for the first time, his voice weary. "I wish I had better news."

"How?" Adam asked desperately.

"Our plane was attacked by these people," Simon complained, eyeing Demetrius and Charlie with uneasiness.

"To be fair, you weren't invited here," Demetrius explained calmly.

"Didn't know I needed an invite. We came just to see if this place really existed."

"So you could get your evidence and expose our hidden paradise to the world," Demetrius said.

The king's words silenced Simon, since that part was actually true.

Looking from the king to Simon, Adam insisted, "So where is he then?"

"By the sounds of it, he is probably in Draconia," Charlie announced with dread.

"What do you mean, Draconia?" Adam said, searching each person's face for any clues.

There was an uneasy silence.

"You came here together. He has to be with you. I knew you were up to no good!"

"When we bailed out of our plane with our parachutes, we got blown in different directions by the wind," Simon said, motioning in the air with his hands. "That had nothing to do with me! Okay?"

"What?" Adam turned to Charlie, pleading. "If he's in Draconia, what does that mean?"

"Well, if they found him, I have a feeling that they will try to use him," Charlie said. "Your father's body and mind can be useful in many ways to the demons living there. If he is forced to help them, it's very bad news."

"No way! He'll never agree to do that!" Adam shouted. "We have to save him now."

"Agreed," Demetrius cut in. "We will rescue him for your sake, Adam, but after that, we are sending both Simon and your father back to the surface immediately."

"Thank God," Simon mumbled under his breath. The guards escorted him out of the room.

"What are we going to do about my dad?"

"The Draconians have much to fear from us," Charlie answered with certainty. "If we fly over there and snatch your father, I doubt there would be much objection; none that we couldn't handle, anyway."

"Are you coming with me?" Adam asked, concerned that he had to go alone.

"Of course," Charlie said. "We'll bring a guard as well, if that meets with your approval, Demetrius."

The king was in deep thought. "Of course," he said slowly. "And ... take Lena with you too."

"What?" Lena, Charlie and Adam cried in unison.

"You heard me," Demetrius said loudly.

Adam and Charlie looked at each other in astonishment.

"Are you sure?" Charlie asked cautiously. He was completely confused. Draconia was much worse than the surface world.

Demetrius said to Adam with confidence. "Don't let me down. You should go immediately. Charlie and Lena, go to the transporter. Adam, meet them there in five minutes."

"Um ..." Adam stammered. "Sure."

"Take this crystal bracelet to help strengthen your courage." The king handed it to Adam.

Adam slipped the Telos bracelet over his wrist as everyone left the room, leaving him alone feeling quite perplexed. Right now, what mattered most to him was getting his dad safely out of Draconia.

❁ ✳ ❁ ✳ ❁ ✳ ❁

Figuring his way out of the palace's maze of rooms and corridors was trickier than he had realized. Anxiety overtook him when he found that so many rooms led into each other or dead ends. He couldn't find any turbo lifts anywhere.

Relief replaced anxiety when he eventually found Kozbi wandering in one of the halls, searching for him. Kozbi escorted him out of the palace.

Charlie, Lena and a guard, who had been assigned to help, were waiting for Adam by a transporter. Its rounded windows protruded to a point around the center. They all hustled into the aircraft.

"Hurry, Adam," Charlie shouted and scurried past him. "Let's go!"

Adam looked at Charlie with apprehension. He climbed the steps onto the transporter. Once on board, he saw about twenty over-sized seats arranged in a circle. In the middle stood a large, round platform with a control panel. The pilot took his place behind the controls and started the engine.

Adam naturally chose the seat next to Lena, who was looking out the window unaware of his presence or seemed to be ignoring him. He figured maybe she was mad at him for getting her into trouble. Or maybe she was just scared, since she had never left Telos. She looked different somehow, maybe because she had removed her small crown. He wished he could read her mind. It would sure come in handy now. Oddly, his gift was failing him.

The engines made a soft whirring sound as they took off. Within seconds they ascended straight up and then forward, racing through the cloudless sky. Adam watched through the window as the horizon darkened from a tranquil blue to gray, and then to terracotta orange.

We must be getting close, he thought.

A few minutes later, the aircraft slowed, hovered and descended. When they landed, Adam spoke to Lena to break the silence, "Do you think we are there already?"

"Yes," Lena said curtly. She stood and headed toward the exit. Charlie remained seated.

"Aren't you coming?" Adam asked when Charlie didn't move from his seat.

"Not yet," Charlie said. "I'm sending you and Lena with the guard. The Draconians have sensors here to warn them when any adults from the surface arrive, but they won't pick up children. I cannot go unless I am absolutely needed."

That doesn't make any sense, Adam thought. Everyone is acting so strange. He worried that maybe they thought he was a part of Simon's plan. Stepping out of the door, Adam took a deep breath and sprinted down the walkway. Lena was waiting for him at the bottom, looking quite serious.

"Let's go," she said fearlessly, pointing to a lifeless mountain silhouetted against an orange and greyish sky. "That dreadful place is just over the hill."

"How do you know?" he asked with concern in his voice, knowing she had not traveled outside Telos.

"My father showed me a map earlier." Her voice sounded heavy and dead-like without any sparkle of life at all.

Adam led the way, struggling through the steep path on the charred mountainside as the two others followed behind. Adam's annoyance showed on his face. Wasn't a guard supposed to walk in front of them in case anything happened?

He stopped to catch his breath. Sitting on a large boulder, he inhaled deeply and instantly regretted it. The air burned his throat like hot smoke. Unfortunately, no one had brought any water.

Without warning, Lena let out an ear-piercing

scream that echoed across the empty landscape. Adam jumped up instinctively and glanced back. He realized something hideous had grabbed her. Tall, green and scaly, the thing was like something out of a nightmare. It had wrapped one grotesque arm around Lena and hissed with its repulsive forked tongue. She dangled like a ragdoll held high in the air by its clutches.

As Lena gasped and struggled to escape, the scary monster lashed out with lightning speed at Adam and the guard.

Before Adam could think rationally about his predicament, he saw the beast swing at the guard with a massive claw, striking him hard across the chest. The poor guy flew to the ground with a thud. He staggered to his feet and fled.

Adam's brain seemed frozen from fear. He had to save the princess! Think, Adam! There was no other option.

"Stop!" he shrieked to the monster. "Let her go!"

The beast started wobbling away, ignoring his plea.

"Put her down," Adam shouted in utter desperation.

Looking around frantically for a weapon, he spotted a long charred branch lying on the ground. He snatched it in mid-step without a second thought, his brain flowing with adrenalin. He ran toward the monster, quickly gaining on it. He came within reach and took a leap, clumsily swinging the branch. It smashed into pieces on the beast's head.

The beast turned its head around as if on cue. Adam noticed a sinister grin playing across the monster's demented features. The creature didn't even blink. Its smirk grew wider as it let out a high-pitched mocking laugh, giving Adam goose bumps. While he moved slowly backwards, staring at the beast, he tripped on a rock.

"Thinksss yousss can harmsss me humansss," the monster hissed, as the words slithered off its forked tongue. Adam saw Lena's body dangle helplessly in the monster's grip. "Sssurface sscum," it blustered in anger, knocking Adam to the floor with one swift swing of its free arm.

Adam hit the ground hard. With a flash of pain pounding through his skull, he felt blood trickling down his chin. He wiped it off with the corner of his dirty sleeve. His knew his strength was running low, but he couldn't quit.

As the creature turned around to face him, Adam propped himself on his elbows weakly. "She's the princess of Telos!" he choked. "If you take her, you're dead."

The creepy creature turned slowly and looked at him with its huge, yellow eyes. Adam's determination prevented him from giving in. He saw the full figure of this thing. Adam lowered his eyes, trying to avoid seeing its grotesque face again.

"A princesssssss?" it hissed in amusement. Its foul breath almost made Adam vomit. "Ssshe doesn't ssssmell like a princesssss."

Adam noticed Lena was running out of time. The monster had her in such a tight grip that her face was turning blue.

"Yes, the princess!" Adam roared. "Now let her go!"

"Isss that ssso?" it hissed again.

Adam remembered what Charlie had told him; that demons feed off the good energy of people's souls.

"She is a princess," Adam repeated, standing his ground. "The Lemurians are strong. They will come and find you!"

"I'm ssstarving. I'll rissk it," it said as it started to leap away.

Adam could not let the monster take her.

"Wait! Take me instead!" Adam called desperately and gulped as the creature stopped and turned around to face this human pest, with Lena hanging limp at its side.

"What did you sssssay?" it hissed at him.

Adam glared as he spoke. "You heard me!"

The thing threw Lena to the floor. Adam tried to move towards her, but the monster snatched him up before he could get to her. Adam breathed in deeply and closed his eyes, hoping it would help prevent the inevitable. To his surprise, the demon dropped him and suddenly hobbled away.

Adam rushed to Lena's side, hoping she was still alive. Her face looked lifeless. Shaking her fragile body, he realized she wasn't responding. He wished he could remember what he had learned in the CPR class he had taken last summer.

He held Lena's hand, staring with despair at her motionless body. He jumped when he felt a hand touch his shoulder.

"Adam, it's okay now. Well done," Charlie said excitedly.

"No, it's not," Adam cried. "I tried to save her, Charlie, I did. Lena is gone!" Adam lowered his head in defeat. His heart couldn't have sunk lower. Why was it supposed to happen this way? They were going to save his father—Lena and him together.

Adam took her hand and rubbed it against a tear on his cheek. "Oh, why did she have to come with us only to die?"

Charlie pulled the boy away from Lena's body. "Listen to me, Adam. That is not the real Lena."

"You liar! I saw her die right in front of me! How can you say that?" Adam said, wiping away the tears from his eyes.

"Take a deep breath, Adam. I know what you saw, but this Lena was only a hologram."

Adam looked back and forth between Charlie and Lena.

"What?"

"That's not Lena," Charlie repeated.

Adam stared at her as she faded away into nothingness. "What's going on here?"

"Demetrius wanted to see if you were willing to sacrifice your life for another. You passed his test. I am proud of you."

"What?" He was outraged at this cruel trick. Adam sat down on a rock, exhausted from the ordeal. "We were supposed to get my father!" he shouted. "You said time was everything, so why did Demetrius slow us down? He had to test me now and make me think his daughter was in danger and dying? What's wrong with him? Is he normal? Here I am crying like a fool because I thought I just witnessed the death of the Princess of Telos. What other tricks are you guys going to play on me before I am good enough in Demetrius' eyes?"

Charlie took Adam's anger in stride. "Do not worry about your father. We will save him. As for Demetrius' reasons, do not trouble yourself with them. You needed this test. We wanted to see how you would react to danger and if the Telos band and watch helped," Charlie assured him. "Kind of like a test run. See, it worked!"

Adam felt duped. He had no more energy to argue. His entire body went limp like a wrung-out towel.

"So you mean Lena is alive?" Adam muttered, sitting on a rock.

"Alive and watching the whole thing in Telos," Charlie confirmed and picked up the small hologram from the ashen ground. "See."

He took the little piece of crystal from Charlie, looked at it and threw it onto the ground.

Resentment raced through Adam's mind knowing that he was being watched and practically graded on his conduct. Lena's involvement, of all people, in this so-called test run angered him even more.

When they rode the Pegasus together down by the beach, his heart felt a strong attraction, as if they were somehow supposed to be connected. He craved that feeling again so badly, but this act of betrayal ripped those feelings to shreds. He didn't know exactly what he felt toward her anymore. He tried to push the hurtful thoughts out of his mind, but that didn't work.

It never does.

Love wasn't so simple after all.

Chapter 26 –
SOS

For the first time since college, Larry was having the time of his life. This party was such a blast. The laughter and vibration from the pumping music poured out of the windows of the Draconian castle and across the parched landscape.

He was quite drunk and drugged on some strange concoction Lillith had given him. He realized he was heavily under the influence of something, but at this moment, he didn't really care.

He couldn't think straight and forgot why he had come here in the first place. Feeling so high, he thought he could fly. He danced the night away as the hypnotic strobe lights flashed to the beat of the music.

The Draconians made Larry the guest of honor and the unofficial "king of the night." They even placed a crown upon his head and bowed to him.

Lillith took Larry to an adjacent balcony outside to have a private chat. She showed him secrets of the powerful evil world. Peering into this mysterious dimension, he noticed an alien power surge through him. It slowly enveloped his conscience, blocking any logical thoughts. This sinister intruder surrounded his psyche, convincing him that there weren't consequences for any actions.

His mind was suddenly able to understand the incredible power of the Vril; something that he had yearned to comprehend. It was quite complex, as he saw the many dimensions of existence, the past, present and future, flash before him.

He felt a sense of freedom, forgetting about any boundaries and responsibilities of an earthly being. He was surprisingly comfortable with the newly opened pathway in his mind.

He even had to admit, Lillith was truly an amazing woman!

When they returned to the party, the music stopped as loud horns blared. A host of about twenty dragon-like creatures of various sizes and colors paraded into the room. They hissed and moved through the crowd, spewing green mucus on the floor. They looked toward the huge, vaulted chamber doors as Sarus, the king of Draconia, entered.

His whole body was covered in lumps and scales, except for an enormous ridge of bony spine that ran down his back between his two webbed wings. They spread out in either direction and arched over his head like an umbrella.

Everyone in the room bowed their heads in reverence to Sarus. Larry looked around and noticed Sarus staring at him, so he lowered his head to show his respects too.

"Welcome, welcome! Larry, I am Sarus, and I am so glad to see you are enjoying yourself in my palace! I hope my daughter has made you feel comfortable here with us," he bellowed, directing his words towards Larry.

"Oh, she is quite the hostess," Larry said in his most charming voice. His face was flushed and his eyes flashed wide open.

Sarus raised his goblet and made a toast, "Here's to Larry, our new friend and leader. I hope this is the beginning of a long and prosperous friendship!" All the creatures howled and hissed. "Now, on with the party!"

In a normal state of mind, Larry would have been frightened to death by this creature, but he wasn't the least bit disturbed. In fact, this gigantic monster seemed like his new BFF.

As the chaotic music started again, Larry belted out a loud howl and began dancing a clumsy imitation of a break dancer, occasionally stumbling and slipping in some slimy mucus.

Sarus invited him to leave the party for a private tour of his castle. A brilliant plan had been brewing in the king's mind.

"You know, my dear friend, so many great nations joined us over the centuries, and look at all the power they got. Life is supposed to be enjoyed freely—not controlled, wouldn't you agree, my friend?"

"Sure," Larry answered.

"Guilt is what prevents people from life's pleasures. We need a genius like you to help us rid the world of this guilt. In return we will offer you wealth, health and power. You would lead our revolt, freeing the people of responsibility and restrictions," the king said happily. "We will put you in the power seat. Bottoms up to you!"

Larry should have disagreed with Sarus' bad advice. But instead, he robotically nodded, agreeing with everything Sarus suggested, then finished off the concoction in his cup.

Larry looked flattered and his ego was clearly convinced, thinking how influential and rich he would soon be.

"Power! That's what you'll have!" Sarus shouted enthusiastically. "If you join us today, as a special offer, we will enable you to access Hades, the master of the underworld, and his thousands of slaves. They will fulfill your every desire when you get back to the surface world, and you won't have to tolerate your wife anymore. We can easily get rid of her for you!"

"Well—" Larry's voice quivered.

"Not sure? Who needs her? All you get is constant aggravation and pressure. Family is a burden around your neck!" Sarus said. "Am I wrong?"

"Um—" Larry said, staring at Sarus.

"Power! Power, pleasure, respect and riches,

Larry. It's all yours for the taking. Just imagine all the women fulfilling your every command!"

"So how do I sign up?" Larry stammered, forcing the words out of his mouth.

"Let's get back to the party and I'll show you."

Once Sarus and Larry returned to the ballroom, the cunning king announced that he had some good news.

The music stopped.

"Everyone, pay attention! Larry is ready to join us. Lillith, darling, isn't that amazing news?" Sarus asked rhetorically, focusing his gaze on his daughter.

Lillith approached Larry and batted her overly long eyelashes, putting him once again under her mesmerizing stare. "It will be unbelievable. Together, we will be in charge of the world," she said in a forced, breathless tone.

Sarus smiled and nodded at her to proceed.

"Now, we just need to make it official," she said. "Just repeat after me. Say, 'I, Larry Mason, accept you, Lillith, the Princess of Draconia, into my body to take control of my soul.'"

Lillith waited for Larry to repeat her request.

"What was that?" Larry asked warily.

"You need to repeat what I tell you." She looked

blankly at Larry. "Say, 'I, Larry Mason, accept you, Lillith, the Princess of Draconia, into my body to take control of my soul,'" she said, staring deep into his eyes.

He slurred, speaking, "I... Larry Mason, accept you... I'm so sorry. What's your name again?"

"Lillith, Princess of Draconia!" she snapped. "Start over. Start with 'I, Larry Mason.'"

Larry tried to focus. "What? Oh. I, Larry Mason, the Princess of Draconia..."

"No. No. No! Stop," she interrupted.

"I'm sorry," he quipped. "It's kind of a long sentence. I am really tired, and—"

"Not to worry. Let me write this down for you." She tried to hide the irritation rising in her throat. "What an idiot," she said under her breath glaring at her father. She snapped her fingers. Instantly a quill feather, a piece of paper and a dish with red ink appeared. She wrote down her spell for Larry to read.

"Here, Larry. It's one little sentence. Just read it out loud. That's all you have to do and we will be soulmates forever," she purred. "Now, don't disappoint me, okay?"

He had no idea where his reading glasses were. Larry squinted at the paper. Slowly he proclaimed, "I, Larry Mason, accept you, Lillith, the Princess of Draconia, into my body... to take control," Larry gulped and stopped as he silently recited the rest of the spell in his mind.

"—of my soul, you fool," Lillith interrupted. "I thought you were supposed to be brilliant," she hissed. Her patience had run out.

"Soul? Forgive my ignorance, but what's a soul?" Larry asked, looking around with his bloodshot eyes at all the creatures gathered around them.

"Just repeat it exactly as I wrote it," she snapped. "Start again! You have to say the whole thing without stopping in order for this to work!"

"For what to work?" he asked, momentarily gaining his sanity.

Lillith was riddled with rage at this stage and ready to slap him, but she mustered her willpower and decided to try another tactic instead.

"Larry, my darling, we are going to be soulmates and we will control the world together. Imagine it. Soon you will be rich and famous. Don't you want that, sweetheart?" she said in her most convincing voice.

"Yes!" he said enthusiastically.

"So, there is just one little detail we need to work out before that can happen. Just read this, darling. Just read the whole thing and the world will be yours," Lillith said invitingly and waited.

Larry looked at her and then noticed that everyone in the room was staring at him with anticipation.

"If you would rather not, I understand," she said

in a malicious tone.

"Okay," he said, hoping to regain their respect and not be killed. He cleared his throat and read the spell aloud, "I, Larry Mason, accept you, Lillith, the Princess of Draconia, into my body to take control of my soul." He immediately regretted it, but it was too late.

"Thank you!" she said breathlessly. She opened her arms, evaporated into a thin, green mist and flew into Larry's mouth. Larry's deep laugh echoed throughout the room, as he looked over his new community of demons.

"What a good friend you are, Larry!" Sarus exclaimed, removing Larry's wedding ring from his finger. "Well done. Bring us the finest wine!"

Sarus immediately placed the ring on his pinky finger and held it out in front of himself to admire it.

The loud music started, and they began to celebrate this momentous occasion; the seduction of another soul.

Chapter 27 –
The Rescue

Adam glanced back one more time, scanning for any trace of chasing demons. The coast seemed clear. As he hurriedly climbed into the transporter, the stairs retracted, and the silver craft took off. Within moments the ship zipped over the charred, scorched landscape deep into the heart of Draconia.

As Adam sat motionless, his face looked sullen and his heart ached. He couldn't wait to tell Lena that he regretted ever meeting her. By doing this, he thought it might ease his emotional pain. Better to be an owner of a lonely heart than owner of a broken one, he realized.

He also wanted to tell that awful, pompous king that he could take his stupid mission and shove it where the sun didn't shine. But if he did that, then surely the king wouldn't help him save his dad. Adam's mind was muddled with fear, and he felt worried about everything.

While Adam anxiously peered out the window to scan the scenery below, he spotted a dot that broke the steady barrenness of the desert land. As the ship neared the ground, the dot grew bigger. Adam took a second look and noticed that this dot had a cathedral roof.

Adam pressed his nose against the window, wondering what the structure could be. Maybe it was a house where he would find some people. As the transporter moved closer to the ground, the inevitable truth became clear to him. This residence was no house. It was something far more sinister and foreboding. It was at that point that the ship landed.

"Well, this is it," said the pilot, powering down the engine.

"This," Charlie said, pointing out the window, "is most likely where your father is being held captive by the infamous Lillith."

Adam could see a look of disgust spreading across Charlie's face.

"Who is Lillith?" Adam asked.

"Lillith is the Princess of Draconia," Charlie said. "Princess is too nice a word for her. Evil demon queen would suit her better."

"How do you know this?" Adam asked.

"Oh, every so often a human accidentally finds his way to this pit of hell. This happened to me, unfortunately, so I know how she operates. She preys upon the poor soul she finds, luring him into joining demonic forces with her. She needs to borrow a human body so she can return to the surface and spread her havoc. You have your watch, right?"

"Yeah. Why?"

"Keep in touch with me by pressing the red button," Charlie answered. He took out a crystal wand and handed it to Adam, explaining, "Here, keep this in your pocket for when we need it. This is going to be a perilous mission, and we will require all the help we can get."

"What about protecting yourself?" Adam asked.

"If I need it, hand the crystal to me immediately," Charlie said. "But for now, I may need to use myself as bait. With the crystal on me, whatever Lillith is trying won't work. You must stay in the ship with the guard until I am inside. The guard will protect you and help you sneak in unnoticed."

As Charlie opened the hatch, a wave of hot wind rushed into the cabin. They gasped for air.

Loud, pumping music blasted out of the castle.

"It sounds like a party. Not good," Charlie said.

"Why?"

"Why do you think they would be celebrating?" Charlie answered with a stare.

Adam watched as the brave man exited the craft and cautiously walked towards the castle.

Stepping into the brutal heat, Charlie felt like he was melting. Walking closer, he was engulfed in the dark shadow of the massive structure. No path or steps seemed to lead to the huge, vaulted doors.

As he stood outside thinking of a way to get in, he noticed a large, black iron bell. He rang it, even though the deafening music just drowned out the dong. Just then, Charlie stepped back in surprise when two demonic creatures appeared next to him. The two monsters resembled the one that Adam had encountered earlier, but these creatures looked much more threatening.

Charlie faced the guards confidently. He bowed his head and said in a polite voice, "I am Charlie Mason. I would like to pay a visit to the Princess of Draconia. She knows who I am."

"We have sssummoned the Princesss. Sshe knowsss you are here," said one of the creatures, with a sizzling rasp. Slime oozed between its teeth and lips. With that, the beast returned to its post and remained silent while they waited.

Lillith did not appear immediately since she was involved with Larry. She wanted to maintain her hold on him, so she divided herself into two parts. One part stayed in Larry and the other part she used to make her appearance to the uninvited guest.

Charlie waited in the miserable heat, dripping with sweat. The ground trembled and the vaulted castle doors cranked open as a long ramp cranked down to the ground. Lillith greeted Charlie with a look of annoyance.

He forgot how beautiful she seemed to be. *She's only an illusion,* he had to remind himself.

"Lillith, so nice to see you again, my dear," Charlie exclaimed, bowing his head. "You look lovely as usual."

"Charlie," Lillith said gracefully, "please come inside and make yourself at home where you'll be more comfortable."

He entered the antechamber of the foreboding castle, and to his dismay, it was even hotter inside. Its four fireplaces in the hall were all lit, adding to the heat and causing his robe to stick to him like glue.

"So what brings you here?" Her voice bounced off the enormous stone walls.

"Well," Charlie said, "there is some business that you and I must settle."

He wiped the sweat off his forehead and tried not to think about the heat.

"Settle?" Lillith gave him a questioning look, her eyebrow raised high. Her movements were smooth and slow, but Charlie knew they were deadly.

She looked at her old acquaintance. "It's really not a good time for me, you see. We are in the middle of a party, but if you want, perhaps you will join us?" she suggested, gesturing her palm toward a winding staircase.

"How can I say no to a party?" Charlie joked cautiously.

She led him up a flight of stairs and into a gigantic ballroom on the second floor, with her two guards close behind. This room was decorated with opulent red jewels and it oozed a thick, evil ambiance. The lights dimmed and the music quieted as the princess and her guest entered.

Sure enough, as Charlie suspected, sitting in the middle of the room on a golden throne shaped like a hand was Larry, staring in a trance. His eyes glowed a brilliant green.

Charlie followed Lillith as she walked lazily around the room and rambled about her beautiful domain.

"Who's this guy?" Charlie asked, inquisitively pointing to Larry.

"He's the latest addition to our family," Lillith boasted.

"He looks like he is having a really good time," Charlie said sarcastically.

❁ ❋ ❁ ❋ ❁ ❋ ❁

Adam noticed that no one was guarding the entrance and the castle doors were wide open. He convinced the Lemurian guard on board the ship to sneak in with him.

Once inside, they ducked behind a black leather couch. He pressed the red button on his watch. Placing the watch to his ear, he was amazed that it worked like a walkie-talkie and he could actually hear Charlie having a conversation with a lady.

Chapter 28 –
The Trick

Charlie sneered, "So, you took over the poor guy's body!"

"What if I did?" she said hauntingly.

"You settled for him?" Charlie asked doubtfully. "Compared to me, this man is a total joke. He's worthless! I'm a much better catch than he will ever be!"

"Well, I couldn't wait around for you forever. And true, he doesn't exactly have your intelligence or good looks, but he certainly has enough to be useful."

"You should have waited just a bit longer. I came here today to tell you that I have decided to accept your offer and join you!" Charlie said, giving a phony smile.

The truth is that Lillith had always been madly attracted to Charlie, and his charm was hard for her to resist.

"I've been asking you for decades," Lillith responded with annoyance. "Why did you suddenly come around now?"

There was a quiet pause.

"Maybe it's because you are jealous," she said smugly. "Is that it? You saw that you weren't the only one I could use. Took a blow to that ego of yours, did it?"

"Take me instead!" Charlie said with a stressed voice. "You know that we could have a lot more fun together."

Lillith considered this for a moment. After all, Charlie was right. Larry really wasn't that smart, after all, or handsome or charming, or as fun as Charlie. Actually, Larry was pretty dull.

Adam listened carefully through his watch, struggling to hear the conversation through the background noise. He couldn't believe his ears, but he knew one thing for sure: there was no way Charlie was on Lillith's side. Adam tried to collect his racing thoughts and peeked around the couch to make sure the coast was clear. He ran up the winding stairs into the ballroom, straight into the party, with the Lemurian guard following behind him.

"Say it first," Lillith said teasingly. "Say you're jealous. Come on, just once!"

"Take me. Enough with the games! I'm sick and tired of them, Lillith," Charlie answered forcefully.

"And what do you want in return for your service?" she asked, still suspicious of the sudden turnaround in Charlie.

"I want to return to the surface with power and riches and do what I want without constantly being questioned," Charlie said. "That's my deal. Make it so!"

Before Lillith had an opportunity to react, Adam rushed over to his dad. "Dad!" he cried and bent down to embrace him. Adam's heart sank when he got no response. He looked at his dad's face. "Dad, it's me, Adam! Are you okay?"

Larry looked at him blankly.

"Dad," he pleaded again, "we have to get you out of here!"

He took his father's hands and tried to pull him off the chair, but his father wouldn't budge.

"Hey. It's your son, Adam! Remember me?"

Larry finally spoke. "You cannot be my son." His voice was flat. "My son's name is Mark."

Those words pierced like a sharp blade into Adam's heart. He dropped his father's hands and moved away from him.

"Charlie, no, don't do it!" Adam screamed.

"You stay out of this, boy!" Lillith shouted, turning back to Charlie. "Deal!"

Charlie took off his Telos watch and threw it underhand towards Adam, shooing him away.

In order to enter Charlie's body, Lillith needed to get her other half of her spirit from Larry's body. She manipulated his movements as if he were a robot. He stood and his arms flew upward as green smoke streamed out of his mouth and shot into Lillith's. Larry collapsed to the floor.

The music stopped playing. Adam saw Lillith joining hands with Charlie as he prepared to make a pact with the devil herself.

Lillith peeled back her lips, revealing her gross teeth. "Ready?"

"No, Charlie, stop!" Adam yelled.

"I told you to stay out of this, you pest!" Lillith snapped and pushed Adam to the floor.

From across the room, Larry weakly looked over to him and said hoarsely, "Adam."

"I'm all yours," Charlie said bravely.

"Say 'I, Charlie Mason, accept you, Lillith, the Princess of Draconia, into my body to take control of my soul!'"

What? Adam thought. This can't be happening.

"I, Charlie Mason, accept you, Lillith, the Princess of Draconia, into my body to take control of my soul," he recited without delay.

Lillith dove into Charlie's mouth, her own image discarded onto the glistening ground.

Adam gasped as he watched Charlie, who was now staring at him with glowing green eyes. Charlie laughed with a familiar wide grin. "I don't have much time," Charlie struggled to say to Adam. "Put the Telos watch on me and get the crystal wand from your pocket and give it to me."

Adam watched the struggle between Lillith and Charlie as his eyes turned from brown to bright green and returned to brown. Adam quickly stood, eager to follow Charlie's instructions. Frantically grabbing the crystal wand from his pocket, Adam shoved it into Charlie's hand and placed the Telos watch into his robe pocket. Charlie raised his hands in the air. Green smoke began to leave from Charlie's mouth for a few seconds before trying to shoot back in.

Charlie fell to his knees, desperately fighting the evil entity that was taking control of his body. Then he shouted with all his might, "I order you, Lillith, the Princess of Draconia, to leave my body now!"

His arms flew in the air and black smoke shot out of his mouth, forcing the hideous Lillith to reappear next to him, shrieking with rage.

Charlie dropped to the floor.

Looking over at Lillith, Adam realized that she was in a state of confusion. All the creatures stared in awe. Taking advantage of the situation, Charlie ordered his guard to carry Larry out of this dreadful place, as he and Adam followed right behind. They all fled together down the stairs, out of the castle foyer and safely back to their ship.

It was a narrow escape as they flew at full speed back to Telos.

Chapter 29 –

Encouragement

Upon returning to Telos, Charlie, Adam and Larry were taken to a small healing clinic. Smokey quartz crystals were placed on the three of them to remove all the negative energies they had absorbed in Draconia.

Crystabol, the Healer, a sweet, older gentleman with a glistening smile ran the place single handedly. He wore a simple white robe and donned many colored necklaces and bracelets.

Adam was barely awake, letting a sliver of light enter through his partially opened eyes. He noticed something that made him happy. He saw Lena waiting by his bed, smiling.

She spoke first, "Welcome back. Glad you made it. That was a close escape from Draconia, and I am so grateful to see that you are safe."

"I thought you really died back there," Adam said, annoyed.

"See, I'm fine. But more importantly, you passed my father's first test," she beamed.

"First test?" Adam said angrily, sitting upright in bed and fully awake.

"My dad just wanted to see if you would run away from the monster, or if you had the courage to at least try to save me."

"Oh, what? By making me think that you died?"

"Sorry it was so harsh."

"More like cruel. I actually thought you liked me," Adam said in a hurt tone, looking away from her loving eyes.

"My dad made me do it. I am so sorry. Now I realize what a hero you truly are."

As Lena said those words, any anger he felt toward her instantly melted away.

"Sometime soon I will rule Telos." She crossed her arms over her chest. "So my father wanted me to see what is going on in Draconia."

Adam didn't know what to say to her. He looked confused. Was he talking to another hologram, or was she really there? They all seemed to be the same Lena to him—beautiful and regal.

Crystabol approached Adam, putting his hand on the boy's shoulder. "You should be fine now. When you are ready, you are free to go. I am checking on your father next."

"Thank you very much," Adam said to the man.

A few minutes later Lena left the healing center, leaving Adam alone lying on the white bed, staring at the high ceiling and feeling quite restless. He decided to find his dad and Charlie. He wandered down the hall and peeked into the next room. There Charlie was resting, surrounded by blinking colored crystal rods.

"Adam," Charlie beamed weakly as the boy walked in and took a seat by his bedside. Charlie sat upright leaning against a pillow, looking completely drained.

"How's the hero?" Adam asked.

"What hero?" Charlie joked, looking around the room. "Oh, me? Not too shabby, considering everything. I'll be just dandy."

"What happened to you in Draconia?" Adam asked.

"What do you want to know?"

"Well, you said that once someone gives up his soul, it is almost impossible to get it back. But you and my father got your souls back. Also, why did Lillith want my father in the first place? Plus, why would she ever fall for your silly trick?"

"It's all quite simple," Charlie began. "Lillith pestered Nicky for years to join her, but once he died he lost his body and became an angel, she stopped trying. Then she turned to the next available body— me—since Nicky gave me all of his hidden secrets.

"She tried for years to convince me to join her, offering me anything I wanted in the world. It sounded all very tempting, but I wouldn't agree to it. When your dad came down from the surface, Lillith was presented with another brilliant mind and available body. Not as useful as Nicky, but definitely valuable enough for her ghastly deeds."

Adam was confused. "Why would you and Nicky go to Draconia?"

"We certainly didn't intentionally mean to go there. But when a person dabbles in quantum physics, sometimes they enter inner space. While in that empty space, there is no time, and there the Draconians can piggyback on a person. I was one of many handfuls of people that got intercepted by Lillith and other cunning demons while we travelled in inner space."

"So why would she take you instead?" Adam asked.

"Her ego got in the way. Even though I rejected her and she knew that I would never join her, she had her group of demons watching, and she wanted to show off."

Adam digested this information for a moment. Charlie continued, "She recognized the rare opportunity that I finally agreed to hand over my soul to her, so it was hard for her to resist.

"First she needed to imprison my soul to enter my body. I never intended to let her take control over me. Even as her spirit entered me, I was fighting with every ounce of power I had. It was really tough. Without the crystal and Telos watch, I doubt I would have had the strength to resist her."

"Why?"

"Because the watch has protection from evil forces infused into the quantum chip, and the crystal magnifies a person's inner intentions. I fought to control my soul by admitting she had no power over me. If you really believe that, it will be so. Your dad, on the other hand, never could have fought her. He was under her power even before she took over his soul. When Lillith voluntarily left his body to enter mine, he was freed. That's about it in a little nutshell."

"Wow. The whole thing is unbelievable. Thank you so much for saving my father."

"You are very welcome. Besides, he is actually my family in an odd way. Now go to your father. I'm sure he'll be glad to see you."

Chapter 30 –
Giving Advice to Dad

Adam saw his dad sitting in bed speaking with Crystabol when he entered the small room. Larry's face beamed, noticing his son's presence.

"Adam!" he said with enthusiasm. "This is my boy who I was telling you about." He motioned for Adam to come closer.

"We have met. A special child you have there."

"Thanks," Larry said, giving a boastful smile.

"You are doing much better and should be ready to leave later today."

"Great," Larry said weakly.

Cristobal left the room.

Adam noticed his dad had large black and blue circles surrounding his eyes. "How are you feeling?"

"Not so good. I guess I deserved what I got, though," Larry said sadly.

"What are you talking about? It could have happened to anyone. You were tricked," Adam exclaimed.

"Well, you should be ashamed of me," he scoffed bitterly. "I can't believe I got myself into that mess." Tears rolled down his bruised cheeks. "I'm so sorry... I'm so embarrassed."

Adam stared in disbelief. His father was crying.

"Tell them all that I'm sorry; tell your friend…" he trailed off realizing he didn't even know the name of the person who saved his life.

"Charlie."

"Yes. Charlie."

"Dad, no one blames you. Lillith fooled you. You couldn't have known. You were completely controlled by her, and it wasn't even you anymore." Adam waited for his father to compose himself.

"You have changed down here, Son." He reached out for Adam's hand and pulled him near. "You seem to have found your voice."

"I always had a voice, Dad, but you never heard what I had to say."

"You scared me. You were good, but you were in your own world. I couldn't understand you."

"I thought the same about you." Adam smiled warmly.

There was a pause.

"The doctor just gave me a spiritual health checkup. Apparently, I'm in pretty sad shape," Larry said with concern.

"Really? What did he say?" Adam asked.

"According to his Indigo Meter," he said, grabbing the paper to read it, "I have a congested heart, a blocked love chakra, unresolved anger stuck at about age five—whatever that means, and get this: I have holes in my cosmic lineage from past lives."

He tossed the paper onto the nightstand next to his bed. "Sounds like rubbish to me. What are they talking about?" Larry asked rhetorically. "This is not what I expected to find down here, to be honest with you. These people are really different, the few I have met so far."

"I know. They are so nice and loving. I wish I could move here for good."

"So how in the world did you get all the way down here, by the way?"

Adam paused and glanced into the corner of the room, trying to find a place to start his tale. This adventure defied all science and logic. He flew away to a far-off land; discovered a long-lost father from another time zone; found the girl from his dreams; was reunited with Nicky; and felt real happiness for the very first time with his dad. So where in the world should he begin?

Chapter 31 –
The Mission

After leaving the healing center, Adam, his dad and Charlie were taken to three adjacent rooms in the palace. They each received personal invitations to join the king and queen for an honorary dinner.

Larry was relaxing in bed when he heard three taps. Excited to receive some company, he opened the door with anticipation. A tall, lanky man offered Larry a neatly folded, light blue robe and a rose quartz necklace.

He cleared his throat. "This is for the dinner tonight. King Demetrius requested that you wear it," the man said.

Larry took the robe and necklace, thanked the guy and shut the door. Realizing that he couldn't insult the king, he removed his own clothes and slipped the free-flowing robe and necklace over his head, glancing into the mirror. "You've got to be kidding me," he moaned and looked away, shaking his head back and forth.

He heard another knock. Cracking the door open with hesitation, he peeked out into the hall. Outside his door Larry found three grinning faces. Adam, Charlie and Simon seemed to be amused with something Larry couldn't quite see.

"Dad, look at you!" Adam exclaimed.

He blushed. "Stop it! I am horrified I have to wear this dress. I feel like a monk. Should I shave my head too? Is this some joke?"

Simon's expression indicated his discomfort as well, wearing a light yellow robe and a yellow citrine necklace.

"Are they setting us up to be fools?" Simon asked with raised eyebrows. He had already experienced the king's wrath when he intruded on the city. He really didn't trust Demetrius' motive for inviting them to a dinner party.

"If you haven't noticed, this is how they all dress down here. At least it's comfortable," Adam pointed out. He shifted around inside his own attire and held it out to show its roominess.

Charlie interrupted them and said, "Come, let's go to dinner. We shouldn't keep them waiting."

As they walked, Simon whispered into Larry's ear. "Good news. I got some DNA samples."

Larry smiled and nodded encouragingly. Adam knew they were chatting, but he couldn't hear a word.

They took the turbo lift up to the majestic dining hall.

As they entered the room, the royal family was waiting for their arrival. Lena waved to Adam, causing him to smile and blush.

"A well-deserved welcome," Demetrius said as he rose to greet Larry and shake his hand. "We assume you must be Adam's father."

"Yes, I am. It's a pleasure, uh, to be here," he said skittishly, trying to be as pleasant as possible.

"I'm King Demetrius. The pleasure is most assuredly all mine. We are sure you are proud of your son for accepting such a difficult task."

"I am," Larry said with a look of happiness, although not really sure what that task involved. He placed his hand on his son's shoulder, calming his own nerves.

"Even though your visit was unexpected, it has evolved into a fortuitous event," Demetrius said. "What an arduous journey to show Adam your support."

Larry's smiling face turned panic-stricken when he realized everyone in the dining hall was probably aware of his true intentions for coming to Telos. He looked down to avoid all the eyes staring at him.

Chimes sounded and everyone took their appropriate places at the ornate tables. Servers carried in massive plates filled with vegetarian food that had made Adam cringe before. He pitied his dad who also hated most veggies. In fact, Adam held himself back from cracking up when he saw his dad close his eyes and spit a bite of food into a napkin while making a sour face like he was about to gag.

"I'm on a fruit diet down here," Adam said to his dad under his breath. As all the plates were placed on the table, he chose the reddest, biggest grape and stuffed it into his mouth.

The king briefly explained to Larry and Simon about Adam's mission to help bring peace to humanity.

Larry couldn't help but say something intelligent.

"No offense to your plan, but do you really think that by simply giving out crystals to kids, that it can change our world? I mean, I am sure you are aware that there is so much hatred up there. How could Adam change any of this? Furthermore, how can you expect Adam to challenge the powerful forces that control our world, encouraging war?" Larry stared down into his lap, hoping he hadn't insulted the king with such direct questions.

"My friend, we are not fools," Demetrius said patiently. "We are quite aware of what you speak. We have to start somewhere, wouldn't you agree?"

"Well, sure," Larry said.

"So please take note, that there are two types of despair in your world. The first type of despair is from people who feel hopeless, as they struggle to gather enough for their families to eat each day. They also worry about disease and poverty.

"The second type of despair is from people

who have more than enough of everything they need. They have every gadget and gizmo they desire, but often they suffer from boredom and impatience, struggling to find purpose in their full, but meaningless lives. This feeling leaves a nagging emptiness in their hearts. Hoping not to notice, they occupy their time with fleeting pleasures.

"Both types of despair are equally destructive. We can only help the second type of people initially, giving them a purpose to life. Once we have a large army of children willing to donate a portion of their free time and money to helping others in need, then poverty will begin to evaporate. As you say, kill two birds with one stone, even though that's a dreadful saying." The king gave barely a trace of a smile.

"And Adam is going to lead the so-called army?" Larry said with a sarcastic look, even though he was quite proud that his son would be involved in something so lofty.

"That's the plan," the king replied.

"Sounds great, but impractical," Larry said bluntly with a doubtful look.

"It may seem impractical, but you see, my friend, even a tiny burning candle can light up a dark room with its radiant sparkle. When that little light shines, the darkness in the whole room vanishes. That is an example of how light destroys darkness.

"As long as there is even a small amount of goodness bringing light into the world, wickedness stands no chance. You see, world peace actually starts in our own hearts.

"If kids are willing to open their hearts even a little to receive the light, they can transfer that beacon of light to others. The crystals magnify that light and will assist them. On December 21, 2012, the world will ascend into a higher dimension, but with it comes more darkness to the people who don't choose to go towards the light. On that day, the crystal bracelets that your son will give out will be activated to connect all who have them and help those who are stuck, removing the darkness of confusion."

Larry broke his stare with the king and glanced over to Adam who looked somewhere between proud and unsure.

"Why not adults? I mean, Adam is just a kid."

"We have lost hope with adults. Our future relies on your son's generation, but they are in terrible shape. They have this awful entitlement attitude. As I'm sure you know and frequently witness, many surface children lack a good path to follow and often follow the wrong ones. By appointing Adam as our messenger for peace," the king smiled and gestured towards Adam, "we want to offer children leadership by giving them hope and inspire them to create a better world. Children are the perfect vessels to accomplish this as long as we stay under the radar. Does that make sense to you?" Demetrius paused, looking solemnly ahead.

Larry blinked a few times, trying to process the king's answer, and responded, "Interesting." He had heard enough about this simplistic peace idea and wanted to change the topic. "Well, all right. You talk about peace, but didn't you guys destroy the world a long time ago in a big war?"

"We did, indeed. We have learned from our experience," the king reassured him. "We are here to make sure we never repeat our mistakes again."

"Why do you guys live so much longer than we do?" Larry asked, since he was on center stage asking questions.

"Your people used to live long lives as well until the world changed."

"How so?" Larry interrupted.

"It is an issue you really should take up with Mother Earth," Demetrius said in a straightforward tone. "We indeed have our differences. Interesting fact, we don't acquire the same diseases."

"So you don't get cancer down here?"

"Heavens no!" the king said.

"How interesting...Then I assume you wouldn't have the cure either," Larry asked.

"The only cure is merely strengthening your body's own ability to ward off the disease," Demetrius explained, matter-of-factly. "Kind of like having the cure for the common cold."

Larry and Simon stared at each other in

bafflement, not wanting anyone to notice. They avoided any eye contact with all the happy Lemurians present in the dining room and remained quiet until the king clapped his hands together, calling the meal to an end.

Larry was hoping for a moment to ask the king some questions about the Vril, but it didn't seem to be the right time.

"I must speak to Adam alone now. Please excuse us for a few minutes," the king said to the smaller group that accompanied him at the head of the table. "Come with me, son."

Walking towards the door, Adam looked over his shoulder at the table for a second. Charlie grinned, Larry gave him a proud nod and Lena beamed her encouraging smile.

Adam felt brave knowing that everyone was on his side, but what in the world could the king want now?

Adam followed Demetrius out of the room, feeling a knot tighten in his stomach.

Demetrius led Adam into his private chambers down the hall. The king gestured for him to take a seat. Sitting down stiffly in a big, green chair, Adam waited for the king to speak.

"My son," the king started, "you have pleasantly

surprised me. To be willing to sacrifice your own life is a quality that we rarely see. You proved me wrong and Charlie right. He believed in you from the beginning. I now have confidence in you too."

Adam beamed with pride.

"Unfortunately, Adam, I feel the need to test you further."

Adam's smile vanished and his face turned red. "Another test? Why?"

"Think of it more like a quest to discover who you really are and further seek what greatness lies inside yourself," the king said with sympathy, seeing the boy's concern.

"What's the test?" Adam asked warily.

"Look here," Demetrius instructed, and he pointed out the window. From a distance, Adam saw a magnificent amethyst mountain. A waterfall cascaded down a steep cliff, disappearing into the purple mist below. "That is the Shangri Li Mountain," Demetrius said, gesturing towards the grand scene, towering into the sky. "A few centuries ago we built steps in the mountain leading to the top of the waterfall."

"That's pretty high. I can't even see where it ends," Adam said.

"Well, it doesn't quite end there. At that point, caves and tunnels go up to the surface world."

"Wow!" Adam said.

"The stairs that we built are a couple thousand

stories, and your test is to climb to the top of the waterfall," Demetrius said. "And you must do it alone."

Adam swallowed hard.

"When you reach the top, I shall know that you are ready for the enormous responsibility you have agreed to do. Once you finish, our transporter will be waiting to bring you down."

Adam felt quite intimidated looking at the gigantic mountain.

"When do I start?" he asked.

"Tomorrow morning. A guard will bring you to meet me at the bottom of the mountain. Good luck."

The meeting was apparently over.

The king left Adam alone in the room, staring out the window. "He's a total nut. I can never do that," he said to himself. He shook his head and felt doomed before he even started.

❁ ✳ ❁ ✳ ❁ ✳ ❁

That night in bed, Adam tossed and turned as end-less, unanswerable questions tortured him, pre-venting him from sleeping more than a few winks.

What if I don't make it? Would I just go home and forget about everything? What would Lena and Charlie say? Will I ever see them again?

This festered more fear and anxiety inside him. Nevertheless, he had to try to put those feelings aside for now. Tomorrow was going to be the most important day of his life.

Chapter 32 –
Test Two

Demetrius met Adam at the foot of the mountain. Charlie and Larry showed up for moral support. At the bottom of the stairs, Adam looked upward. The task seemed even more impossible. He tried to appear confident as the king spoke to him.

"You start your climb here," Demetrius said, "You shall have only a flask of water and this sword to help you."

The king handed the items to Adam. He took the sword gingerly, unsure of why he might need it or how to hold it.

"If you finish or get into trouble, to contact us just press the red button on your watch. Are you ready, lad?" Demetrius asked, glancing at the boy with concern and admiration.

Of course not, Adam thought. "Yes," he said humbly.

"Very well, then," Demetrius said. "Good luck. I will be watching you from my chamber's window."

"You will do well!" Charlie reminded him. "You know that, right?"

"Yeah, sure," Adam said doubtfully, still not sure why he had to do this.

There was not much Charlie could do to bolster Adam's faith in himself at the last minute. It was all in Adam's hands now. Charlie patted him on the back and gave him a sincere, warm smile, Charlie repeated firmly, "You can do this."

Adam looked at Charlie and nodded slowly.

"Give it all you got," his dad said encouragingly.

That was a first. Adam couldn't believe his dad was cheering him on. He looked up at the long, winding stone stairs and took a deep breath. "Here goes," he mumbled to himself and started his trek.

He wasn't sure if he should run up the steps as fast as he could to get it over and done with, or take his time so he wouldn't tire too soon.

Charlie and Larry looked around for a place to rest and watch. Over to one side was a lavish date palm that beckoned them to sit under its plush foliage.

Larry figured that maybe Charlie might know how the Vril worked, so he broached a subject surely they both loved to talk about. Science.

"You know, it's amazing how much we have in common. We both are scientists and we both came all the way down here, and of course, our dear Adam. Oh, Adam," Larry said, giving a hearty laugh and the most charming smile he could muster. His mind searched for just the right words to ask Charlie about the Vril. "My research tells me that the Lemurians know how to use the Vril down here."

Charlie wanted him to get to the point. He had other things on his mind and this talk wasn't one of them.

"They do. The Vril is a powerful force. The secret of how to use it has been hidden down here for centuries because it was abused by the nations of the surface world," Charlie said.

"Ah! You know about the Vril? Do you know how it works exactly? Lillith explained it, but it's as if I forgot everything she had taught me."

Charlie wasn't in the mood to give over a science lesson, but it really wasn't that complex. He gestured his palm upward and, like a magician, focused all his thoughts toward his hand. A ball of white energy appeared.

"Now how do you do that?" Larry exclaimed.

"It's no trick," Charlie said and winked. "But it starts with ridding yourself of all anger and ego, then finding that inner space within your heart. Once you find that special place, you can tap into the Vril. It's a neutral energy that forms the basis of every dimension of existence. You understand quantum physics, don't you?"

"Yes, I understand that, but how do you mold it and use it to do something?" Larry asked.

"Although you have the power inside of you, I can't teach you how to use it sitting here right now. It takes years to master."

"Years!" Larry exclaimed, disappointed. He tilted

his head while he thought about it, looking upward to find his son somewhere gradually ascending the mountain.

For a good hour, Adam quickly trekked through the steps without stopping. He was making great progress until he felt a sharp cramp in his left side. His heart pounded and he gasped for air, as sweat dripped down his forehead.

Stopping briefly to rest, he immediately regretted that decision. All the muscles in his legs burned in protest.

He gulped down all his water he had. He was still thirsty and already feeling tired. He hadn't realized how out of shape he was. With a very long way to go, how in the world did they expect him to make it?

With renewed strength after his rest, he forced his legs to climb upward. He decided to walk backwards, then sideways for a while, using different leg muscles. With this technique, he managed to climb another chunk of the mountain.

He struggled not to think of his thirst or fatigue as he walked up the steps that snaked through the winding stone path. He stopped to rub his legs and stretch them out. His head began spinning.

"I can't give up," Adam panted.

He looked around for a shady spot to rest.

Off to one side of the steps, he noticed a big cave overgrown with green moss. He wandered into the mouth of the cave thinking he could rest. Inside, he noticed a trickling stream. He dropped onto his belly and cupped his hands to drink down the refreshing water and fill up his flask, while a white mist cooled his body.

Hearing a grinding sound, he turned his head and saw the mouth to the cave closing.

"Hey!" he cried desperately and jumped up. He attempted to make it out of the cave, running as fast as his aching body could move, but it was too late. The opening had shut. He banged his fist uselessly on the wall, shouting and kicking. It was nearly pitch black in there with only a crack of light shining in and no apparent means of escape.

Maybe I should use my watch to call Demetrius and Charlie. Surely they would understand my situation and try to help me, he reasoned.

He couldn't bring himself to do that just yet. Only as his last resort. He wanted to get out by himself.

Cautiously feeling his way along the cave wall, he searched for any openings or cracks. He stopped when his hand encountered something round and smooth like a button. When he touched it, a faint light began to flicker across the room.

To his delight, he saw that the cave was filled with crystals. Some were black, deep purple and navy blue, ranging in size from a penny to a beach ball.

His eyes were drawn to a mirror that rested against the cave wall. It reflected a dim light that bounced around the jeweled room.

He walked over to the far wall, gently touching one of the massive black crystal stones. He instantly regretted this decision, feeling a powerful force sweep him off his feet. It tugged at his skin, sucking him into the stone head first. He felt himself swimming in a thick void of emptiness. It penetrated into his skin's pores, reaching the innermost part of his being.

Then the nightmare began.

Adam's body filled with waves of terror as the realization that he was totally alone hit him. Shameful memories and repressed fears tried to escape through his throat, strangling him mercilessly with an invisible hand. The years of behaving like a coward and looking incompetent flashed in front of his closed eyes.

This was one movie that Adam did not want to watch.

The raw brutality of war, which he had never experienced and didn't understand, raged in his mind. He witnessed people starving and searching the barren land for food. He saw himself hung on a rope around his neck, swinging while everyone witnessed. He saw swords clashing and body parts flying in the air. Disembodied hands reached for him, tugging at him for help.

A cold, empty feeling replaced the space where his heart should have been. Adam felt a severe pain in his chest. He heard disturbing laughter and deafening screams prodded at him from all sides. Voices filled with anger and ordered him to get out of this place and take revenge on the people who had brought him in here.

Suddenly, the coldness left him, but with little relief. A fire immediately engulfed his body. He was being burned alive, feeling hotter by the second. Then there was no pain at all. He pleaded silently for help.

Finally the fire was extinguished. The gloom revealed more than just darkness. He found himself in the presence of putrid, glassy-eyed demons. He watched as they screamed and peeled off their deformed bodies to reveal what was inside. They wailed louder as Adam noticed that under their flesh was blackness.

He shouted with what little energy remained, trying to scare them away, but to no avail. A sound hardly escaped from his mouth. Fear choked him, paralyzing every inch of his body. The events shot rapidly and unexpectedly through his mind, bombarding him with new, disturbing images.

What is this all about? None of these things had ever happened to me, he thought.

Adam tried as hard as he could to think of Lena's smile and love glow. He took that glimmer of hope and imagined the good in the world. Thoughts of happiness and peace began shooting from the center of his heart like a beacon of light out into the heavy blackness. He thought of the surface world and the people who needed him.

"I'm strong! You have no power over me!" he shouted over and over again to all the miserable images, as if in a chant. Slowly, as he struggled, the dark veil started to lift and the evil began to withdraw.

The black stone that had engulfed him spat him out onto the cave floor. His body shriveled into a ball. He could feel the repressed, salty tears escaping his eyes and the constriction in his throat releasing.

✿ ✳ ✿ ✳ ✿ ✳ ✿

Around him, dim lights reflected off the crystals and a gentle voice echoed through the cave, comforting him.

"Adam, you're safe now. Such knowledge about what is inside one's self is difficult to face, but a blessing to discover. Go look in the mirror."

He weakly stood and did as instructed. Reaching the mirror, he saw his reflection. He noticed that his image swirled and then faded from his view. In place of his own face stood another figure looking directly at him. Adam recognized Peter, the boy he had been in his previous life with Charlie.

The voice continued, "You were Peter Mason and you were killed in a fire before you could accomplish your mission, and now you have returned to Earth to do so."

Peter's image disappeared, and a tall man replaced him. He was about twenty years of age, handsome with long sawdust-colored hair. He seemed dignified and important. Adam stared at this stranger in awe, and the image stared back at him with a forlorn expression.

"Adam, this too was you. You were Prince Absalom, King David's son, over three thousand years ago. Your mission was to bring peace to your world. You let your handsome looks get to your head and your ego intensified. There was no room for anyone else in your heart. You rebelled against your father, and you were killed. You failed your mission and your people. Now it is time for you to finish."

"Me? I don't understand," Adam muttered to the soft voice echoing through the cave.

Adam attempted to reach out to touch Absalom. The man's image disappeared and Adam's reflection reappeared before his glazed eyes.

Is that really me in the mirror? He tried to touch

his reflection, fearful that he would disappear again.

With no warning, the entrance to the cave opened. Adam scrambled to get out, nearly tripping on his way and leaving behind his sword and flask of water.

When he inhaled the fresh air outside, he knew that it wasn't just the cave door that had been opened. It was his heart and mind.

The adrenalin was pumping with full force. With unexpected vigor, he started up the stairs again never looking back to the moss-covered cave. He knew he had a long way to go but pushed himself nonetheless.

This time he went slower, giving his legs time to rest, but this only prolonged the completion of this ridiculous test. Soon, he was drenched in sweat and ready to collapse again. He had also lost track of how much farther he had to climb. He just kept moving one step at a time. Each rough block of stone seemed harder to climb than the last.

He had to be pretty high by now. Lush foliage blocked his view below. He had been climbing for quite some time. He decided to call Charlie to see how much more of this torture he had to endure. He pushed the red button on his watch.

"Hello?" Charlie answered immediately.

"It's me," Adam shouted to make sure he was heard.

"Who else? How's it going?" Charlie asked with

concern, thinking something was wrong.

"Okay, I suppose," Adam said breathlessly. "I just lost count of how many stairs I've climbed, and I was wondering if you could tell me how much farther I have to go."

Charlie sighed with relief. "You're almost halfway."

"That's it?" Adam cried with despair. "I don't know if I can take much more of this."

"Don't worry," Charlie prompted. "Just keep going. You are doing great, and soon—"

The connection was lost.

Chapter 33 –
Pushed Beyond Limits

Adam took another deep breath, saying, "Only halfway! I've got to stop for a while. Demetrius didn't put a time limit on me," he said to himself, collapsing where he stood. He decided to rest and start again later.

Lying perfectly still on the cool stone steps was such a relief. His eyes closed and his body relaxed until he heard a hiss. His eyes popped open and without moving, he glanced around.

To his disbelief, he saw a huge snake slithering from under a rock and moving towards him. He yelled, jumped up quickly and ran several more steps to safety. Normally snakes back at the pet shop didn't worry him, but this thing was enormous, with a red streak on its skin, usually indicating it's poisonous.

That sword would have come in handy now, Adam thought.

Wiping the sweat from his forehead, he stopped when he reached what he thought was the halfway point. Nothing mattered to him now except to rest. He placed his head on a step, absolutely still. Nothing, not even snakes, could get him to move another inch. He hoped they would leave him alone so he could get some rest.

A few moments later, he felt a tap on his shoulder.

"Adam," a voice whispered. "You passed the test."

Slowly opening one eye, Adam saw Charlie standing over him.

"Adam, come on. You've done it!"

Adam looked up weary and confused. Next to Charlie stood his dad in front of a transporter.

"My boy, you did it," his dad said joyfully. "We're going to take you back down now."

Adam could barely lift his head off the ground, much less think clearly.

"But I only...only made it halfway," he whispered. "I didn't make it to the top, but I'll try again. I promise. Just let me rest now."

Charlie's expression turned to worry. "Are you okay, Adam?"

"I don't know," he said weakly, and then passed out.

❀ ✳ ❀ ✳ ❀ ✳ ❀

Adam awoke. It took him a minute to realize where he was. He found himself back in the palace in a comfortable bed.

I'm dreaming again, he thought.

"Ouch!" he moaned, sitting up, feeling pain in every inch of his body. He remembered his test. The journey through the mountain was no dream.

Sitting beside him, his dad beamed, "You completed the test, Adam! I'm so proud of you."

Adam looked to his other side where the king, Lena and Charlie all smiled at him.

"But I didn't finish."

"No. You did, Adam," Demetrius said. "All I needed to see was that you would do your best. And you did it. By the way, most people could never make it all the way to the top. We wanted to see if you would try the impossible."

A huge smile burst across Adam's face. "So I passed your test?"

"Not only did you pass," Demetrius said jokingly, "you get extra credit. Actually, you passed the third test as well. I did not anticipate you enduring the cave without calling for help. We were about to rescue you, but you succeeded all by yourself."

"What happened in there?" Adam's dad asked.

Adam shook his head. He didn't want to talk about it. He saw Charlie and Demetrius looking at him with sympathy, and he knew that they understood what he had gone through dealing with the demons inside of him.

"Most of the cave is filled with obsidian crystals, the most powerful healing stone of all. It is merciless in bringing up your repressed emotions, fears and character flaws, stopping at nothing until it gets to the core of your very soul," Demetrius explained.

"You know, I may not be ready for the mission," Adam responded as his eyes became teary, "but … I want to be." He couldn't express all the emotions he felt at that moment.

The room was silent.

"That," Demetrius said, beaming, "is all I needed to hear."

Chapter 34 –
The Gifts

The next day, Adam, his dad and Simon were getting ready to leave Telos and return home to Mount Shasta. They had dressed in their own clothes rather than the soft Telosian robes.

Demetrius asked Adam to join him for a quick chat.

Uh-oh. What does he want now? Adam couldn't help thinking, as he followed the king to his office.

When Adam sat down, he watched the king place a golden pyramid key, a crystal bracelet and a map on the table in front of them.

"Integrity and courage, that is what will keep you on the right path," the king began. "Your integrity, which means being true to yourself, connects you to your intuition, which connects to the source of all good. Your courage gives you the strength to succeed and do the right thing. If you compromise your integrity, such as by lying or stealing," he continued, leaning forward, "your intuition will become confused, and that is the beginning of the end of your success. Understand, lad?"

Not really, Adam thought to himself. "I think so," he said, staring out the window.

"This diagram indicates where we have hidden

the millions of crystal bracelets all over the world," Demetrius explained and motioned to the neatly folded parchment. "Open the map, Adam."

Adam unfolded it carefully and noticed that there seemed to be nothing on the page.

"It's blank," he said. He flipped it over to check the other side.

"The map has special ink that will appear when you place the pyramid key over here in the corner," Demetrius said, pointing to the spot. When he placed the small golden pyramid on the page, the parchment lit up.

"Look carefully. If you want to go to Stonehenge in England, move the key this way," he said, making a swift movement with his hand. "Move it in the other direction, and it takes you to the Pyramid of Giza in Egypt. Move it down and it takes you to Atlantis, which is under the Atlantic Ocean."

Adam smiled widely. "Wow! And how do I get to all these places?"

"The carpet, lad," the king said.

"Oh, I get it."

"Once you are on the carpet you become invisible. You can get into any of these places and then retrieve the crystal Telos bracelets that we hid. Don't misplace the key. If it gets into the wrong hands, our plans will be at risk. And remember, the Draconians are always looking for a way in."

"I hate to admit it, but I lose everything," Adam

explained. "I mean, I would lose my head if it weren't attached onto my shoulders."

"Oh, my Mother Earth," Demetrius said. "In that case, come here."

The king took Adam's palm and placed the key on it. He put his hand over the key and said a few words under his breath. Adam felt a slight burn in his hand. When he instinctively pulled away, he was mesmerized to see that the key had melted into his palm. All that remained was the raised, golden imprint of the pyramid.

"Now you won't lose it."

"Wow, that's amazing," Adam said, staring at his hand.

"I do have one other present for you," the king said. He removed a large book from a velvet bag with a strap.

Adam's eyes widened with anticipation. He loved getting presents, especially from a king.

"This is the *Book of Wisdom*," the king said. "Most people live and learn from their mistakes. Wise men learn first and then live what they learned. Understand?"

"I think so," Adam said, skimming through the thick book. He noticed a slight problem.

"How am I supposed to understand this when it's in another language?" he asked, perplexed.

"When the time is right, the angels will teach you. Everything will come together from there. Do you have any more questions?" asked the king.

"I guess not," Adam said.

He graciously thanked the king for everything and folded the map, placing it along with the bracelet into the velvet bag. He left the chamber feeling like he had just received a million dollars.

❁ ✳ ❁ ✳ ❁ ✳ ❁

A pang of sadness ripped through Adam at the thought of leaving. It had been tough, but wonderful. He had learned more about himself here in a few days than he had ever learned from the surface world his whole life. He was actually eager and excited to start his mission.

"I'm not going to say good-bye," Lena told him, "because I'm sure we will be together again soon."

"Really! But your dad…"

"Shhhh!" she said, placing her finger over her lips. "Leave that to me. Just take care of yourself."

He wanted to hug her good-bye, but he couldn't bring himself to do it with everyone watching. He stood there awkwardly, shifting his weight from side to side until Charlie announced, "Nicky's coming with your carpet."

Everyone gathered around to watch as Nicky arrived. The carpet gracefully landed on the palace lawn with Nicky holding Gypsy closely. Adam was thrilled to see them again. He scooped his dog up and looked around to show Lena his buddy, but to his disappointment, she was nowhere to be found.

"Larry," Demetrius said, "we hope you got most of your questions answered, but we must ask you to leave behind anything that you have collected while in Telos."

"Of course," Larry said, giving a genuine smile. He took some envelopes and test tubes out from his bag and handed them over to the king. "I wouldn't dream of telling a soul about your perfect paradise."

Simon looked at him with horror thinking, There goes our proof.

Adam couldn't believe how much his dad had truly changed.

Larry turned to Charlie, stared into his brown eyes and said, "Thank you for saving my life and helping my son."

"You're welcome," Charlie said. He gave a firm handshake to Larry and pulled him close to give him a stiff hug.

"This is Nicky, a dear friend of ours," Charlie explained to Larry.

Nicky, Larry and Simon all exchanged firm handshakes.

"Thanks for everything, Charlie," Adam said, choking back tears. As he hugged Charlie, he noticed that there were tears in his eyes too.

"And thank you. You have no idea how glad I am to see you at last," Charlie spoke with the softness of someone who had loved and lost someone dear. "I will miss you, my son. Now I can go to your world and help you without living in fear."

"Really! That's great. You can stay with us at our house—I mean, your house. It's big enough," Adam boasted.

"It sure is," Charlie said, setting the time on Adam's watch so that it would be in sync with the surface world.

Larry and Simon sat closely together Indian style on the carpet and gripped the handles tightly. Adam sat in front of them with Gypsy in his lap.

Adam secured the *Book of Wisdom* in the velvet bag around his chest. He searched again to see if he could find Lena in the crowd that gathered around them, but he couldn't see her.

Where did she go? he thought.

Finally ready to depart, Adam spoke his home address aloud three times. The carpet rose and sped off in a flash of light. Instantaneously, the mysterious land of Telos, along with the entire underworld, was far below them.

Chapter 35 –
The Return

A dam awoke with Gypsy licking his frozen ear. His coat partially covered his body. He was sprawled out on the carpet, in the exact same spot on the cottage floor where his journey had begun. The velvet bag's strap was still wrapped around his chest.

He checked his watch, 12:01, with the moon symbol showing.

He jumped up in a daze, struggling to remember what had just happened to him. Within a moment, it all came back. He had left Telos with his dad and Simon. He stared out the window at the bright, full moon looking for them.

"Wonder where my dad and Simon went."

Gypsy barked.

"Gypsy, what did you say?" Adam said excitedly.

Gypsy barked again.

Adam couldn't believe his ears. It was as if he could understand what Gypsy had said.

"Did you see my dad or Simon?"

No, Gypsy whined.

"No? Where could they be?"

He touched one of the crystals bordering the carpet. It was still hot from the journey. Because his dad and Simon had not arrived with him, Adam decided to leave the carpet in place, thinking maybe it would help them return. Adam picked up Gypsy and headed outside toward the house.

❁ ✳ ❁ ✳ ❁ ✳ ❁

In the darkness, he stumbled on some rocks while searching for the back door. Fortunately, it was unlocked, or he and Gypsy probably would have gotten frostbite being stuck outside for the night.

He went through the back stairway as quietly as he could. His legs ached as he approached the top step.

He peeked into Mark's room. His brother was sitting in his bed reading a book.

"Hey, twerp. Are you okay?" Mark asked, looking over his glasses.

"Yeah, but where is everyone?" Adam asked.

"What do you mean?"

"Where's Dad and Simon?"

"Ah, Dad is still on his trip. He'll be back sometime next week," Mark said with a condescending look on his face. "Plus you owe me ten bucks, remember? The carpet didn't work." He held out his hand with a gesture indicating to pay up.

"Why? I made it there! I really saw it. It was amazing! You should have come!" Adam shouted as he motioned toward the cottage.

Mark laughed in disbelief. "Are you serious? Come on, you dummy. You fell asleep while waiting for that stupid carpet to take off. Then you started screaming, and I just couldn't take it anymore. Plus, it was freezing, so I decided to cover you with your coat. I felt bad leaving you there. I figured the cold would wake you up sooner or later. You must have had some kind of wild dream."

"Well, it wasn't a dream."

"Adam, you were asleep."

"How long was I sleeping?"

"Don't know. Ten minutes," Mark said.

"You were right there when I left on the carpet, remember? You told me to get off as it started to take off," Adam argued.

Mark crossed his arms and stared at him with a little smirk. "Adam, get real. It was only a dream."

Adam was totally confused. That whole experience couldn't have been a dream. It felt so real, so exhausting, and his muscles still ached from the climb. "No, it wasn't a dream!" he insisted. "What day is it?"

"It's still Tuesday night," Mark said, raising his eyebrows.

"Tuesday?" Adam asked, surprised.

"Yes. I really got a good laugh, though," Mark teased.

"I saw Dad down there."

Mark gave a doubtful grin.

"Really! And look at this book the king gave me," Adam said, attempting to show his brother the *Book of Wisdom*.

"You've lost your mind. Get out of here," Mark said, waving his hand and returning his eyes to the computer. Adam stared at him, who was obviously not interested in hearing any more of his tale.

Adam walked out of Mark's room, looking at the floor trying to make sense of what was happening.

When he entered his room, he locked the door, placed the velvet bag on the table and went under his bed covers with Gypsy to warm up.

"Was I dreaming?"

Gypsy whined no.

"I knew it wasn't a dream."

He thought about all the events that had taken place and then remembered what Demetrius had given him. He quickly stood and looked at the imprint of the pyramid key in his palm. He reached into the velvet bag where he found the folded map and the Telos band. Placing them onto his desk, he shook his head.

"I knew it! But where's Dad and Simon? Maybe they fell off the carpet on the way. What do you think, Gypsy?"

Adam realized that the dog only responded to 'yes' or 'no' questions, so he needed to ask questions that could be answered in that way.

"Is my dad in trouble?" he asked nervously.

Gypsy barked yes.

He panicked. Where was Lena when he needed her? Where were Nicky and Charlie now? He remembered Charlie saying he could push the red button on his watch if he were in trouble, so he decided to try it. He pushed the red button and called, "Nicky! Charlie! Can you hear me?"

There was a long pause. Adam felt a sense of hopelessness. It was useless. The watch didn't work. He closed his eyes and sighed. Then his watch beeped and a light flashed.

Adam quickly pushed the red button and heard Charlie say, "We're here, Adam."

"Charlie, hi!" Adam said, feeling relieved.

"Great to hear your voice," Nicky said.

"Oh, hi, Nicky. Gypsy and I made it home in one piece, but where's my dad and Simon? They're not here."

There was a pause, and then Charlie answered, "Uh … your father's not there? Are you sure?"

"Well, I woke up on the carpet and I was alone with Gypsy. Gypsy didn't see him either." He felt so odd saying it like that, but it was true.

"Maybe he left before you woke up," Nicky reasoned.

"I don't think so. My brother saw me leave and now he says I never took off and I just fell asleep. What's going on? Now what do I do? Where do I start?"

"Just wait for the first sign," Charlie said. "In the meantime, we'll make our own inquiries about Simon and your father."

Just then, Adam heard a gentle knock on the door.

"Got to go now. Bye."

He quickly unlocked his door and saw his mom standing in her PJs half asleep, yawning.

"Sweetie, who were you just talking to?"

Adam wanted desperately to tell her everything, but he decided against it for now. She most probably wouldn't believe him either.

"Oh, just mumbling to myself, you know, just talking to Gypsy."

"It's the middle of the night."

"Well, I couldn't sleep." He paused, then said, "Mom, thanks for everything. I love you so much. I really missed you." He hugged her tightly for a moment. "I'm so glad to see you."

"Ah, you too," she said. "Adam, you're cold as an icicle."

"Really? I don't feel cold. Did you hear from Dad yet?" Adam said, changing the topic.

"Not yet. Why?" she asked.

"Oh, nothing."

"What does that mean? What's wrong?" his mom said with curiosity.

"Nothing, really! Why?"

"Well, it is the middle of the night, you are having

a conversation with yourself and you're totally frozen. Are you coming down with something?"

"No. I just took Gypsy out for a walk." Adam knew somehow that his mom didn't buy his story, but luckily she was far too tired to pry for any more information.

"Go to bed, please," she firmly ordered, closing the door behind her.

Adam fell back into bed next to Gypsy.

Wow! That was a close call.

Chapter 36 –
To Believe or Not to Believe

A dam knew that there was no way he could sleep. When he thought of the unbelievable events he had experienced, it was just too much to comprehend.

I can't believe Mark didn't see me leave on the carpet. He was right there when I left. Maybe it was a dream. But no, I have the Telos crystal band, the map and the *Book of Wisdom*. I just don't get this.

Back and forth in his mind he tried to sort it all out. He couldn't tell anyone what had happened. No one would believe him anyway. He just had to figure out what he was supposed to do next.

He remembered dreaming about the cave, the treasure, the princess and the fire. Now it all began to make sense to him. He had found a real treasure. He had found his true purpose in the world and the courage to fulfill it.

While he contemplated his future, Gypsy cuddled against him and he fell into a deep, peaceful sleep. Just as quickly as he fell asleep, the morning arrived. His eyes flew open as he heard his mom speaking to him.

"Adam, get up. Gypsy's owners are here."

"What owners? There's got to be a mistake." He

sprung up out of bed.

"Yeah, well, the dog pound gave them our address. They're so grateful. I'm sorry, sweetie, but you have to give Gypsy back to them."

Just then her cell phone rang, and Adam raced down the stairs two at a time to see this impossible news for himself, Gypsy trailing behind. He found two men standing in the kitchen with their backs towards him. His worry melted instantly when they turned around and he recognized who they were.

There stood Charlie and Nicky.

Charlie put his index finger to his lips to silence Adam's shock and whispered, "We have a little problem. Your dad is stuck in Draconia and Simon is with him!"

"What?" Adam exclaimed. "How?"

"When you were returning home on the carpet, the Draconians snatched him back. And because Simon was holding onto your dad, he got pulled down there too. The Draconians must have had something that belonged to your dad in order to drag him back."

"My dad told me his wedding ring was missing."

"Lillith probably stole it from him and pulled him back using the ring with some black magic," Charlie exclaimed. "This is just dreadful."

"Now what?" Adam asked with a look of concern.

"We have no choice. We'll have to return and rescue them."

Adam swallowed hard and stared at the two men in bewilderment.

"Oh, no! Please tell me I am dreaming again," Adam begged.

"Sorry, kid, but it's the real deal," Nicky said.

"I don't get it. My brother saw me leave on the carpet, and when I got back last night, he told me that I had never left, but instead I had just fallen asleep on the carpet. He saw me though. He was right there when I left for Telos."

"When you travel on the carpet, you enter into the quantum zone, where there is no time. When you returned, we simply sent you back a minute before you left, which to your brother looked like you had fallen asleep on the carpet," Nicky said.

Adam looked utterly puzzled by Nicky's answer. "Really? And now?"

"And now we are here to help you get started," Charlie reassured him.

"Get started with what?" Suzie interrupted their conversation, walking into the kitchen.

Nicky paused and smiled sincerely. "Get started on our way home. We realized that Gypsy loves it here so much that if it's okay with you, your son can hold on to her until we get back from our vacation.

"Well—" Adam's mom said.

"Really! Thanks so much! Please, mom! Just until Dad gets back! Then we'll ask him. Please…"

"We are actually going out of town for a week

and we were going to get a house sitter. We'll even pay you," Nicky said.

"Oh, that's not necessary," Adam's mom said, walking the men towards the foyer.

Adam waved to them as they exited the front door. He realized he didn't know what he was supposed to know, and he didn't know what he didn't know. But one thing he did know for sure was that he would never be the same kid again.

<   The end of book one   >

Admiral Richard E. Byrd's Diary
(Feb. 19, 1947)
The exploration flight over the South Pole
The Inner Earth, My Secret Diary
(published online)

I must write this diary in secrecy and obscurity. It concerns my Antarctic flight of the nineteenth day of February in the year of Nineteen and Forty Seven.

There comes a time when the rationality of men must fade into insignificance and one must accept the inevitability of the Truth! I am not at liberty to disclose the following documentation at this writing ...perhaps it shall never see the light of public scrutiny, but I must do my duty and record here for all to read one day. In a world of greed and exploitation of certain that mankind can no longer suppress that which is truth.

FLIGHT LOG: BASE CAMP ANTARCTIC, 2/19/1947

0600 Hours- All preparations are complete for our flight southward and we are airborne with full fuel tanks at 0610 Hours.

0620 Hours- Fuel mixture on starboard engine seems too rich, adjustment made and Pratt Whittneys are running smoothly.

0730 Hours- Radio Check with base camp. All is well and radio reception is normal.

0740 Hours- Note slight oil leak in starboard engine, oil pressure indicator seems normal, however.

0800 Hours- Slight turbulence noted from easterly direction at altitude of 2321 feet, correction to 1700 feet, no further turbulence, but tailwind increases, slight adjustment in throttle controls, aircraft performing very well now.

0815 Hours- Radio Check with base camp, situation normal.

0830 Hours- Turbulence encountered again, increase altitude to 2900 feet, smooth flight conditions again.

0910 Hours- Vast Ice and snow below, note coloration of yellowish nature, and disperse in a linear pattern. Altering course for a better examination of this color pattern below, note reddish or purple color also. Circle this area two full turns and return to assigned compass heading. Position check made again to base camp, and relay information concerning colorations in the Ice and snow below.

0910 Hours- Both Magnetic and Gyro compasses beginning to gyrate and wobble, we are unable to hold our heading by instrumentation. Take bearing with Sun compass, yet all seems well. The controls are seemingly slow to respond and have sluggish quality, but there is no indication of Icing!

0915 Hours- In the distance is what appears to be mountains.

0949 Hours- 29 minutes elapsed flight time from the first sighting of the mountains, it is no illusion. They are mountains and consisting of a small range that I have never seen before!

0955 Hours- Altitude change to 2950 feet, encountering strong turbulence again.

1000 Hours- We are crossing over the small mountain range and still proceeding southward as best as can be ascertained. Beyond the mountain range is what appears to be a valley with a small river or stream running through the center portion. There should be no green valley below! Something is definitely wrong and abnormal here! We should be over Ice and Snow! To the portside are great forests growing on the mountain slopes. Our navigation instruments are still spinning, the gyroscope is oscillating back and forth!

1005 Hours- I alter altitude to 1400 feet and execute a sharp left turn to better examine the valley below. It is green with either moss or a type of tight knit grass. The Light here seems different. I cannot see the Sun anymore. We make another left turn and we spot what seems to be a large animal of some kind below us. It appears to be an elephant! NO!!! It looks more like a mammoth! This is incredible! Yet, there it is! Decrease altitude to

1000 feet and take binoculars to better examine the animal. It is confirmed - it is definitely a mammoth-like animal! Report this to base camp.

1030 Hours- Encountering more rolling green hills now. The external temperature indicator reads 74 degrees Fahrenheit! Continuing on our heading now. Navigation instruments seem normal now. I am puzzled over their actions. Attempt to contact base camp. Radio is not functioning!

1130 Hours- Countryside below is more level and normal (if I may use that word). Ahead we spot what seems to be a city!!!! This is impossible! Aircraft seems light and oddly buoyant. The controls refuse to respond!! My GOD!!! Off our port and starboard wings are a strange type of aircraft. They are closing rapidly alongside! They are disc-shaped and have a radiant quality to them. They are close enough now to see the markings on them. It is a type of Swastika!!! This is fantastic. Where are we! What has happened. I tug at the controls again. They will not respond!!!! We are caught in an invisible vice grip of some type!

1135 Hours- Our radio crackles and a voice comes through in English with what perhaps is a slight Nordic or Germanic accent! The message is: 'Welcome, Admiral, to our domain. We shall land you in exactly seven minutes! Relax, Admiral, you are in good hands.' I note the engines of our plane have stopped running! The aircraft is under some strange control and is now turning itself. The controls are useless.

1140 Hours- Another radio message received. We begin the landing process now, and in moments the plane shudders slightly, and begins a descent as though caught in some great unseen turbo lift! The downward motion is negligible, and we touchdown with only a slight jolt!

1145 Hours- I am making a hasty last entry in the flight log. Several men are approaching on foot toward our aircraft. They are tall with blond hair. In the distance is a large shimmering city pulsating with rainbow hues of color. I do not know what is going to happen now, but I see no signs of weapons on those approaching. I hear now a voice ordering me by name to open the cargo door. I comply.

END LOG

From this point I write all the following events here from memory. It defies the imagination and would seem all but madness if it had not happened.

The radioman and I are taken from the aircraft and we are received in a most cordial manner. We were then boarded on a small platform-like conveyance with no wheels! It moves us toward the glowing city with great swiftness. As we approach, the city seems to be made of a crystal material. Soon we arrive at a large building that is a type I have never seen before. It appears to be right out of the design board of Frank Lloyd Wright, or perhaps more correctly, out of a Buck Rogers setting!! We are given some type of warm beverage which tasted like nothing I have ever savored before. It is delicious. After about ten minutes, two of our wondrous appearing hosts come to our quarters and announce that I am to accompany them. I have no choice but to comply. I leave my radioman behind and we walk a short distance and enter into what seems to be a turbo lift. We descend downward for some moments, the machine stops, and the door lifts silently upward! We then proceed down a long hallway that is lit by a rose-colored light that seems to be emanating from the very walls themselves! One of the beings motions for us to stop before a great door. Over the door is an inscription that I cannot read. The great door slides noiselessly open and I am beckoned to enter. One of my hosts speaks. 'Have no fear, Admiral, you are to have an audience with the Master...'

I step inside and my eyes adjust to the beautiful coloration that seems to be filling the room completely. Then I begin to see my surroundings. What greeted my eyes is the most beautiful sight of my entire existence. It is in fact too beautiful and wondrous to describe. It is exquisite and delicate. I do not think there exists a human term that can describe it in any detail with justice! My thoughts are interrupted in a cordial manner by a warm rich voice of melodious quality, 'I bid you welcome to our domain, Admiral.' I see a man with delicate features and with the etching of years upon his face. He is seated at a long table. He motions me to sit down in one of the chairs. After I am seated, he places his fingertips together and smiles. He speaks softly again, and conveys the following.

'We have let you enter here because you are of noble character and well-known on the Surface World, Admiral.' Surface World, I half-gasp under my breath! 'Yes," the Master replies with a smile, 'you are in the domain of the Arianni, the Inner World of the Earth. We shall not long delay your mission, and you will be safely escorted back to the surface and for a distance beyond. But now, Admiral, I shall tell you why you have been summoned here. Our interest rightly begins just after your race exploded the first atomic bombs over Hiroshima and Nagasaki, Japan. It was at that alarming time we sent our flying machines, the 'Flugelrads', to your surface world to investigate what your race had done. That is, of course, past history now, my dear Admiral, but I must continue on. You see, we have never interfered before in your race's wars, and barbarity, but now we must, for you have learned to tamper with a certain power that is not for man, namely, that of atomic energy. Our emissaries have already delivered messages to the powers of your world, and yet they do not heed. Now you have been chosen to be witness here that our world does exist. You see, our Culture and Science is many thousands of years beyond your race, Admiral.' I interrupted, 'But what does this have to do with me, Sir?'

The Master's eyes seemed to penetrate deeply into my mind, and after studying me for a few moments he replied, 'Your race has now reached the point of no return, for there are those among you who would destroy your very world rather than relinquish their power as they know it...' I nodded, and the Master continued, 'In 1945 and afterward, we tried to contact your race, but our efforts were met with hostility, our Flugelrads were fired upon. Yes, even pursued with malice and animosity by your fighter planes. So, now, I say to you, my son, there is a great storm gathering in your world, a black fury that will not spend itself for many years. There will be no answer in your arms, there will be no safety in your science. It may rage on until every flower of your culture is trampled, and all human things are leveled in vast chaos. Your recent war was only a prelude of what is yet to come for your race. We here see it more clearly with each hour..do you say I am mistaken?'

'No,' I answer, 'it happened once before, the dark ages came and they lasted for more than five hundred years.'

'Yes, my son,' replied the Master, 'the dark ages

that will come now for your race will cover the Earth like a pall, but I believe that some of your race will live through the storm, beyond that, I cannot say. We see at a great distance a new world stirring from the ruins of your race, seeking its lost and legendary treasures, and they will be here, my son, safe in our keeping. When that time arrives, we shall come forward again to help revive your culture and your race. Perhaps, by then, you will have learned the futility of war and its strife...and after that time, certain of your culture and science will be returned for your race to begin anew. You, my son, are to return to the Surface World with this message.....'

With these closing words, our meeting seemed at an end. I stood for a moment as in a dream....but, yet, I knew this was reality, and for some strange reason I bowed slightly, either out of respect or humility, I do not know which.

Suddenly, I was again aware that the two beautiful hosts who had brought me here were again at my side. 'This way, Admiral,' motioned one. I turned once more before leaving and looked back toward the Master. A gentle smile was etched on his delicate and ancient face. 'Farewell, my son,' he spoke, then he gestured with a lovely, slender hand a motion of peace and our meeting was truly ended.

Quickly, we walked back through the great door of the Master's chamber and once again entered into the turbo lift. The door slid silently downward and we were at once going upward. One of my hosts spoke again, 'We must now make haste, Admiral, as the Master desires to delay you no longer on your scheduled timetable and you must return with his message to your race.'

I said nothing. All of this was almost beyond belief, and once again my thoughts were interrupted as we stopped. I entered the room and was again with my radioman. He had an anxious expression on his face. As I approached, I said, 'It is all right, Howie, it is all right.' The two beings motioned us toward the awaiting conveyance, we boarded, and soon arrived back at the aircraft. The engines were idling and we boarded immediately. The whole atmosphere seemed charged now with a certain air of urgency. After the cargo door was closed the aircraft was immediately lifted by that unseen force until we reached an altitude of 2700 feet. Two of the aircraft were alongside for some distance guiding us on our return way. I must state here, the airspeed indicator registered no reading, yet we were moving along at a very rapid rate.

215 Hours- A radio message comes through. 'We are leaving you now, Admiral, your controls are free. Auf Wiedersehen!!!!' We watched for a moment as the Flugelrads disappeared into the pale blue sky.

The aircraft suddenly felt as though caught

in a sharp downdraft for a moment. We quickly recovered her control. We do not speak for some time, each man has his thoughts....

ENTRY IN FLIGHT LOG CONTINUES:

220 Hours- We are again over vast areas of ice and snow, and approximately 27 minutes from base camp. We radio them, they respond. We report all conditions normal....normal. Base camp expresses relief at our re-established contact.

300 Hours- We land smoothly at base camp. I have a mission.....

END LOG ENTRIES.

March 11, 1947. I have just attended a staff meeting at the Pentagon. I have stated fully my discovery and the message from the Master. All is duly recorded. The President has been advised. I am now detained for several hours (six hours, thirty-nine minutes, to be exact.) I am interviewed intently by Top Security Forces and a medical team. It was an ordeal!!!! I am placed under strict control via the national security provisions of this United States of America. I am ORDERED TO REMAIN SILENT IN REGARD TO ALL THAT I HAVE LEARNED, ON BEHALF OF HUMANITY!!! Incredible! I am reminded that I am a military man and I must obey orders.

30/12/56: FINAL ENTRY:
These last few years elapsed since 1947 have not been kind...I now make my final entry in this singular diary. In closing, I must state that I have faithfully kept this matter secret as directed all these years. It has been completely against my values of moral right. Now, I seem to sense the long night coming on and this secret will not die with me, but as all truth shall, it will triumph and so it shall.

This can be the only hope for mankind. I have seen the truth and it has quickened my spirit and has set me free! I have done my duty toward the monstrous military industrial complex. Now, the long night begins to approach, but there shall be no end. Just as the long night of the Antarctic ends, the brilliant sunshine of Truth shall come again... and those who are of darkness shall fall in its Light... FOR I HAVE SEEN THAT LAND BEYOND THE POLE, THAT CENTER OF THE GREAT UNKNOWN.

Admiral Richard E. Byrd
United States Navy
December 1956

Nikola Tesla
The Forgotten Wizard

Nikola Tesla was one of the most brilliant-minded scientists the world had ever known, even though he has been virtually forgotten. He was born in 1856 in Croatia, Russia at the stroke of midnight during a wild electrical storm. Tesla showed his aptitude for science at an early age. He experimented with complex ideas that eventually formed many of today's modern technologies like electronic devices, cell phones, radar technology, and alternating currency, just to name a few.

It is rumored that most of his information came from an esoteric knowledge given to him by the Lemurians and other extraterrestrial beings.

Tesla sailed to America in 1884, arriving in New York with nothing more than a pocketful of hope of selling some of his hundreds of intricate inventions that were way ahead of his time. After briefly working with Thomas Edison, Tesla created a mind-blowing power plant that could provide endless energy for the entire world everywhere for the price of nothing.

Unfortunately, there were two major setbacks that prevented his technology from reaching the public. Some greedy investors wanted to capitalize on his new-found energy plant and distribute it for a costly price. Investors took advantage of Tesla's poor business skills.

We can thank them for our electricity bill each month.

These shrewd investors teamed up with Tesla for the sole purpose of gaining access to all his hundreds of revolutionary inventions, and then they systematically discredited him for his discoveries and pushed him into seclusion.

The sad part of this story is that Tesla died disgraced and discouraged, while his 700 plus inventions sit to this day in the custody of the United States government.

We brought Nikola Tesla back to life as a guardian angel in the Quest to Telos to show him our appreciation for his contribution to society and honor him for the angel he truly was.

Weblinks

Below are a few of my favorite links to websites
found on QuestToTelos.com that I feel will give you
some food for thought to research the book and come to
your own conclusions.

Journey to Middle Earth
http://www.youtube.com/watch?v=47NDX6PBoqk&feature=r
elmfu

Article on Hollow Earth
http://www.v-j-enterprises.com/holearth.html

Article Hollow Earth Heaven or Hell?
http://www.librarising.com/hollow/heavenorhell.html

Hollow Earth Pictures
http://www.youtube.com/watch?v=ekDWZzWUG3s&feature=
related

Documentary on Hollow Earth
http://www.youtube.com/watch?v=_ifa6um-iiI&feature=fvsr

Untold War with UFO's in the South Pole
http://www.youtube.com/watch?v=97YkOWwUE2Y

Documentary on Admiral Byrd's Diary
http://www.youtube.com/watch?v=Rn0prGhLCR8&feature=r
elated

History and Messages of Lemuria
http://www.youtube.com/watch?v=H7mGQvM4VsY

Documentary on Nikola Tesla (Nicky in the book)
http://www.youtube.com/watch?v=eoY_7mbm5ng

Story of Nikola Tesla
http://www.youtube.com/watch?v=XMhAIdqH0Cs

Rachel Albert has been a certified court reporter and business owner for over 25 years, although her passion has always been the storytelling of bizarre, mystical tales. Even as a young child she would spend hours acting out all the parts to a scene she had created in her mind. Her dream was to become an author and producer someday. But, like many children, she struggled to read, making her dream seem impossible.

"I would get lost in the words and couldn't follow the storyline. It was very frustrating, and I avoided reading. So I can feel the pain that reluctant readers go through. My profession has forced me to read my transcripts and overcome my difficulties."

Rachel noticed the same aversion to reading in her own children until she converted them into accomplished readers.

She has transformed her difficulties into a unique writing style that simplifies complex topics. She hopes that her debut novel will appeal to the avid reader as well as to the alarming number of middle schoolers who hate reading. She has interwoven philosophy and magic with factual events and intriguing historical figures, including Nikola Tesla, the South Pole's secret connection to Telos, and Admiral Byrd. This story will stay with her readers long after they finish the book, creating a catalyst for literary and personal growth.

She lives in Miami with her husband and four kids.